UPPERDOWN

On a sunny morning in June a bomb goes off at Upperdown school. As the investigation procedures take place, we meet Upperdown's gallery of colourful characters: Charles Melfort, the smooth and arrogant son of a banker, his housemaster 'Killer' Rhage who once caught Melfort smoking pot, Detective Chief Superintendent Albert Crump, tubby and ailing, his repulsive assistant, Detective Sergeant Slicer and finally the glamorous Dutch girl, Elkie van Horning who is more than just an au pair. They are all linked with the bombing in ways which the presumptuous Crump had never imagined.

UPPERDOWN entertains all the way, offering both high comedy as well as great suspense.

'A debut to be applauded'

Yorkshire Post

'Mr Cook has a refreshing turn of phrase and some very strong characters'

Oxford Times

About the Author

Stephen Cook, journalist on *The Guardian*, comes from Yorkshire and now lives in London with his wife and son.

Upperdown

Stephen Cook

CORONET BOOKS
Hodder and Stoughton

Copyright © 1985 by Stephen Cook

First published in the United Kingdom in 1985 by
Hodder and Stoughton Ltd

Coronet edition 1986

British Library C.I.P.

Cook, Stephen *1949–*
    Upperdown.
    I. Title
    823'.914[F]   PR6053.0524

    ISBN 0 340 40122 2

Printed and bound in Great Britain for
Hodder and Stoughton Paperbacks, a
division of Hodder and Stoughton Ltd.,
Mill Road, Dunton Green, Sevenoaks,
Kent (Editorial Office: 47 Bedford
Square, London, WC1 3DP) by
Cox & Wyman Ltd., Reading.

'Beware the fury of a patient man'
Dryden

1

The explosion happened at half past six in the morning of a perfect shining day of early summer, violently shaking the heavy leaves of the chestnut trees in Blunt's Copse. When its hard reverberations had thudded away through the surrounding downs, the gentle early birdsong had changed to a flapping discord and gusts of dirty smoke stained the clear colours of sky and landscape. More to the point, though, a lot of the front wall of 'Killer' Rhage's ivy-clad house had been blown off and tossed into the front garden, where it inflicted heavy casualties on his wife's prized lobelias.

The best view of this most sensational moment in the long history of Upperdown School was enjoyed by Smithson A. J. and Nimmo Senior, who were returning across Great Sward from an illicit early-morning outing, walking briskly in order to re-pyjama and get back in bed before the rising bell rang and prefects started flexing their petty authority. The two had been lounging in the broken-down barn on Rifle Hill, smoking cheap cigarettes, chatting about exploits with girls – mostly imaginary – during the recent holidays, and swotting sporadically for their forthcoming O Levels. The bang halted them in their tracks, and they gaped first at the spectacle before them and then at each other. They could see, as the smoke cleared, straight into the front upstairs rooms of the house.

"Christmas," Smithson A. J. gasped eventually. "Killer's still alive. And he's absolutely bollock naked."

Nimmo Senior appeared to be in a wide-eyed trance. Then suddenly he started out of it, remembering Killer's habits of punishment, still savage despite the fact that the twentieth century had by now more or less wrested Upperdown from an earlier, darker age. Getting up early was a particularly serious offence since the previous summer,

7

when a spot check at five in the morning by a sleepless and ill-tempered Killer had found a dozen members of the senior dormitory engaged in wide-awake activities like frying sausages in their studies and playing poker and billiards in the dayroom.

"Cave!" said Nimmo, urgently if rather absurdly, given the obvious fact that Killer had a lot else on his mind and nothing on his back. "He'll see us!"

The two schoolboys, as one, darted furtively to the adjacent cover of the music-school hedge to watch from there as the drama of the bomb took its course forty yards away. Overtopping the privet were only their stretched-open eyes and fashionably punk-ish hairstyles – modestly strange cuts were tolerated, but no artificial colourings allowed, in today's comparatively relaxed barbering regime.

It was doubtful whether Rhage could even see the hands which he was at that moment stretching shakily in front of him like a blind man whose cane has been snatched. Thrown violently out of the warm torpor of his conjugal bed, deafened and half-blinded by the blast, he dragged his mind through swells of pain into a groggy consciousness – a consciousness not of the immediate present, however, but of the worst times of his commando days, when he had first earned the self-explanatory soubriquet which was still firmly attached to him despite his greying hair and the approach of his sixtieth year. As he now climbed to his feet in his customary night-time nakedness and groped towards the place where the window had been, he was reliving the Dieppe raid and the shells were bursting around him on the beach.

"Back to the boats!" he croaked urgently. "Jerry's on to us, the C.O.'s bought it – back to the boats!"

He stopped only a step away from a fall which would have taken him neatly into a small monkey-puzzle tree which, though damaged by fallen masonry, would probably have given him a worse mauling than the Germans ever managed. And fortunately for his standing among the boys of the school, who generally feared and even revered him, Smithson A. J. and Nimmo Senior were too far away to hear his deluded mutterings. The visual excitement was fairly terrific anyway, without the soundtrack, and was just now moving into a sensational phase. Another figure, less massive than Rhage and wearing a baby–doll nightdress, fluttered towards him along the sagging upper floor of the half-demolished house, throwing its hands jerkily in the air and emitting sounds – this time audible to the secret spectators – like the squeals of a frightened hamster.

"Fuck me," breathed Nimmo Senior, who was a sober boy and rarely moved to obscenity. "It's Elkie."

"Fuck her, more like," replied Smithson A. J., who had an unfortunate mid-pubescent tendency to confuse obscenity with wit. "She's got practically nothing on, too. D'you think Killer will throw her down in the rubble and stuff her?"

"Couldn't possibly," said Nimmo Senior, whose temperament was less fevered and who was probably destined for the civil service. "His wife's in there somewhere, and she wouldn't let him. Besides, he's just been blown up. He couldn't get a hard-on."

"You've got to take your chances when you get them," persisted Smithson A. J., picking excitedly at a spot built with perfect red-and-white symmetry round a single angry whisker on his chin. "I could stuff her, anytime."

If Nimmo Senior was destined for Whitehall, there were already hints that Smithson A. J. might one day be selling motor-cars or plying the trade of the more popular end of Fleet Street.

Nimmo gestured impatiently for his prurient companion to shut up. The bitter, hot smell of the explosion had drifted over and tainted the fresh morning air in their nostrils. The two figures they were watching – the big, lumbering one of Rhage and the small, fluttering one of his Dutch au pair girl – appeared now to be conferring together, moving forward and back, gesticulating, turning their heads, touching each other, stepping away again.

"Funny time to tango," said Smithson, with a small leer. He had recently signed on at dancing classes, where matrons and masters' wives patiently allowed their feet to be trodden on by blushing would-be Lotharios. Nimmo Senior turned to him with sudden contempt.

"You've got a horrible little mind," he said severely. "This is serious, you know, it's a real explosion, not just something on TV. We ought to be helping."

"But then he'd see us and we'd get punished," objected

Smithson, who had now only just caught up with Nimmo's initial perception of their danger. "He'd gate us at least, and probably beat us too, knowing him. There was that special warning he gave out at the beginning of term about getting up early."

"But he's hardly going to be in any fit state to punish us, is he, bonehead?" Nimmo's mind was once again far ahead.

"You never know," said Smithson, whose scarred buttocks gave him reason not to underestimate Rhage's powers. "Besides, they don't need us to help them now – look at that lot."

His arm swept round to indicate the great brick flank of Paine House, studded with small windows like the portholes of an ocean liner. At more and more of those on the two upper floors, peering in some cases through shattered panes, heads were appearing, accompanied variously by parts of arms and upper bodies in standard green-and-white Upperdown pyjamas. It was a bizarre and growing audience for the black farce developing on the rough suspended stage which had been blasted into existence a few yards away from them.

Smithson's hand then swept round again to indicate events in the school's main avenue along the front of Paine House. A group of variously shaped men in dressing gowns and slippers were hurrying anxiously towards the outrage. They looked like a motley crowd of down-and-outs who had raided a costume wardrobe and were now making a confused escape, staring wildly about them, hair sticking up, bits of unappetising flesh peeping out – a hirsute ankle here, a grey tummy there. They ranged from 'Fat Pat' Connolly, the egg-shaped history master in stained paisley, to 'Clod' Stevens, the stolid and muscular woodwork teacher, sporting Marks and Spencer's towelling which exposed his chest to public view. And last of all came the headmaster himself, Archibald Webb, a tall figure jerking along like a stick insect in a hurry, draped in a flapping, fading blue-and-maroon silk number which had evidently once had Noël Coward pretensions.

"God, it's like an open day at the loony bin," sniggered Smithson, giving his pimple some heavy, excited punishment.

10

Nimmo jogged his arm and pointed urgently. Rhage and Elkie had disappeared on to, and then behind, the huge double bed at the back of the exposed bedroom. Smithson's eyes began to glow as he geared up for some lewd remark. Then suddenly the two shell-shocked figures appeared again, dragging a body with them. This was Rhage's wife, a young woman of good breeding whom he had married some ten years before. She was swathed in a voluminous floral nightie and, it seemed, unconscious. They laid her on the floor and bent over her. The cries of children now filled the air as the more enterprising dressing gown rescuers, who had got into the house by breaking glass on the ground floor, handed the two Rhage offspring, three and four, kicking and screaming, through the sitting room windows. They were laid on the front lawn and anxious heads bent over them.

"You all right, Rhage?" quavered the headmaster, standing among the shattered flowers with his turned-up face sheltered by a hand from the brightness of the morning sky. His grey curls, normally so strictly flattened across his head, were sticking upwards in tufts, as if from a burst mattress.

Killer was now halfway back from Dieppe.

"Could be worse, skipper," he managed slowly but firmly, thrusting his large smoke-stained face over the edge of broken brickwork. "Shock, blast-burns, that kind of thing. Field dressings applied. Glad to see the offspring are OK."

"Yes, they're fine, old boy," said Webb, who was already more worried, now that he knew no one was dead, about the consequences of this affair for his headmasterly career. "What d'you think it was – gas?"

"*Gas?* There's no bloody gas on the premises, man. It was a bloody bomb. B-o-m-b."

The noise made by the children was quickly overwhelmed by a police-car siren, followed before long by the irritated bell of an ambulance. The two policemen in flat hats who jumped out of the big patrol car ran back and forth, shouted at each other and the anxious bystanders, and disappeared several times through the windows into the damaged house, only to reappear again in seconds, waving their arms. The

11

ambulance men calmly put the children in their vehicle and climbed into the house carrying folded-up stretchers to bring down the adults. For a moment, the front lawn of the house was all but deserted.

"Quick," said Nimmo Senior, nudging Smithson A. J. "If we get round to the back now, we can get up to the dorm without anyone seeing us."

They made their way swiftly to the left, dodging from tree to tree, until they reached the safety of Blunt's Copse. This gave them cover to move forward until they were virtually behind Rhage's house, and had only to cross fifty yards of exposed asphalt to reach the back door of Paine. The coast seemed clear; they breathed in and ran for it, their heavy shoes ringing on the hard surface.

Just at this moment, however, the back door of Rhage's house opened and two of the ambulance men began edging out carrying a heavily laden stretcher. Nimmo, for all his careful planning, had failed to notice that the front door had been virtually blocked by the fallen wall. From the red blanket covering the stretcher there protruded a large, solid-looking foot and an ankle with a smoke-blackened edge of dressing gown hanging round it. It was Killer all right, his head raised alertly. His bloodshot eyes fell immediately on the furtive figures of Nimmo and Smithson.

"You two!" his voice cracked at them like a pistol shot. They skidded to a halt and the ambulance men also froze: something told them that the tone of command in this voice was to be ignored at their peril. The two boys' eyes, the whites showing fearfully, shifted on to Killer's craggy, dirt-stained face.

"Why are you two dressed?" he snapped. "The rising bell hasn't gone, has it?"

"No, sir," was all they could manage in a weak, defeated chorus, staring at their housemaster fixedly. He looked as if he was being evacuated after some daring night-time strike behind enemy lines, but still had the resources to inflict hard discipline. He was the last, and toughest, of the die-hard old guard at Upperdown.

"You're gated," said Killer, in a grim but gratified tone. "And see me in my study as soon as I get back."

"Yes, sir."

Killer looked up impatiently at the still-stationary ambulance men.

"As you were, you two," he said, motioning forwards with his hand. "Carry on. We haven't got all day, you know."

2

"A right nasty business, this," said Detective Chief Super-intendent Albert Crump, sinking into a leather chair in the headmaster's study and accepting a tot of brandy with unconcealed relish. DCS Crump was a grey-faced northerner with the taut, all-over body fatness of an over-inflated balloon; he tended to move slowly, breathe heavily, think spasmodically, and anger easily. He had emigrated to the inhospitable south largely under the impetus of the driving ambitions of his troublesome wife. She had once dreamt of him being the first ever Commissioner of the Metropolitan Police to hail from Slack End, Cleckheaton. Such ambitions had long faded, however, and she had resigned herself with ill-grace to being the wife of no more than the CID chief of one of the less significant Home Counties.

"Very nasty," agreed the headmaster in a trembling voice. "The times we live in, eh?"

"Indeed, sir, indeed. Have you talked to the hospital yet?"

"My wife got through about ten minutes ago. Nobody's badly hurt at all, apparently. Thank God those two children weren't sleeping on the same floor as the explosion." He sighed and shook his head briskly, as if to expel from it a vision of mutilated babies. "No, just severe shock and a few cuts and bruises. Probably be out in a couple of days. Bulldog breed, that family, of course."

DCS Crump sucked gratefully at his brandy, which was warmly, magically, bringing some sort of order to the agitated, if limited, thoughts in his brain. An explosives case was bad enough – the first in his time with the force. The pressure would have been ten times greater, though, if it had involved death or serious injury as well. The Yard sticking their nose in, pressure from politicians, the Chief

14

having hernias, that sort of thing. An explosion by itself – he hoped – they could just about handle. Happening in one of the county's many public schools, of all places, the media interest would be hysterical, of course; there was probably a fair sprinkling of aristocracy among the boys, and titles were guaranteed to send the tabloid hacks running around in ever-diminishing circles. There would probably be reporters climbing up drainpipes into dormitories and pumping half-witted sheep-shagging domestics and ground staff about 'security'. But at the same time, with luck, it would virtually solve itself, rather along the lines of a domestic crime, a family affair featuring some internal grudge that wouldn't be too hard to locate. Not the IRA, anyway; he groped urgently for another cigarette at the very thought. As he lit up, he became aware of the head-master, squinting hopefully at him through the fog of exhaled smoke.

"Well," Crump said bluffly. "That's something to be grateful for, at any rate. The next question, of course, is who did it? Can you, for example, think of anyone – any-one at all – who might have wanted to plant a bomb in that house? Any threats or warnings of any kind that you know of?"

Webb, known to his youthful charges as 'Spider' because of the unfortunate coincidence of his name and his arachnid appearance, walked behind his desk, sat down, leant back, and rested the tips of his fingers together against his lips. It was an attitude he had devised years ago for times when he wanted to give the impression that he was thinking, incisively and impartially; in fact his mind was usually, at such moments, scampering round like a frightened creature in a trap, intent on self-preservation and desperate for escape. This was just such a moment; he wished he had Bernard Briggs, the deputy he hated and feared, on hand to give advice at such a tricky time – Briggs had a better 'feel' for these rather political matters. Publicity was very much on Webb's mind as well as the policeman's – and its effect on future admissions. His stomach was whirling with the secret nausea of mild panic.

"Who indeed? This is something that's been exercising me ever since I rushed down the avenue and saw poor

Rhage staggering around trying to put on his dressing gown minus the front of his house," he said, hoping that he sounded judicious. "Naturally, one's mind lights on all sorts of things – Baader-Meinhof, IRA, PLO, the rather dramatic sort of thing one reads about in the papers. We're not far from London, after all, and there are quite a few Army establishments in the not-too-distant neighbourhood. One or two Middle Eastern chappies have got their sons here. But on calm consideration, I can't for the life of me think it can really be that kind of thing. We're not even a school with much of a military tradition, like Wellington and one or two others. The IRA might just be barmy enough to go for one of them, but I can't see them seriously hoping to get anything but bad propaganda out of it, and that's what they're supposed to be interested in. One of the international groups, perhaps? Well, who knows? I've no doubt they'd regard it as a coup – body blow to bastion of privilege and oppression, that sort of tommy-rot. All seems a bit far-fetched, really. No, I have to admit, Chief Superintendent, I'm, er, rather floundering at the moment."

DCS Crump pressed his thumb and second finger against his eyeballs and rubbed them, hard enough to produce a slight, stimulating pain. God help us, he thought, here we go again. All his life, Crump had accepted that people like him, the nuts and bolts people as he liked to think of the breed, should do the running repairs which kept the figureheads and symbols of society fixed firmly in place. He was happy to do the fudging and covering-up and cutting of corners because he believed that the alternative would be galloping chaos. But he had to admit, especially on a low morning like today, that he got a little tired of the people appointed to the responsible, example-setting positions in .life being so bloody feckless. He would never turn against them, oh no, he had too much invested in the established order to dare ever to shake it; but he did sometimes get, well, a bit bloody fed up with them. A good few of them lived on his patch, too, cruising up to town each day from their ostentatious mansions in their chauffeur-driven limousines. This time it was the headmaster of one of the country's best-known if minor schools who was going to have to be steered away from making an idiot of himself.

Baader bloody Meinhof! Why couldn't they be a little more down to earth? This wasn't some bloody Continental country with a revolution every other half-century. It all sounded rather more like Stinky the fifth-form chemistry wizard overreaching himself with a little experiment.

Crump had rubbed his eyeballs so vigorously during this vehement train of thought that when he opened the lids again and looked at Webb, the head's face was fuzzed by curdled blobs and streaks of yellow, red and green. He looked as if someone had vomited on him. Crump ruthlessly suppressed the unfamiliar surge of laughter which rose suddenly inside him.

"I think we *might* have a bit more luck pursuing a few more immediate lines of inquiry, if you see what I mean, headmaster," he said, blinking exaggeratedly, like an owl, to clear the disconcerting technicolor. "Is there anyone in the school who might have wanted to plant an explosive device of this nature?"

"In the *school*?" Webb now also blinked hard, in surprise. The thought had not occurred to him that it could have been an inside job, as the jargon went. It did not fit in with the cosy fiction, to which he was helplessly addicted, that all his chaps were more or less pulling together and were virtually incapable of catching a crab.

Crump sighed.

"Not a pleasant thought, headmaster, I know," he said gently, staring over Webb's head at a Victorian gentleman in mortar-board and gown looking severely down from a dark picture, flexing a cane in his hands. "But there can be a bad apple, even in the best of families. It's even been known in the police force, I'm sorry to have to admit."

The metaphor of family was one that immediately struck a chord in Webb; he used it a lot himself, and was considering dusting it off and bringing it out during the special school assembly he had called for the late morning for the purposes of morale. He nodded approvingly, thoughtfully, then sprang out of his chair and paced the study again, watched with badly concealed irritation by Crump. Eventually he stopped, face to window and back to room, clasping and unclasping his hands behind him. Below him was his domain, its very heart – the main quadrangle and stone-built cloisters, a few black-suited boys carrying books. The bell for chapel began to sound, the sun still shone. It looked – it *looked* like a normal day. Then a large police van crawled slowly and self-importantly down the avenue on the way to Paine. On its side: 'Mobile Incident Room'.

"Well, sir?" prompted Crump. Webb began to rock on his heels, just a little, as if a slight swell was just entering his anchorage.

"There has been some unpleasantness in Mr Rhage's house," he said hesitantly. "But I can't for the life of me . . ."

"Involving who?" cut in Crump, immediately wondering, since he was in the presence of a schoolmaster, whether it would have been more correct to say 'whom'.

"Involving Mr Rhage himself and one of the boys."

"Which boy?" Crump was getting excitedly brusque.

Webb turned abruptly round, as if taking the decision to face up to facts, look them in the face. It was, after all, a course which he often recommended without mercy to distressed pupils and indecisive masters.

"Chap called Melfort. Senior boy, outstanding sportsman, bright fellow, good background. Father the chairman of Grosswort Hedges."

Crump nodded impatiently.

"What happened?"

Webb stalked over to his desk and sat down again. Crump wished the man would keep still, and stubbed out his cigarette in the onyx ashtray which matched the elaborate penholder on the desk. Webb's fingers were together in front of his lips again.

"Well," he said waveringly. "It was, I'm afraid, an affair involving, er, a prohibited substance, shall we say. Cannabis resin, to be precise. At least, I believe that to be the technical name. Do correct me if I'm wrong. The boys call it dope, I understand – rather crude, don't you think?"

Webb paused, with the hint of a grimace of pain and distaste on his face, sighed regretfully, and continued.

"A school like this cannot stay entirely invulnerable to the degeneration of the society outside, Mr Crump, as I'm sure you'll understand" – Crump closed his eyes, nodded briefly in understanding acquiescence – "and I'm afraid Mr Rhage, while making his rounds at an unaccustomed late hour one night last term, discovered three of his senior boys lounging around in one of the bathrooms smoking this obnoxious substance. Quite intoxicated they were too, by all accounts – very noisy, incoherent, and rather rude, none of which exactly helped their case. It was the racket they were making, in fact, which had woken Rhage's wife and prompted him to make his rounds in the first place."

"And young Melfort was one of these three, then, was he?"

"Unfortunately, yes. I say unfortunately because he was due to be head of the school this term, and probably all next year as well, not to mention captain of cricket. Rather a fine bat, you understand, in a generation where such attributes are a little bit thin on the ground. Rhage had been deliberately grooming him, as it were. Almost a sort of, well, personal favourite."

"I see. And how were these offences punished? I don't recall any member of my police force being involved in the investigation and prosecution of these particular infringements of the criminal law."

There was a slight flush climbing Crump's grey neck. Webb's eyes skated furtively round the room for a moment.

"No, er, well, you have a point there, of course, Mr Crump. However, it was deemed better for the sake of all those involved that we should try to deal with it informally, without involving the law as such. Rhage insisted on beating them all, of course. Personally I renounced corporal punishment some eight years ago, but I felt unable to withdraw the sanction from my masters en bloc and Mr Rhage is, I'm rather afraid to say, the only one who still regularly practises it, almost as an article of faith, er, as it were. He was generally not very happy with the onset of a more liberal, less traditional regime, you see. Blames things like this cannabis affair entirely on the erosion of discipline, as he calls it."

Quite right too, thought Crump, whose own daughter Amanda, now a police cadet herself, had not been spared the rod until the age of fifteen. But a light was now beginning to flicker in the back of his mind, the glimmer of a motive: had this young gentleman perhaps turned nasty, tried to get his own back for the thrashing – thought himself superior to that sort of thing, perhaps, especially if he was due to be head boy or whatever they called it? Webb, pacing again, ploughed on.

"Anyway, the other two were leaving at the end of last term anyway, and they were sent home a couple of weeks early under something of a cloud. Melfort presented rather a trickier problem. He was due to stay on at least until next December – take his entrance exams for Oxford, you see – and probably for two terms after that as well."

"And so?"

Webb sighed.

"Well, we found a way out of the difficulty, but young Melfort wasn't entirely happy with it. The basis of it was that, well, it seemed wrong to spoil such a promising career. Melfort's family would certainly have been very upset. We reached a compromise that he should be rusticated for the rest of term, like the others, but should be allowed to stay on for this term only to take his A levels in the hope of getting into another university, perhaps taking his Oxbridge entrance from outside later on. The condition was, of course, that he should be debarred from any position of authority in the school. Far from being the head of school, he is now not even a prefect."

Crump nodded smugly. I see, he thought, usual cosy little stitch-up behind the scenes. He had come to believe such deals to be the way of the world – he encountered them often enough in this part of the country with its unfair share of the rich and influential. Their passions and motives were just as venal and commonplace as everyone else's, of course, but Crump found them more worthy of protection and privacy. An affection, born of familiarity and warmed by brandy, rose in him at Webb's slightly embarrassed narrative. The warmth was increased by the hope that he was about to step on to the first tee and hit a hole in one.

"How did young Melfort take all this?" he asked.

"Badly, I'm afraid, even though he has been allowed into the eleven – couldn't do without him, quite frankly – and scored a century in the very first match against Branleigh House. You'd think that would be some kind of consolation, but no. He seemed to think that once he had been beaten by Rhage – a formidably painful experience, I'm given to

20

understand – he should not only be allowed to stay on indefinitely but should also take what he regarded as his rightful place as head of school and captain of the eleven. Rather arrogant, I'm bound to say, and totally unrealistic in the circumstances. Crime must be punished. Anyway, there has been a constant friction and even a few outbursts of rather nasty bad temper between Melfort and his house-master. Nothing more than insolence, of course, nothing really serious. And that, in a word, is why I've mentioned the whole story to you – in confidence, of course."

"Of course, headmaster." DCS Crump put his glass down on the leather-topped desk, an almost imperceptible smile on his fat features. "I shall have to interview this youth, of course."

Webb grew immediately flustered, as if realising that he had planted a seed in a mind which might not have too many tracks.

"I did not mean to imply, Mr, er, Crunch, that Melfort is responsible for this morning's event. Couldn't possibly, oh no, too far-fetched altogether. Don't know why I went into such detail, on reflection. But since you asked – it might possibly help to shed some light on something . . ."

"Don't worry, headmaster," said Crump, squashing his lambent desire for more brandy and pushing himself to his feet with a small grunt. "I think we'll have a result for you fairly soon. Just leave it to us."

3

What has happened at Upperdown, that this trauma has come about? What has this distinguished school, with over a hundred years' service to its country, done to deserve this? How has this cowardly currency of the late twentieth century been smuggled in beneath that imposing Victorian wrought-iron gateway, which carries forbiddingly the school shield and motto – a simple red cross with a quill pen in one corner and a rugby ball in the other, and the words 'Abjure the self' beneath?

This school, after all, has nurtured a man who was Prime Minister – only for seven months, admittedly, but nevertheless, he was Prime Minister. It has sent forth innumerable luminaries of the Indian Civil Service, a late nineteenth century explorer of Upper Java, and an eccentric aviator of the nineteen thirties who perished in mysterious circumstances in Nigeria (some say he had 'gone native'). On the academic front, it has produced the author of *Qualitative Aspects of Morphological Investigation*, a seminal work, though admittedly little known to the general public. It has formed the youth of two Chief Constables, and recently even, yes, an up-and-coming charismatic trade union official. (After agonised debate, it was decided this should, "in this day and age", be seen as distinction rather than shame.) So why, now, has this alma mater of eminent men – and of others not so eminent, over whom a veil is usually drawn – been singled out for this dastardly act of terrorism? Surely it is innocent of any social crime, beyond upsetting a few pinkos and hairies who are jealous of its status as a centre of excellence? Who could possibly sink so low as to inflict such vicious damage on this seedbed of distinction, this forcing-house for the flower of Britain's youth?

These were the inflated questions swimming alongside

opiates and tranquillisers in the brain of Rodney Rhage as he lay in his hospital bed, soothed and bandaged by a nurse in a cheekily short skirt, and skidding off every so often into pleasant fantasies of the mediaeval penalties he would inflict on the culprits. They were the questions which turned in the anxiety-racked mind of Archibald Webb as he struggled to cope calmly with the burdens of the day – working out what to say to the school about pulling together in a crisis, co-operating with the police and their endless demands for interviews and special catering arrangements for their men with the school kitchens, soothing agitated governors and fending off nosy reporters on the telephone, trying to compose a reassuring letter to be sent to all parents. He felt as if the channels of his brain were going to rupture and leak like the filaments of an overheated car radiator.

These were also the questions which buzzed around the staff room as the masters gathered after chapel into excited, speculative groups. The science masters, at the request of the police, bustled off officiously to examine their store cupboards for the disappearance of any potentially explosive substances. All the others strained their minds to remember any strangers they had seen, any suspicious movements around Paine House and the housemaster's residence attached to it. They felt alive, important, elevated above the mundane repetition of their normal lives. One felt moved enough to confide with modest excitement to a close colleague that they were all on their way to becoming "a footnote in history, if not part of the text itself".

Mr Rattray, however, the ageing, eccentric senior English master who had gradually achieved a certain mystical and bitter wisdom over the forty years it had taken him to become the longest-serving member of staff, eschewed the hubbub, whistled up Boodle, his Jack Russell, planted his little green woollen hat over his wispy, silvering locks, and set off for a meditative stroll through the chalky downland during two conveniently free teaching periods. He liked to meditate through communion with nature; he would hope for a dream.

The customary slight smile dwelt on his thin lips as he ruminated on his instinctive feelings about the history and traditions of the school, which today, in the late nineteen seventies, was so sadly and obviously bound up with the vices and vicissitudes of the world outside. The events of the morning were to him only the logical, almost inevitable culmination of a process that had begun in the near-insurrectionary atmosphere of the nineteen sixties, when everyone had seemed paralysed and tongue-tied as the blast of radical rhetoric had torn through the corridors and halls of every institution in the land. Only the other day, he remembered, the new Prime Minister had referred to it all as "trendy claptrap" – quite right, too. Like automata, wearing vapid smiles, everyone had gone along with the collective self-delusion of 'liberation'; they had been unable to gather their forces and find the reasons to stand their ground. The school had abandoned fagging, compulsory CCF and most punishments; the sixth-form syllabus had been infected by alien concepts such as 'humanities' and 'liberal studies'; dances were frequently organised with nearby girls' schools, occasioning immorality under library tables; and they had even – O tempora! O mores! – considered admitting girls to the school itself. Indeed, this could yet happen. Rattray came to a halt at a wooden fence above the railway cutting and watched a blue-and-grey train of the Southern Region lurch and clatter its way up towards Victoria, towards the Babel which had no doubt spawned the obscene indignity which was the modern England.

And yes! After the so-called progressive and liberal sixties, which had turned the world upside down, had come the confusion and stagnation and degeneracy of the early seventies: persistent runaway inflation, the pernicious erosion of the coin of the realm, was the most tangible result. The school, stripped of its moral stiffening, had been unable to take the strain. Its spine had collapsed. Disintegration, disorientation, drink, drugs, socialism, nihilism, the very concept of moral fibre backed into a corner and fighting for its life – and now, a terrorist outrage. Rattray turned sadly as the clacking of the train finally died away, and leaned against the fence to gaze back towards Upperdown, distinguished and gleaming, as in the day of its foundation in times of smiling Empire, on the green slopes of the far valley. You could believe, standing here, that nothing had happened; twenty years ago, nothing *would* have happened. If only someone had drawn the line, pointed out the collective nakedness of all the emperors. But – too late; there was nothing he could do. He was an old man now. Rattray whistled up Boodle again and consoled himself with his favourite lines of the curse of Timon of Athens, which had recently become his almost daily incantation to his gods of doom and disillusion:

> Instruction, manners, mysteries and trades,
> Degrees, observances, customs and laws
> Decline to your confounding contraries
> and let confusion live!

He spoke the words aloud, jabbing a pale, bony finger at the distant school. As he hurled out the word 'confusion' he abruptly realised that a heavily built farm labourer with a big round head stood by the fence twenty yards away, watching his ranting approach with trepidation. Rattray's face softened into a vague academic smile.

"Morning, morning," he murmured as he passed the worker, who shrank back into the hedge, the fear of the unknown glinting in his pale eyes.

4

There was a knock on the door of the junior housemaster's study and DCS Crump looked up nervously. He didn't feel comfortable surrounded by piles of red exercise books, shelves full of French grammars and other such mysteries, and fading framed pictures of teams of boys exposing large naked knees and wearing decorated blazers and tasselled caps. He liked to interview people on his own ground, in a room in the station without decoration or unnecessary furniture, where the atmosphere reflected the task in hand – breaking down someone's story, getting to the essentials. It was clearly impossible to transport all the boys to the station, however, and the headmaster had set this place aside for the use of the police; it would do for the present.

"Come in," he called.

A tall, handsome boy of about eighteen entered. He had black glossy hair, a pale and perfect complexion, and the only irregularity in his smooth features was a slight snubness to the nose which gave him a look of youth and appealing mischief. His bright, dark eyes seemed calm, slightly arrogant. His blazer, collar and tie sat perfectly upon him.

"Morning, sir. I'm Melfort."

The voice was controlled, and seemed edged with the contempt and indifference which Crump felt came naturally to the well-heeled. Too controlled? he wondered, as he leant back, narrowed his eyes, and looked Melfort up and down. It was a tried and tested softening-up technique. The boy did not shift or shuffle under the scrutiny, but stared expressionlessly back, as if he were scrupulously observing some fascinating but rather unpleasant natural event in the garden. Crump recognised the aura of confident superiority projected by the ruling class and picked up so effortlessly by their offspring, and fought down an instinctive impulse to give ground, to defer. He was in charge, he told himself firmly, and this young man was in hot water.

"Ah, Mr Melfort," he said brashly, his northern vowels extra-round and chewy. "I'm Detective Chief Superintendent Crump and I'm in charge of the investigation into this morning's, er, detonation."

Melfort stared at Crump for a moment, his eyes widening as if in amazement that the man had actually produced, actually articulated, a statement of such devastating obviousness. His eyes shifted to the window and rolled a fraction upwards. Most Upperdown boys soon became past-masters in dumb insolence.

"I know," he said with flat, ill-concealed exasperation.

Crump cleared his throat. Suddenly he badly wanted to assert his authority, to use words like 'whippersnapper' and 'young pup' and tell Melfort in clear terms that he wasn't going to put up with any of his cheek. But the patrician eyes of generations of school teams bore in upon him; he didn't dare.

"Er, sit down, Mr Melfort," he said gauchely.

Melfort sighed indulgently and did so. Crump attempted to regain the advantage he felt he had lost by rising and pacing up and down the room, moving occasionally behind the lounging figure of the schoolboy. He, however, showed no sign of being unnerved by this manoeuvre. Crump settled on the brusque approach.

"Know anything about it, Melfort?" he threw in suddenly.

Melfort gave him a withering glance, half over his shoulder.

"Of course not, sir," he said with contemptuous patience.

"Of course not? What do you mean, of course not? Someone must have done it, you know. It didn't just happen of its own accord. That device didn't just appear, just materialise, in that house, now did it? It wasn't an act of God."

Melfort studied Crump languidly, then considered his own fingernails.

"You're not suggesting I did it, are you, sir?" he asked ingenuously.

"I'm not suggesting anything, Mr Melfort. But I am

interested in information. Someone must have seen some-thing, heard something. We need witnesses. That's why we're interviewing all the boys in the house. Starting with you, since I'm told you cut something of a, shall we say, figure, round these parts."

Crump felt pleased with this little thrust, and the trace of a smirk touched his lips. Melfort looked back at Crump, however, as if he could not believe the banality he was hearing from this man. His eyes slid down Crump's rotundly stuffed form, noting the sparse, badly plastered–down hair, the pale mounds of the face, the blue suit with its shiny seat and elbows and sagging knees, the nylon shirt, the scuffed suede brogues. Crump stood his ground, defying a com-pulsive desire to sit behind the desk again, to cower from this withering scrutiny.

"Well, Mr Melfort?" he prompted severely, but with a voice slightly faltering.

"I'm sure you and your chaps will sort it all out soon enough, sir," said Melfort, gesturing towards the window which looked out over the Rhages' front garden. "There seem to be enough of them about, doing all those scientific things. They call it 'forensic', don't they, sir? I've read about that sort of thing in the papers."

"They do indeed, Mr Melfort, very good," replied Crump, recruiting sarcasm to lift his spirits in the face of this languid, seemingly impenetrable arrogance. "Our men out there will go through all that rubble and mess and remove for examination any material which might yield evidence. And you're quite right, Melfort, we'll soon sort it out. In the meantime, however, I would be grateful for all the co-operation I can get from you and your, er, fellow-pupils."

Melfort stared out of the window, as if considering this request. A small blue van had just drawn up outside the Rhages' house and a man with long hair and a moustache was standing at the back of it putting on overalls and rubber boots. Other men with expressionless faces, wearing blue suits like Crump's, moved in and out of the wrecked house; some wore rubber gloves and held plastic bags, while others were shaking the hedges or kneeling and studying the dusty, sunlit lawn. Melfort turned to Crump as if he had made a sudden decision to help, to tell all he knew.

"Well, sir, naturally we've been wondering about it our-selves a bit in the house, and how it could have happened. Maybe it's the terrorists or someone, you know, the Jackal or the IRA or someone. It almost seems like somebody's got a grudge or something, doesn't it? I mean, I know Killer – er, Mr Rhage that is – I know he's got a reputation as a bit of a hard man, but most people in the school rather like him, actually."

"Do *you*, Melfort?" Crump narrowed his eyes, hoping to look lynx-like and unconsciously pandering to what he thought Melfort would expect of a detective.

"Me, sir? Well, yes, actually we get on very well."

"Oh, you do, do you? And what about the affair of the cannabis?"

Melfort stayed impassive, but was suddenly a little less languid.

"The what, sir?"

Crump put on his best 'don't-come-that-with-me-sunshine' expression and ambled loosely, threateningly, over to Melfort's chair. He leant forward, placed his hands on the arms, and projected his sour tobacco-breath into the boy's face in a controlled shout.

"Cannabis, Mr Melfort. MARRY-JEW-ARNER, if you prefer!"

Crump paused, watching closely for effects.

"Just go back through that leaky memory of yours to last term. Yes? All right? With me, are you? Coming back to you now, is it?"

Melfort turned his head to one side, flushed with disgust at the policeman's proximity and with shame at being caught out, almost accused. He nodded quickly. Crump stood up straight, pulled the jacket of his suit smoothly over his breasts with a satisfied air, and returned slowly to sit at the desk. The suspect was now thoroughly off balance and on the defensive; he would begin to talk. Most of them did. Melfort clasped his hands in his lap and squirmed his shoulders in sullen discomfort.

"I don't know why you're bringing all that up again, sir," he said. (Crump preened inwardly every time he heard that 'sir'.) "It was all settled last term, I thought. I got beaten for that, you know, and lost all sorts of privileges and things."

29

Crump nodded smilingly.

"I know," he said. "I know."

"Well, I don't see how it could have anything to do with this, as I said. It's all over and done with, isn't it?"

Crump continued for a while with his falsely benign smile — another little interview-room ploy, calculated to increase his victim's nervousness by implying that more was known about him than he thought.

"But Mr Melfort," he said eventually, in tones suitable for use with the mentally backward. "You said yourself that somebody must have a grudge."

Melfort's nicely cut lower jaw dropped a fraction and his pale, aristocratic-looking skin went paler. He looked from side to side, his initial composure crumbling by the second. A little warm glow came pleasantly to life at the back of Crump's stomach. He rewarded himself with a cigarette, ritually tapping it on the box and lighting it with sensuous care.

"But sir, you're not suggesting . . ."

"I'm not suggesting anything, Mr Melfort. Certainly not. It would be quite unprofessional for me to do so — at this stage, at any rate. As I told you earlier, what I want is information. Information, please, Mr Melfort. Speculation is easy. Any old toe-rag can speculate."

"But I don't know anything about it, sir. How could I? I was just woken up by the explosion, like everyone else in the house."

"Mr Melfort." Crump stood up briskly, as if about to lose patience, but give the victim one more chance. He paced behind the desk, rolling and tubby. "You are a senior inmate, if I may use the term, of Paine House, to which Mr Rhage's residence is attached. You know your way around, I would assume. Now, what about access from the boarding house to the housemaster's house? Just for instance."

"Well, sir, there are doors on the ground floor and the top floor . . ."

"And where do they lead, exactly?"

"Well, the ground floor one goes straight into Killer's — er, Mr Rhage's — study; and the top one goes from the landing outside the senior dorm into a sort of landing in Ki . . . Mr Rhage's house. The landing outside his bedroom."

There was a certain hesitation before the final sentence which Crump did not miss.

"Precisely, Mr Melfort. And not only Mr Rhage's bedroom, in fact."

Melfort blushed suddenly again, his white neck glowing rose.

"What do you mean, sir?" he asked nervously.

Interesting, thought Crump, watching the subject ever more closely.

"There's another bedroom on that floor, isn't there now, that of Miss van Horning, the au pair girl, as I believe such people are known. And the two young children have bedrooms on the floor below."

"Er, yes, sir," said Melfort, regaining some composure and sitting still again.

"Just so that we get it right, Melfort," said Crump, looking at him hard. "Now then, the door. Is it locked? Not the one on the ground floor, we know that Mr Rhage locks it from the inside every night so that you horrible lot can't get in there and start poking through all his papers. Very sensible precaution, if I may say so. Still locked this morning, too, or so my men tell me. But what about the one on the top floor?"

"That's locked too," said Melfort.

"Always?"

"Well . . ."

"Yes?"

"Except when someone opens it."

Crump stopped pacing, placed both hands on the desk and leant over it towards Melfort, who was now suffering from incipient panic at the way circumstances seemed to be starting to point at him as the culprit, a criminal. The set of circumstances, anyway, that were being selected by this aggressive policeman. He might, like any schoolboy, have his secrets, but they were not to do with violent crime. He tried to hold on to his composure, telling himself there was nothing to fear from the truth, but knowing he was unable to reveal it to this man. Crump would have to find out for himself. Little cameos were now flashing through his mind – himself, passionately declaiming his innocence and his affection for Killer from the dock of the Old Bailey, his

proud father and tearful girlfriends embracing him as he a
last walks free from the courtroom, vindicated. Crump's
voice cut rudely into this reassuring fantasy.

"Thank you, Melfort, for that statement of incontrover-
tible truth. I can tell you're a scholar."

Melfort eyed Crump with distaste. The phrase 'you nasty
little man', which he had often heard his father use to denote
ordinary members of the working population, was onl
millimetres from his lips; but he controlled himself and
continued.

"No, sir, what I mean is that there's a key."

"Oh yes. And where is it?"

"Well, it's a latch, you see, sir, so Mr Rhage can just open
it at any time and come in and do his round in the dorms
and we have a key so we can go through from our side and
wake him up if there's an emergency or anything. You
know, someone ill or something."

"*We've* got the key? Who's we?"

"Well, the prefects, actually, sir."

"But you're not a prefect, are you, Melfort, after the little
affair of the illegal substances which were not, I might add
duly reported to the police."

"No, well . . ."

"You know where it is, though?"

"Yes . . ." Melfort was blushing again.

"Ever use it, do you?"

"No, sir, I just know where it is, that's all." Melfort's fac
was glowing like a rosy sunset. "Because I'm friendly with
the prefects. I ought to be one, strictly speaking, you see
sir."

"I see, Melfort. You appear to refuse to accept th
punishment you were given. But never mind that. I w
only interested, you see, because that landing outside M
Rhage's bedroom is where the device which exploded th
morning appears to have been placed."

"Was it, sir?"

"Why are you blushing, Mr Melfort?"

"I'm not, sir."

"Oh yes, you are." Crump looked sarcastically round th
room. "We'll be needing a fire extinguisher soon, at th
rate. You look to me as if you're about to burst into flames.

Melfort was silent, fighting to look calmly out of the window, to distance himself from this incipient nightmare. Crump allowed the silence to continue for a few seconds before asking lightly, almost jovially: "Study chemistry, do you, Mr Melfort?"

"Yes, actually, I'm doing A Level . . ."

"Smells, bangs, gases, that sort of thing?"

"Not really, sir, it's all a bit more sort of, well, serious, than that."

There was a pause, and a small, twisted smile on the purple-tinged lips below Crump's hard and careful final stare.

"Yes, Mr Melfort," he said. "It is indeed – serious, I mean. Thank you, you can go now."

Melfort looked at Crump, hesitating, feeling he should stay, insist on explaining himself, exonerating himself from the guilt the detective appeared to be loading on to him by this carefully chosen selection of fact. But Crump was now sitting again, looking down at some notes.

"Er, Mr Crump . . ."

Crump did not look up.

"Off you go, Melfort, there's a good chap. We'll have another talk later, when you've thought things over a bit."

Melfort stood up and walked slowly to the door. For probably the first time in many weeks, his self-possessed bearing had degenerated into a shuffle, confused and awkward. As he was about to close the door behind him, Crump called out.

"Mr Melfort."

"Sir?"

Crump spoke without looking up. "There's a detective sitting at a table in the corridor. He's going to take your fingerprints."

Quite outside the rules, of course, but Crump had long ago discovered that one of the best things about being a policeman was that few people knew their rights. Crump knew without watching that Melfort's features fell still further. He smiled to himself as the door clicked tamely shut. Young pup, he thought.

5

To pause and reflect, as Rattray had done during his walk, is
to touch upon the core of the Upperdown experience. For
the place he chose to stand and rummage in his long and
melancholy memory is a place familiar to all those who have
known the school: a stile at the top of a rise in the chalk
downs, looking on one side towards the railway line, toy-
like, its clattery sounds floating upwards out of the cutting,
and on the other, across the dip of the rich landscape towards
the distant magnificence of the best profile of this respected
institution. All who have known this place remember it
moreover, with that distinctive public school mix of pride
and pain. It is the spot where runners in the school steeple-
chase, having toiled blindly up the hill across a ploughed
field, pause on the flat summit before plunging on into the
green and slippery gloom of Keats Wood. Every boy is
obliged to run in this event every year, and cover the course
several times in training, unless declared unfit by the school
doctor, a crew-cut, red-faced man with all the bedside
charm of a sergeant-major. They have endured terrible
exhaustion as the sticky loam snatched at their failing legs.
Their eyes have misted in sweat and pain, they have
questioned life itself; they feel they would welcome death.
Why must they do this? Why can they not be at home with
their mothers and fathers? A longing for relief fills their
bruised young hearts.

And suddenly they reach the top and magically,
mysteriously, the answer to their doubts is there before
them, gleaming in the weak autumn sunlight like a distant
Valhalla – Upperdown! Their substitute home, the fate
thrust upon them by ambitious parents, the ideal held up
before them by stern and blinkered beaks, the microcosm of
the nation and museum of its superannuated values. The

e suddenly uplifted by the vision, their chests loosen and
their feet are lighter, the pain in their hearts is subtly diluted
by a noble pleasure, and down they plunge into the wood,
nurturing a mystical inspiration to do more battle with the
mud. In the short term they will suffer, taking orders and
obeying them, submitting to the tyranny and punishments
of masters and prefects alike, biding their time; and the
certain knowledge seeps into them that, in the longer term,
they will get their own back – they will one day be prefects
themselves, and then pass out into the world to organise and
threaten and chivvy the lower orders, to take an unfair share
of the world's goods, to strive to keep the foreigner in his
place, and to carry forward the cause of class division by
sending their own sons to Upperdown.

Consider an episode from the not-too-distant past, a time
when Britain was enjoying prosperity, the socialists had not
yet had their second post-war episode of power, and youth
culture still meant no more than beatniks. Across our near
horizon appears a column of Upperdown boys in brightly
coloured rugby jerseys, staggering and dragging their mud-
laden plimsolls like surgical boots through the clinging
slough, their faces either blotchy and red or deathly pale
with effort. Some of the boys are tall and have an autocratic
bearing; they are outside the general column, like the guards
who supervise a prison work-party, and every so often they
call sharp instructions to the others. The others are smaller,
their striped shirts still have the crispness and creases of
newness in them and their faces wear expressions of – could
it be fear? Yes, fear. They are the new boys, the squits, the
new intake of this pre-liberal year at Upperdown, and they
are on their way to the fulfilment of one of the school's most
hallowed and outlandish rituals, a throwback perhaps to
some ancient Saxon rite. It is designed to test at once their
resilience, their submissiveness, their willingness to take
punishment with a good grace, to embrace a hostile fate in
good Upperdown spirit. They are not sure exactly what is
going to happen to them; they have only been told by some
of the gloating seniors back at their houses that they are
going to Keats Wood, and terror pumps redly through
many a delicate twelve-year-old heart. The sudden sight of
Upperdown, across the autumnal valley, only intimidates

them further; but they will learn before long to love it - hate it. Delicate boys, but not for many days more.

The panting, jogging column, breath clouding the d air, comes to a ragged stop and mills around as each waits his turn to be herded over a stile into the dark int of the wood. Here, though the term is only a few old, the brown fallen leaves have already been broken pulped into the mud by scores of other toiling, run schoolboys. One of the squits stumbles and falls at the and is casually kicked by a prefect. The boy picks hir up with an exaggerated nonchalance, but he is blin too frequently, holding back tears. The column disapp into the damp green interior to meet its fate.

"Stop here!" barks a prematurely balding senior, w peers have been overheard unkindly referring to hir 'Bonehead'. The squits slide and skid to a halt and nervously about them. Their eyes fall on a stretch of mu water, studded with clumps of rotten-looking rushes, w lies below a long and slippery bank beside the path. The a pause, and the live silence of the wood falls upon ther quietness broken gently by a breeze passing through canopy of branches, the rustle of a bird in the bushes; tw the prefects smirk at each other, then stare with vulpine at the squits. The squits look uncertainly at each other the prefects, at the pond; and just as the horror dawns u them, it happens. With sudden barbaric shrieks, the se boys grab the squits and hurl them like baggage on to muddy slope, where they flail and slide messily towards foul, knee-deep water. Their tormentors, hitherto ren and contemptuous in their bearing, have metamorphe into caterwauling hooligans and leap into the mud a their victims, dunking them and daubing them, roll them over and plastering their hair with fistfuls of filth. squits quickly become indistinguishable brown mumr forms from which their white and terrified eyes gle forth. Their rugby jerseys, bought for them and so admi by mothers who told them in their home-leaving to thin all the 'advantages' Upperdown would bring them, filthy rags. Many of the boys are sobbing as they struggl escape, wading towards the edge, but stumbling, be caught and dragged back with whooping and arm-twist for more daubing, more ritual humiliation. The seniors are getting their own back, with interest.

One boy, however, one squit, that is, has decided the way to survive is to enter into the spirit of the thing, to enjoy it bravely, even to fight back a little, to join the older boys in their suppression of his peers. Miraculously, he has kept his large, round face clean of mud. He is short-bodied, a good fighter, skilful at throwing and ducking the clods of slime and mud. After ten minutes he is still standing there proudly, knee-deep in the water, panting, while the other squits, like wounded infantry crawling in the shell-holes of no-man's-land, attempt to scrabble their way up the muddy banks. He turns to Bonehead as the prefect wades towards him; he smiles, this squit, expecting congratulation for his spirit, his guts, hoping for acceptance in the ranks of the select.

"Congratulations," says Bonehead sarcastically. But one of his hands is behind his back, and as the squit looks up at him with the glow of success, a large cold clump of muddy reeds appears and is thrust accurately into his round, white face and worked, like a brush, into all its orifices. This boy has got it quite wrong; you cannot jump the gun or buck the system, no matter how good you are. As one housemaster once said confidentially to a new colleague when explaining the school's 'approach': "We drop them in the shit to teach them how to stay out of it."

6

Elkie van Horning lies in her hospital bed, her golden hair dishevelled on the pillow, her face as pale as the crisp sheet pulled chastely up to her chin. Her eyes flicker open occasionally and she looks sleepily out from her drug-induced doze. Her mind is running a slurred and crazily edited home movie on the back of her beautiful china-blue irises, and when she opens her eyes the harsh neon-lit hospital objects around her are also pulled hazily into the dream-like jumble. A woman in a dirty dressing gown walks past, looking curiously at Elkie; Elkie, though, is a little girl now, looking through the wooden bars of her parents' garden gate at the strange, big passers-by. The chrysanthemums at her bedside, delivered by Webb's wife and looking monstrously organic and colourful in the sterilised white room, lean over her like the huge chestnuts outside her bedroom at the school, whispering, protecting and threatening her by turns. Then the explosion, its convulsions still active in her nerves, sends her mind tumbling and crashing slowly round and round, and she moves her head, moaning, on the pillow. Her eyes open a fraction and before her is the round, pale face of the nurse, the sounds from her moving mouth drowned by the continuing echoes in her head. But now Elkie is looking up at the moon on a crisp, dewy night, another movie is slithering and jerking behind her aching eyeballs, lifted from the vaults by a whim of her disorientated brain. She is confined in a small, dark car, trapped by a man who has his mouth against her ear, whispering urgent phrases from which she understands only a few of the obscene words. Elkie is hobbled by her panties, and she is wishing she had stayed in her warm little room, watching television to improve her English and taking comfort from her childhood teddy-bear. The man is trying to do some-

38

thing she finds painful; the explosion feels as if it is going to happen again. "No, no," she murmurs urgently, her voice charmingly marked by the slightly sibilant, guttural accent of the Netherlands; she is swivelling her head from side to side and banging it on the pillow. "No, please, no."

"There, there, dear," says the nurse, still bending over her tenderly. "That's right, no more injections now."

The nurse smoothes the sheet folded down over Elkie's breast. Elkie stares widely and briefly at the chrysanthemums, focusing for a short moment, but this time they offer no comfort, they are only the high trees visible through the raked and rapidly steaming-up window of the car, with the moon throwing an eerie gleam through their branches. She is still terribly agitated, squirming to escape from the hands grabbing her breasts in the loose, thin blouse, from the pulverising echoes of the blast. All the recent terrors of her life are now fusing and blurring together in a confluence forming a torrential, tumbling river. There is a sudden memory of a tremendous, tearing thrust, and she gives her small, hamsterish squeak. The noise she emits jars inside her own drugged head, threatening to trigger to explosion yet again.

The middle-aged woman in the dirty dressing gown pauses in her return shuffle down the ward and studies Elkie with reproachful, half-witted eyes. Elkie, however, is oblivious of her fellow-patient, caught up in her still-running flashbacks. She remembers being thrown out of bed, she remembers kind Mr Rhage putting a blanket around her near-naked body, she remembers helping him to find his wife behind the wrecked bed. Then the passing-out, the hospital, the needles, injections, peering faces, peering like the lust-blind face of the man in the car, like the other faces which have leered at her in her short adult life. Her body runs hot and cold, hot with the blast of the explosion, cold with the air of the early summer night as she crashes her way through the little kissing-gate and back over the damp, musty-smelling playing fields. Her mind swirls around again, she sees the flowers at her bedside once more, and remembers his stiff penis snagging her clothes as she tries to escape. She mutters angrily in Dutch, then suddenly lies still and wide-eyed, as if she has remembere something very important.

"Mad English buggers," she mutters gutterally.

"There, there," says the nurse, returned again, slight shocked at the vehemence in Elkie's voice. "We're not th bad, dear, honest. Now I want you to sit up a momer there's a love. There's an important man to see you."

Elkie, her eyes loose and slightly bloodshot, is raised ar propped against the pillows. The nurse solicitously rearrang her bed gown to hide her delightful breasts, and runs comb carefully through the tangles of her golden hair.

"You've got lovely hair," she says enviously. "You impress this nice man who's come to see you. He's a polic man, but you mustn't be upset, all right? It's only abo catching the people who did it."

Elkie nods without comprehension, but when the m approaches her and sits by her bed, leaning forward to lo closely at her with widening eyes, she stares at him briefl the horror in her face suddenly intensified, and hurls hers to the far side of the bed, forming herself into a foetal ba covering herself with the bedclothes. The explosion brea and rolls through her disjointed mind once again. The nur shakes her head at the man, who has mastered his surpri and stands up, perhaps a little eagerly.

"It's a bit early," says the nurse in a stage whisper. "Sl hasn't recovered from the shock yet. I'm afraid she's pr bably a bit delirious. Perhaps you'd better come back anoth time."

7

The whole school was released from the last teaching period before lunch to go to the special assembly. There was an air of excitement and festivity as the boys jostled noisily through the wooden-floored corridors, spilled into the quadrangles, and pressed into Big Hall. Masters stood around the door, wearing their gowns and concealing their own secret stirrings of delight and excitement by holding their faces in severely serious expressions, trying ineffectually to calm the noise and agitation. Mr Crichton, the music master, was quietly playing 'I Vow to Thee, my Country' on the large but bronchitic organ, hoping this would calm troubled waters and turn boys' heads to nobler thoughts. His own head – two piles of mousey curls springing madly up on either side of a fiercely imposed parting – could just be seen, swaying gently, above the wooden parapet of the organ loft.

The section of Big Hall which belonged to Paine House was in greater disorder than other parts. The reason was that Nimmo Senior and Smithson A. J. had not been able to restrain themselves from letting it be known how they had witnessed the big bang. They had calculated that Killer was going to punish them anyway in due course for their early rising, and that they risked nothing further by talking openly about their sensational experience. The stir this created, the admiration and envy it attracted from their peers, was in some way an advance compensation for the four strokes they would doubtless eventually receive on their grey-flannelled buttocks from the shiny brown cane which stood by the fireplace in Killer's study. Nimmo Senior's account was typically factual, rounded, thorough and neutrally related, but Smithson A. J. went for maximum mileage, and his tale grew and ramified in the telling.

"And then Elkie sort of appeared in this cloud of dust," he was excitedly telling a gaggle around him. "And she was absolutely *starkers*!"

From five yards away, where he was relating matters to a less excitable group, Nimmo heard this lying word and sent Smithson a withering glance intended to tell him what a worm he was. The word drew an eruption of excited questions, however, from the crush around Smithson. In a school where the female population consisted mainly of matrons with grey buns or bow-legs, and Italian maids with moustaches and outlines like logs of salami, Elkie, with her willowy figure and pale blonde hair, was an oasis of desirability, a prime sex object, the fantasy of hundreds of seething adolescent imaginations.

"Cripes, Smithson, how much could you *see*?"

"You mean *completely*? *Everything*?"

"You lucky pig, Smithson."

"Did you get a stiffy, Smithson?"

Smithson basked for a moment before resuming. He did not notice Blair, an officious prefect with slicked-back black hair and a receding chin, bearing down upon him from behind with an impatient, vindictive gleam in his eye.

"Yeah, and then she and Killer sort of met in the middle and just, well, sort of collapsed in each other's arms, just like on the TV. Looked like they'd done it plenty of times before, if you ask me."

The crowd suddenly went silent and parted, as a shoal of minnows for a shark. Blair confronted Smithson and looked him disdainfully up and down: a lumpy, spotty sort of boy was Smithson.

"I heard that, Smithson," he said finally. "You'd better watch what you say, boy."

Intoxicated by his current temporary celebrity, Smithson made a gross error of judgement and answered back.

"I can say what I jolly well like, Blair. I actually saw it happen, which is more than anyone else did."

Blair raised his eyes, with the weary expression of patience severely tried, towards the plaques which held up the gold-painted names of past school heroes and distinguished masters for the admiration of new generations. It was as if he was dutifully consulting them on how to deal firmly, but fairly, with this effrontery and insubordination. He heaved a sigh: duty was painful, it said.

"I think you'd better report to me in games clothes on the back asphalt at two thirty, Smithson," he said resignedly.

"But why, Blair, why? What have I done?" There was a plaintive note, verging on panic, in Smithson's voice, which cracked back into falsetto in moments of stress.

"Done, boy?" Blair seemed genuinely astonished at the question, and his eyebrows slid a great distance back up his sloping forehead.

"Yes, Blair, what have I done?" Smithson was standing his ground, but sinking inexorably further into it. Blair moved suddenly, furiously, into top gear.

"All right, Smithson, I'll tell you what you've done. You got up early, breaking a strict house rule. That's clear for a start. You're making too much noise, you're disrupting assembly, you're spoiling the reputation of the house, you're making a disgraceful exhibition of yourself, you've got your blazer buttons undone, and you're cheeking a prefect. And apart from that, there's your general attitude, Smithson. It's about time you learnt to stop being a bolshy little oik. Now, does that explanation satisfy you?"

Smithson, who realised during this tirade that further resistance was hopeless, drooped visibly into sullen resentment as the organ suddenly swelled into the first phrases of the school song. The headmaster and deputy strode firmly on to the platform with the coloured silk revers of their gowns flowing about them. They took off their mortarboards and took up their hymnbooks. The organ paused on the introductory note and gathered five hundred ragged voices into the well-worn phrases.

> Upperdown! To our creator
> Offer we our grateful thanks
> For thee, our home and alma mater,
> Set 'mong England's woods and banks.

Webb looked nervously around the hall, his face twitching on one side, not concentrating on his singing. He was still wondering what exactly he was going to say to the school. At his side, young Bernard Briggs, the school's up-and-coming 'new man', brought in recently at the urging of the Governors at the age of only thirty-five to consolidate the reforms of the last fifteen years, stood mute: he had been campaigning for the school song to be changed or dropped – too jingoistic in this day and age, he said – and was in the habit of making this protest of silence. Today, however, the familiar complacency of his confident features had slipped into a more anxious cast. His small eyes looked furtive, as if he knew deep down that he, or something he stood for, was responsible for something very serious, and felt guilty about it. Down in the hall, the buzz of gossiping voices was still to be heard in the echoing pause between verses. Spider's face gave an extra little convulsion of irritation.

> Upperdown! Your proud tradition,
> Bears us onward, true and sure;
> Love and service to our country
> Lift our hearts, as e'er before!

The final words of the song bounced and died gratefully away among the high beams above the sea of faces, upturned in the eager hope that a new and exciting twist of the sensation was about to be revealed, or at least that Spider Webb was going to make a fool of himself in some way. Webb grasped a lapel of his gown for reassurance and cleared his throat to speak. His normally sallow cheeks had acquired unhealthily livid blotches. Bernard Briggs watched him slyly from the corner of his eye, contemptuously grateful that he was not now in the shoes which he normally coveted so fiercely.

"Er, I have asked you all to come here for this special assembly for reasons of which you are probably all, er, perfectly aware. Indeed, it probably roused most of you, as it did me. Woke me up, that is. Thankfully, however, the first thing I wish to announce is that the victims of this outrage, for that indeed is what it is, that is, Mr Rhage and his wife and Miss van Horning, the au pair girl" – there was much nudging and winking down in the hall at this point – "are not badly hurt and should be back with us in a day or two. Mr Rhage's children, who were on the floor below the one where the, er, device exploded, are returning from

44

hospital this afternoon to be cared for temporarily by Mr Connolly's wife."

Webb paused and glanced sideways at Bernard Briggs for some sign of reassurance. The expression in Briggs's narrowed eyes, however, had turned from furtiveness to a steely and merciless gaze, reminiscent of that of the lynch mob. Webb, feeling cross and neglected, blundered on.

"So! We can all breathe a sigh of relief and thanks that no one was hurt. I hope to be sending out a letter to all your parents shortly, giving a brief account of today's events and reassuring them. The Post Office has installed an extra telephone line so that we deal more quickly with inquiries from anxious relatives. I hope those of you who telephone home will also make it clear that the situation is not as serious as it might first have seemed from reports on the, er, wireless. Now!"

The last little expletive was Webb's nervous signal that he had concluded one phase of his address and was about to proceed to the next. A wag at the back of the hall, unidentifiable from the platform but immediately pounced on by prefects in a little local flurry, echoed, "When?" It was an old response to one of Webb's many verbal tics, and he chose to ignore the slight interruption and continue.

"Many of you will have noticed that a certain number of police officers are present at various locations in the school grounds. They are, of course, investigating the, er, occurrence, and they inform me that they are confident of reaching a satisfactory conclusion to their inquiries before too long. They have started, naturally enough, to interview and take statements from all the boys in Paine itself."

Blair shoved Smithson in the small of the back and whispered vindictively: "You're the first in there after lunch, Smithson, to tell your little story!"

"Now! They may also wish at certain times to interview members of the staff and other houses, and I would like to take this opportunity to ask you to give them every possible assistance. Treat them, for the moment, if you like, as part of the family, bearing in mind that it is in the interests of Upperdown to have this, er, matter, satisfactorily resolved as soon as possible. Something like this is potentially very damaging to my, er, our valuable reputation and our standing in the eyes of the general public. This is a crisis, school, and I want to see everyone pulling together."

He stared silently round the assembled boys for a moment, trying to issue an inspiration and a challenge through what he hoped were eyes glittering with a fierce and outraged patriotism. From where the other masters stood in the front row immediately below the platform, however, Webb did not look particularly impressive. From this angle, his jowls and nostrils, the latter sprouting grey hairs, seemed the most prominent features of his ineffectual face, and his attempts at ringing tones achieved only a pompous banality.

"Finally, school, a word of caution. It is very likely that newspaper reporters will descend on the school in some numbers to try to discover some aspect of sensation and scandal. Do not co-operate with them if they accost you; do not accept money or gifts from them; do not give them information of any kind. If any of these gentlemen – which I doubt, on reflection, is the correct word – does approach you, ask him to identify himself and refer him politely to me. I will deal with him. Now! Mr Briggs will now make some announcements which would normally be made at tomorrow's regular weekly assembly, which is now cancelled."

Bernard Briggs stood up and waited for the buzzing and shuffling to die down. He liked to think that he gained the boys' attention not by the crude assertion of authority in the old-fashioned way, but through the power of his personality and the breadth of his goodwill.

"On Saturday the eleven will be playing Bunyan's." His light tenor voice bounced sonorously round the heavy plaques and beams. He wasn't interested in cricket himself, but he reluctantly accepted that it was his job to make such tedious announcements. "This is an important match, I am told, and the players will be glad of as much support as they can possibly get. We already have word from the hospital that Mr Rhage will be back in time to cheer the side on. I'm sure it will be an enjoyable match, too, considering the present good form of the eleven; well worth turning out."

The hubbub was growing in the hall. Briggs's conversational manner of addressing the boys as equals only prompted them to treat him as an equal in return – and so

46

ignore him and amuse themselves otherwise if they found him boring. His was a distinctly forgettable style of delivery.

"Next Tuesday is the Whole Holiday. As you know, you may do as you wish and go where you like. I must issue the usual warnings, however, about public houses and certain notorious areas of central London. We would prefer you, naturally, to spend the day in wholesome pursuits, and a certain number of excursions have been organised, including, I am told, an outing to the county match at Tunbridge Wells. Please see your housemasters for details of these."

Briggs cleared his throat, shuffled a step back, and then moved forward again, as if sizing up a fence in front of him.

"Finally, I am told that there has been an increase in various forms of anti-social activity behind the old fives courts on Little Sward. I am sure that I do not need to be more specific since the people concerned must know what I am talking about. It must cease immediately. Thank you. Headmaster."

Briggs sat down again, wearing a slight flush. There were certain things going on in the school which he wished he did not have to mention: it made him rather embarrassed, and it did not fit conveniently with his conviction that Upperdown was now, like the rest of the world, entering an age of enlightenment on a wave of social science and 'sixties thought.

Webb rose again, called "let us pray", and lugubriously intoned a rambling request for grace, favour, deliverance from all enemies, safety for the Queen, and eternal blessing on the hallowed halls and groves of Upperdown. The boys were now very eager for their lunch, however; their appetites increased by the nervous excitements of the morning, they stampeded, almost before the words addressed to the Almighty had vanished Heavenwards, towards the luke-warm smells of mashed potato and weak gravy which had wafted insidiously through the fissures and fabric of the interlocking school buildings into Big Hall.

8

Detective Sergeant Ron Slicer took off his sleekly cut blue mohair jacket and hung it carefully behind the door of the mobile incident room. He had decided to handle his little difficulty in his usual way – by brazening it out and hoping for the best. He sat down neatly on one of the chairs, pulling up his trouser knees as he did so, and loosened his loud silk tie. Even if she had recognised him, she wasn't going to mention it – she'd have done so before now if she was going to. She'd had plenty of time.

"Phew!" he remarked. "It's another hot one."

Crump did not look up from poring over a detailed map of the school which he had borrowed from the headmaster. Slicer, with his sharp little ways, annoyed Crump at the best of times; this was not the best of times.

"Right little cracker, that one, all right," said Slicer lightly, crossing his legs and reaching for a cigarette. "I could do something for her myself, no doubt about it. Rat up a drain job. Any tea come over from those kitchens yet?"

Crump closed his eyes in tight exasperation for a moment before turning to Slicer, who looked back at him with innocently round but deeply cynical eyes.

"*Who* exactly is a right cracker, sergeant? And *what* precisely are you talking about? I was under the impression, correct me if I'm wrong, that you've been undertaking tasks relevant to the serious investigation we have in hand. Would you care to make a report to your superior officer, or are you too busy making crude remarks?"

"So there's no tea, eh?" said Slicer, unmoved, looking around him. "Disgraceful treatment we get sometimes, don't you think? Policeman's lot."

He paused to flash a deliberately boyish smile at Crump. Crump had a pleasing momentary mental image of Slicer leaving the highway at an illegal speed in his noisy black Alfasud while off on his revolting jaunts, and losing out heavily in a confrontation with a fat oak tree.

"Stop drivelling, sergeant," he said curtly.

"Sergeant? Sergeant? Call me Ron, Bert," said Slicer jovially, brushing the back of his fingers along his neat black moustache. "After all, we've got a long way to go together on this one . . ."

Crump banged a hand on the desk and his sluggish eyes flashed wide for a moment.

"Look here, Ron," he snapped. "I've spent all morning interviewing the upper-class twits who call themselves schoolboys round here, and I'm not in the mood for any witty stuff, not in this heat. I've got enough aggravation without you playing silly buggers. Now, did you find anything out or didn't you?"

Slicer drew on his cigarette and was suddenly more serious. That was another thing Crump couldn't stand about Slicer – he could be too bloody good at his job when he put his mind to it, and this was of course not a comfortable state of affairs for his superiors.

"Not a lot to report, really, guv," he said, grimacing slightly. "The housemaster's a bit ropey, his old lady's drugged up the eyeballs gibbering like a monkey, and the au pair's out for the count. Far as I can tell, everyone in the house went to bed in the normal way and were sleeping like good citizens when suddenly, boom, half the house is missing and they're all sitting on their bare arses on the floor in various stages of hysteria. Not exactly the nicest way to be woken up."

"What exactly did they say?"

"Well, Rhage seemed to think it was an episode from the last war and began mumbling on about biffing Jerry back – amazing how these old geezers never forget, isn't it?"

Crump stared at him hard and blankly. He had been in the Army himself for the last two years of the war, in India, but never quite reached the point of any active service; he tried to calm himself by visualising Slicer experiencing everyone's nightmare of those years – toiling, skeletal and diseased, on the Burma railway. Slicer continued blithely, unaware of this sudden seething of Crump's emotions.

"Anyway, I managed to tie him down to last night and he can't remember anything unusual. They never can, can they? Made his rounds at ten thirty, wrote out the team for Saturday's cricket match, had a cup of cocoa with the lady wife, turned in, and that's the last he can remember. Amazing how these people live, isn't it? Tough old stick, though, says he'll be out tomorrow. Runs the cricket eleven, apparently – really determined not to miss a match."

"And his wife?"

Slicer turned down the corners of his mouth and shook his head.

"The quacks wouldn't really let me get at her – not that it would have been much use. She took it all very badly, apparently. No real injuries, not even any cuts and bruises like him, really, but she ended up in the corner with the bed on top of her and she was pretty hysterical by the time the other two pulled her out. So they pumped her full of dope to calm her down. Still squealing like a stuck pig, though."

"And what about the au pair?"

Slicer held up his hands and closed his eyes in silent, blissful tribute.

"She's got a chest on her that you wouldn't believe. It's out of this world, I tell you, Super. Out of this *world*."

He opened his eyes again dramatically on the final word and stared with serious emotion at his superior, who was momentarily fascinated by this apparent strength of feeling but soon recovered and opened his mouth to urge Slicer to stop mincing round like a poof and get back to business. Slicer cut in.

"No, seriously, guv, this little cotton nightie, slightly open at the cleavage, pulled just tight enough to outline the nipples, know what I mean? Skin like cream, hair all golden, falling round the shoulders – unbelievable. A peach. Couldn't take my eyes off her. The bloke who's getting his leg over that is living in paradise, I tell you – bloody nirvana."

Crump wasn't sure what nirvana was and the momentary consciousness of ignorance delayed his release of anger at Slicer's locker-room prurience. So Slicer again got in first, this time by holding up his hands in surrender, and talking fast.

"I know, I know, I'm taking advantage of a poor injured

girl, abusing my position by looking down her nightie, neglecting my duty. But she's not really hurt at all, just a bit shocked and deafened, like the others. And she's just beautiful."

"Yes, Mr Slicer, but was there any information?"

Slicer shook his head.

"Turned over and went to sleep as soon as I arrived. I have that effect on people sometimes. And the medics shooed me out smartish. Apparently her English isn't that good, anyway, so I don't know how easy it'll be to get anything out of her at all. She rolled her eyes a bit for me though, before she keeled over – lovely face, Chief, lovely blue eyes, like a china doll. Well pepped up too, I dare say. It's almost worth getting yourself blown up, strikes me, for all the lovely stuff they pump into you. Zoom, up you go, rolling spheres and that. Anyway, I'll let you go tomorrow, guv, see if she's got anything to say. Special treat for you, how about that?"

Crump studied his junior officer with unmitigated distaste. The dark, neat head, the crisp little moustache, the bright, rodent-like eyes. He detected some particularly deep and devious stroke of insincerity in all that Slicer had been saying, but his thoughts on this score were clouded by the sheer disgust and anger he felt.

"Mr Slicer," he pronounced broadly. "You are a revolting specimen. And a disgrace to the police force. Did you know that?"

Slicer took it as a compliment, smiled a compliant but slightly twisted smile.

"Anything you say, guv'nor," he replied in false humility. "No need to get out of your pram."

Double bluff always worked with a clown like Crump, he reflected quietly and with satisfaction.

9

DCS Crump had a wearying and unrewarding afternoo[n]
interviewing the rest of the boys in the house. The senio[r]
were officious, volunteered too much useless and frivolou[s]
information, and tried to show how much they knew abou[t]
detective investigation – gleaned, Crump fantasised with [a]
mixture of wonder and scorn, from crime novels read illicitl[y]
behind large tomes on Euclid or the Wars of the Rose[s]
during prep. Half the juniors were timid, creeping, cal[f]
eyed, tongue-tied: the rest were cheeky, too bright, an[d]
attempted witticisms which made Crump quickly under[
stand how masters of the old school so soon abandone[d]
words and reached for the cane. For the first time a phras[e]
had crept towards his tongue which had never even occurre[d]
to him in normal police work; but now it emerged fro[m]
some unconscious repertory and he whispered it to himsel[f]
savouring its sibilances and cadences: "I'll thrash you [
within an inch of your life." He had not dared actually use [
during his afternoon's questioning – there was no knowin[g]
who these boys' fathers might turn out to be – but he woul[d]
have liked to. He was making up for it now, though; turnin[g]
his pencil over and over on the desk in the harsh pool of ligh[t]
in the now-shadowy room, he grew bolder, articulated an[d]
tasted each syllable: "I'll thrash you to within an incchh [o]
you lifffe."

There was a mild cough in front of him. The headmast[er]
had knocked discreetly and entered, unheard by Crump i[n]
his near-trance.

"I say, do excuse me, Chief Superintendent," he sai[d]
deferentially. "A heavy afternoon, no doubt?"

Crump leapt heavily to his feet in alarm.

"Who's that? Ah! Er, headmaster. Didn't know yo[u]
were there, er, sir. Forgive me, tell me everything yo[u]

know. Sorry, no, I mean, is everything all right? Any news?"

"Do sit down, old man. Don't apologise. I know exactly how you feel when these blighters get on top of you. Murderous" – he pulled up the knees of his trousers and sat down in the armchair with a sigh of relief – "quite murderous."

"Well, yes, sir, er, it has been rather a trying afternoon." Crump laughed nervously, his thin purple lips like the crack in a pie. "Must say I'm glad I never chose the calling of schoolmaster myself, that much I do admit, headmaster. They, er, try the patience somewhat, do they not?"

"Ha, ha. Quite so, quite so. And I, for my part, am relieved at a time like this that I did not choose your, er, slightly unhappy lot. Constant pressure, eh? Solving cases."

Having ritually sniffed each other's rears, so to speak, the two old dogs, one fat and one thin, got down to their main preoccupation. Webb led off with developments on his side of things.

"I'm afraid to say that this afternoon, our one old-boy MP saw fit to get on his hind legs in the House and ask the Prime Minister some damn-fool questions which only attracts more publicity to the whole sorry business and helps no one at all to sort things out . . . 'Does the Prime Minister think that this morning's bomb outrage at one of the country's most distinguished public schools is to be condemned with horror by all right-thinking citizens and will the PM give the House and the nation an assurance that no stone will be left unturned in the implacable pursuit of the culprits so that they can be brought swiftly to justice?' All very well of course, but what good does it actually do? None. Still, at least you can tell he got a decent education."

"You can never trust a man once he turns to politics," murmured Crump sympathetically and with conviction, remembering the chairman of the local police committee. Webb thought for a moment, then agreed.

"Pompous, windy lot – all rhetoric and not much action."

There was a certain irony, it occurred to Crump, in the headmaster complaining at such characteristics in others. But because he was still slightly off balance and at a disadvantage following the interruption of his too-vivid fantasy on thrashing schoolboys with unbroken voices, he was rash enough to invite Webb to continue.

"What did the Prime Minister say?" he asked.

"What? Oh, usual well-meaning pointless nonsense you get from these people: explore every avenue, deep sympathy for victims and families, noble national institution, that sort of thing. The phrases, the metaphors these gas-bags produce! A rogues' gallery of the English language, an Aladdin's cave of clichés! I wish they'd all just keep their traps shut, if you'll pardon the expression, and let the whole thing pass quietly over. But no. And that's not the end of it either."

Crump, having now recovered most of his aplomb and normal irritability, did not say anything more to prompt the headmaster further. But Webb was now in spate, and there was an unmistakable enjoyment and self-importance in his complaints.

"Every fifteen minutes, the phone rings and it's another blasted newspaper reporter wanting chapter and verse from sunrise onwards, potted history of the school, names of famous old boys, that sort of thing. All very careful about getting my name down, too, correct spelling and all that, you know, asking if there's an 'e' on the end of 'Webb'. Hah! Hardly likely to be, is there? Still, it's nice to see that our national newspapers do occasionally take pains over accuracy, given the gross distortions and falsehoods they perpetrate much of the time. I expect it will be given some prominence tomorrow, something which I'm bound to say I do regret . . ."

"But you'll bow to the inevitable and be famous just this once, won't you, headmaster?" said Crump. His fixedly friendly smile made it impossible for Webb to take this deft jibe as an insult. Instead he simpered, slightly disorientated on his side now, while Crump retained the initiative and went briskly on.

"You've clearly had a trying day, sir, but with no clear information on the crime to pass on to me, if I read you correctly. None of the boys approached you reporting suspicious movements in the grounds last night? None of the masters had any strokes of intuition born of their long experience, eh?"

54

Webb shook his head mutely, like a dog being chastised by its master.

"No, I thought not. Well, my sergeant and I have been getting on with the donkey-work most of the day. I've interviewed all the boys in the house, which makes forty-two young men between eleven and eighteen in various stages of mental incapacity – pardon my rather jaundiced view, headmaster, it's just that they've no idea what a policeman wants. No reason why they should, really, but it doesn't help my temper. None of them saw or heard so much as a dicky-bird. This place of yours seems to run like clockwork, headmaster, if the inmates are to be believed."

While Crump sat down and massaged his eyes, a little animal snarl of painful enjoyment lifting his top lip above his left canine, Webb descended slowly from his self-important fantasy of being quoted in the *Times* making wise and statesmanlike remarks and looked once more into the deep, vacant eyes of this nasty, unsolved crime. It could still be the ignominious end to his career.

"Oh dear," he muttered, looking worriedly sideways at the wastepaper-basket, overflowing with Crump's doodles of pins and arrows stuck into a variety of human and animal bodies. "So, no real progress, then?"

Crump brought his fat fists out of his eye sockets and blinked redly.

"Not so far, I'm afraid. My sergeant hasn't been able to talk to the au pair yet, still too groggy, but it looks as if there'll be nothing from the occupants of the house either. Didn't see anything, didn't hear anything. No, I think young Melfort is our only line so far."

"Melfort?" The headmaster looked haggard. He had hoped that the slight suspicion raised in their conversation of the morning would have been dispelled by now. "Surely not. You interviewed him, didn't you?"

"I certainly did. *And* his behaviour was somewhat nervous, to say the least. *And* he's a chemistry student and quite possibly has acquired the know-how. Anything missing from the chemistry classrooms?"

"The labs, you mean. Ah, yes. Should have said. No. Nothing. Full report by the head of department, gone through it all with a fine-toothed comb, and all present and correct. Down to the last bottle of dilute hydrochloric, it seems. But!"

He raised a finger significantly, dramatically. Crump, who was beginning to lose faith in the value of the headmaster's pronouncements, managed to drag a look of mild interrogation into his face.

"My deputy, bright young spark called Briggs, helped me put through a lot of the reforms round here recently, came up with a minor stroke of genius. He knew, you see, that the IRA sometimes make their bombs from weedkiller, call it Tesco mix or something of the kind. Anyway, he's asked the head groundsman, chap called Thickett, very reliable sort, to check his stock of sodium something-or-other – stuff it's made from."

"Sodium chlorate," said Crump curtly. "Good idea, although I hardly think we're dealing here with co-op mix, as it's more properly called, as stuffed into milk churns and culverts and what-have-you by the bogtrotters. More like concentrated high explosive of some kind. And if our friend Melfort didn't get it from the chemistry classes, I'm sure he's got the sort of connections in high places to procure it elsewhere. Strings to pull, no doubt."

Webb was looking extremely worried by this apparent presumption of guilt by Crump, wondering what effect it might have on the school's image if it were true, when there was a heavy knock at the door.

"Come in!" both men called at once, in the uncertainty over whose terrain this was at the moment. A brown-complexioned man the size of a small wardrobe, wearing dark braces holding up baggy trousers over a white shirt filled the doorway. His sleeves were rolled up over forearms like planks of oak.

"Thickett!" exclaimed Webb. "Talk of the devil!"

The large figure halted and studied the headmaster with resentment.

"What, 'ave I got 'orns on me 'ead or something? I'm 'ere on business, sir, something that might be very much to your advantage."

"No, no, old man, don't take offence," said Webb in the conciliatory tones he might use for recalcitrant pets. "Wha-

56

I mean is, we were just talking about you. Do come along in."

Thickett gestured loosely behind him into the dim corridor.

"I got someone for you out 'ere," he said. "Shall I bring 'im in?"

Webb glanced at Crump, who was tapping his sausage-like finger impatiently on the desk, and made a gesture of apologetic bemusement at the interruption.

"By all means, Thickett," he said, but without conviction.

Thickett disappeared for a moment. Then a small man in a light-coloured trench-coat was catapulted into the room by a push in the back. He staggered to a stop in the middle of the worn rug and looked around him, blinking angrily. He had thinning blond hair and a complexion flushed by his present excitement, the principal cause of which soon became clear. His wrists were tied together with what looked like the belt of his own raincoat.

"Good Lord!" exclaimed Webb. "How extraordinary!"

The headmaster and the policeman stared in mute surprise as the head of the trench-coated figure swivelled uncertainly for a second or two and then settled, pointing towards Webb; it was like a blind creature picking up a nearby object with sound-sensitive antennae. The watery blue eyes then seemed slowly to focus. The bound hands lifted, and one forefinger jabbed aggressively at the headmaster.

"We'll see about that, Jimmy," said the man in a slurred Scots accent. "You'll be the one who's fuckin' extraordinary when I've finished with *you*!"

The last word was given an even greater emphasis than the other ponderous syllables by a rush of breath from the small, wiry body as Thickett thrust him roughly aside and stepped to the centre of the rug.

"Shut yer gob, you," he snapped roughly. Then he turned to the headmaster and the detective, his tone softened, and spoke in respectful, almost sycophantic tones.

"Reckon as 'ow I've got your intruder for you, Mr Webb, sir," he said. "Looks pretty much like a culprit, if you ask me. Found 'im sneakin' over the ring fence in Boundary Copse, sir, just at the bottom of my vegetable patch there."

The small man turned on Thickett with salivary venom.

"If I've told you once I've told you a thousand times, you cloth-eared ignorant bloody straw-chewing yokel," he spat, his drunkenness becoming more evident as his voice lurched over this obstacle course of consonants. "I'm an effin' reporter and I was quietly getting on with my effin' job until you set on me like a mad animal. Now undo my fuckin' hands."

He held up his small, captive fists, panting and glaring at Thickett like a terrier at a bulldog.

"Language, language," tutted Webb. If this man had been a boy, he thought, he might well have to punish him heavily for such speech, even in today's liberal climate.

Thickett showed no sign of having heard the reporter's colourful protestations. He elaborated impassively.

"I was seein' to me beans – runners, they are, doin' very nicely this year – when I hears all this rustlin' and bustlin' and decide to take a look. And there 'e is, stuck on the fence like a pea on a drum, trying to get 'is coat unhooked. Swearin' like a trooper, course, not that I mind that much. Well, mindful of what 'appened this morning, I reckon to meself, 'ere 'e is come back to do it all again for all I know. So I didn't waste no time . . ."

"Too effin' right you didn't, Jimmy," exploded the reporter thickly, eyes beginning to roll a little. "I'll have you for assault and battery. I'll take you to the effin' *cleaners*, Jimmy – and *you*, and *you*. Accessories after the fact, man. I know the effin' law."

The bound hand jabbed a forefinger again at the other two. Crump restrained his reflex, conditioned by long years of squashing insects such as this with a single stroke, to inform him mightily that *he* was the law around here. Again, Thickett continued unperturbed.

"I just trussed 'im up like a chicken, put 'im in the back of my van and drove straight up 'ere. Course, I knew the police officers would still be around, like, and your missus told me where to find you, sir."

There was a silence, broken only by the occasional grunt of effort as the newshound struggled with his bonds. This task seemed to engross him totally for the moment.

"Thank you, Thickett, thank you very much," said Webb, seeming to hesitate between embarrassment and anger

"We're, er, most grateful for your vigilance. I suppose" – he glanced at Crump, whose face bore a slight ironic smile of anticipation – "I suppose we ought to, er, interview this man. Perhaps you'd be so kind as to wait outside, Thickett?"

Thickett produced a vague saluting gesture – a residual forelock-tug – and respectfully and obediently left the room. He had done his bit, now the masters were going to do theirs, which was none of his business. Crump coughed, rose and walked rollingly round the desk to untie the proffered wrists.

"I think you can count yourself lucky you weren't seriously injured, my lad," he began jocularly. This little episode had quite improved his day, given it a little lift in the tail.

"The name's MacPherson," spat the reporter, rubbing his wrists with relief. "Of the *Daily Comet*, if you must know, Jimmy, chief sodding reporter, and I'm going to take you lot to the bloody clean – "

"Yes, yes, son, we heard you first time," interrupted Crump, taking over in a firm policemanly way. He was more used to dealing with this man's style than the kind of behaviour he had been getting from middle-class school-boys all day. "Now why don't you just sit down quietly over there and tell us your side of the story. And show us your press card, there's a good lad."

MacPherson tossed a rectangle of purple plastic on the desk and flopped in a chair, fumbling for a bent cigarette and lighting it clumsily. He coughed nastily, but the nicotine seemed to spring him into a fairly coherent narrative.

"Me and the pack were in a canny little boozer just down the road, very respectable landlord, name of Belper, Kelper, something like that . . ."

"Ah! Whelper!" interrupted Webb. "At the Axe and Stump. Nice fellow, nice little pub."

MacPherson stared hard at Webb as if to kill the inter-jection at birth by sheer silent malevolence.

"And we came to the conclusion," he continued finally, "that we weren't getting anywhere on this story, d'you know what I mean, Jimmy? No hard info, no colour stuff, no quotes, no funnies, no snaps, no bloody nothin', Jimmy, let alone any effin' exclusives. Mickey Mouse story. All we've had all day is this pompous arsehole, some stuffed shirt, at the end of the phone, droning on about the situation all being under control and a rapid return to normality and all this *shit*!"

He glared around him, using both hands for vague stabbing gestures of emphasis. In his unsteady condition he failed to notice Webb shifting resentfully in his chair and trying mutely to extract a supporting glance from Crump over these gross insults to his person. Crump, however, still kept his grim and vindictive little smile.

"I mean, for fuck's sake, Jimmy, there's been an effin' explosion! Right? The sons of the idle rich are blown out of their beds by a bang like something out of the blitz. They must be absolutely shitting themselves, Jimmy. Effin' Prime Minister rabbiting on in the Commons. Heads are going to *roll*! They must be running around like blue-arsed flies! And here's this total effin' arsehole telling us everything's quite normal. I mean, for fuck's sake, Jimmy!"

He pulled in self-righteous outrage at his cigarette spreading his hands in mute appeal for all rational and right-thinking men to join him in his flawless deductions. Crump, still smiling, gestured mildly towards Webb, who looked as if a ripe Aberdeen herring had been wafted under his nose. Arsehole indeed.

"Allow me to introduce Mr Webb, the headmaster," said Crump with a formal gesture. It was a rare stroke of delicate humour for the fat policeman.

MacPherson glared at Webb, not making the connection, and, rested a little now, stolidly resumed his narrative.

"So I decided to pull a fast one on the lads, right? They were all pissed as rats, anyway, couldn't bleeding stand up. The gents is outside at this pub, right, so I let on I'm out for a leak, rest of them still watching each other like vultures, and jump in the old rustbox. Park in the lay-by, very convenient, and find a wee hole in the hedge. Thought the least I could do was get hold of some colour stuff, know what I mean, Jimmy? From Robbie MacPherson, another *Comet* exclusive, the only reporter inside top people's terror-blast school, that sort of crap. Talk to the boys as they settle down to their prep, or whatever it is they get up to at night. Bloody arse banditry up and down the dormitory, no doubt, pity we run a decent family news-paper, none of . . ."

"Now *look* here, Mr MacPherson," interrupted Webb roundly, firmly, having assembled his guns and charged them with a few round phrases to avenge the insults. He had found them particularly wounding since his piles, on top of his other misfortunes, happened to be playing up at the moment; he was going to put this uncouth intruder back in the gutter, where he belonged. "I'm afraid all these foul-mouthed excuses aren't going to get you anywhere, you know. It doesn't cut any ice with me or the Chief Superintendent" – MacPherson's eyes slowly focused on the policeman, widened in alarm as he finally realised his status and exalted rank – "and I don't know why you don't just admit the simple truth: you're a grubby little hack out to capitalise on the misfortunes of others in order to increase the sale of your sordid and immoral little scandal sheet . . ."

MacPherson lurched forward in his chair, his fists balling and his eyes glinting in sudden Glaswegian bloodlust, only to see Crump's hand upraised, like a traffic policeman's, in silent and final prohibition. He paused in mid-movement, then sank back submissively and became limp. Crump held him, as it were, while Webb, with a faint smirk of visceral satisfaction at this unexpected opportunity to vent the tensions of the day without any comeback, continued to hit him.

". . . which you have the temerity, I understand, to refer to as a newspaper. Now I believe I told you, or one of your equally obnoxious colleagues on the telephone, that the affair is under control and being dealt with through the proper channels. That, Mr MacPherson, is all you and your readers need to know. More seriously, perhaps, however, you are trespassing on private property. As it happens, I do not intend to take any action on this occasion, and you can also be thankful that you did not encounter one of our tenant farmers, who are generally out with their shotguns after pigeons at this time of day and would not have scorned the opportunity to shoot a rat."

Webb paused for a moment to see how deep his most carefully poisoned barb could penetrate. He glanced at Crump with a slight, expectant smile, but Crump's gimlet eyes were still single-mindedly pinning MacPherson to his chair. MacPherson seemed to be in a state of nerveless trance, gazing helplessly back at Crump, having recognised his master. He looked impervious to pain and incapable of understanding. Stony ground, thought Webb, and decided irritably to wrap it up; he would happily have continued for some time yet.

"As it is, Mr MacPherson, I hope you have found your experience suitably chastening and will take it as a reminder that the likes of you cannot do as you please, riding rough-shod over the rights of others and contravening the law of the land. I shall be writing a formal letter of complaint to your editor. Count yourself lucky I am not minded to institute proceedings."

He rose to stride magisterially to the door, but one of his legs had gone to sleep during his admonitions and buckled under him at the first step.

"Ooooh!" he moaned involuntarily. MacPherson snapped suddenly out of his torpor into a high-pitched, drunken giggle. Webb glared at him viciously as he limped and struggled to the door and summoned Thickett.

"Mr Thickett," he said, calling on his dwindling reserves of pomposity and noting with mortification that Crump was also smiling. "Show this *gentle*man off the school grounds, if you please."

MacPherson hauled himself out of his chair before Thickett could get to him and headed unsteadily for the door. As he passed Webb, he suddenly stopped, thrust his flushed features up against the head's pale visage, and shouted so that flecks of spittle hit the other's eyes.

"This is cover-up, Jimmy, and I'm going to effin' expose you to the British pub . . ."

The last syllable, however, was swallowed in a gargle as Thickett grabbed MacPherson by the collar and plucked him away, as he might lift one of his rabbits from the hutch. Crump looked on, feeling relieved that he was not in the headmaster's shoes; he knew from experience that the gutter-snipes of the press, for all their apparent powerless-ness, had formidable ways of getting back at you.

10

Rattray had the slightly wild look to his hair and eyes which usually indicated that he had had one of his dreams. His colleagues found him most trying at such times, for he expected them to believe, like him, that these dreams were glimpses into the great collective unconscious of the race, where barriers between past, present and future were dissolved by a single timeless stream of history. It was true he had a certain track record, in that he had dreamed in 1962 of icebergs floating across Little Sward and warned the bursar to institute an emergency programme of pipe-lagging and frost protection: he had been humoured, then ignored, and the great winter of that year had caused bursts and floods which resulted in the entire junior dormitory of Paine House being evacuated to emergency sleeping quarters in the gymnasium. This had then burnt down when a fat boy called Daggers knocked over a paraffin heater during a vigorous nightmare. Rattray often reminded people of this stroke of prescience, quoting the cost of the new gym; this success, however, and most of his communications, as he called them, seemed to concern the spirit and traditions of the school and the way it was run. They usually resulted in a variety of impractical suggestions being pressed upon the headmaster: all boys should learn Greek; school dances should be stopped before there was an epidemic of venereal disease; Bernard Briggs was a subversive paid agent of the state education system. So far, Webb had ignored such things with impunity accompanied by a slight foreboding that his luck might not last.

"You look as if you've been in touch with the other side," said Webb, with a doomed attempt at joviality as Rattray bore briskly down upon him on the Masters' Path next morning.

"I have indeed, headmaster, I have indeed," said Rattray, nodding his whitening head vigorously and grimly. "And the subject matter is so serious, and should be acted upon so rapidly, that I will ignore the thoughtless jibe contained in your flippant choice of terminology."

Webb's attempt at heartiness was chopped down instantly by Rattray's cutting edge and his face fell into the haggard cast of the day before. He sighed.

"All right, Rattray. You have my apologies. I was attempting to keep the cares of the day at arm's length for just a little longer. However, I now see that this luxury is not to be granted to me. Do let me know about your dream."

Rattray's hands were clasped behind him over his old tweed jacket and his slightly milky eyes were fixed on the ground in front of him. Webb took the same position and they walked briskly side by side towards the dining hall for breakfast.

"I believe we have the culprit in our midst," Rattray said with conviction. "A traitor in our ranks. A Quisling. A turncoat who almost certainly intends to strike again at the great institution which has bred him, or which he serves."

Webb sighed and his heart sank further; his face was as long and lugubrious as a door. This was the same theme he had had from Crump. If it proved to be true, it really would be the end.

"Do be more specific, Rattray," he cajoled wearily. "It's a bit early in the day for riddles. You don't mean one of the boys, do you?"

Rattray's forefinger shot warningly, as if spring-loaded, into the air.

"Ah!" he said. "Not necessarily. Could be a master, could be an old boy, could be a servant, or someone working in the school at the moment. The connection is that close, and I must warn you, headmaster: the important thing is that attempts at detection must be directed to that quarter. The very existence, not to say the spirit, of the school could be at stake in the battle against this determined adversary, and I must urge you to act quickly."

"Yes, well, Rattray, we mustn't get carried away. It's the police's job to investigate this affair, you know, and we can't very well start telling them how to go about it. As a matter of fact, I believe from my conversations with them that they are pursuing the particular possibility of it being an inside job, as I believe the terminology goes."

"Excellent, excellent," interjected Rattray, his long, sparse handfuls of hair bobbing with the emphatic motion of his head. "Obviously not as stupid as I thought."

"But I feel it would be indiscreet of me to be more specific: I will, however, pass on your views."

Webb paused in his bureaucratic wrapping-up of the issue and glanced at Rattray cautiously from the corner of his eye. Then he asked with some diffidence, anxious that the inevitable visionary tirade should be one of the shorter ones: "Er, what exactly was it that you, er, saw, in the dream, Ratters?"

Rattray's voice softened and he raised his face to stare mysteriously into the middle distance.

"It all took place in an idyllic Edwardian setting, quintessentially English," he purred; most of Rattray's visions were located in quintessentially English Edwardian settings. "A country house party in midsummer; click of croquet balls, sun glinting on the river, ladies in white with parasols. I am taking a turn in the rose garden, admiring the blooms, when I spy a chap sneaking towards a shed next to the greenhouse. I have my suspicions of him because of the way he loiters around watching everyone with a rather supercilious smile, not taking part in the various activities."

Rattray cleared his throat and fell in more closely beside Webb, his voice falling to a confessional whisper.

"I follow him, taking cover where necessary behind some quite magnificent standards, and peer in through the window of the shed. I can hear the man sniggering as he bends over some sacks containing chemical substances . . ."

"Well, blow me down . . ." put in Webb.

"Blow you up, more likely!" came back Rattray, holding a forefinger in front of the other's face as if to test his eyesight. "Mixing explosives, that was what this chap was doing! To blow up his host and the other weekend guests!"

"Yes, quite so," said Webb brusquely, moving slightly away from Rattray to avoid the finger which threatened to snag one of his hairy nostrils. "The point I'm trying to make, Ratters, is that Bernard Briggs had more or less the same thought."

"Really!" Rattray stopped dead on the path, his face suddenly closed in an expression of suspicion and disgust. He did not like being mentioned in the same breath as that young upstart, that agent of the devil and the Kremlin. Webb also stopped, recognising a certain inner pleasure at the way he had so neatly halted Rattray's flow. He displayed mock surprise.

"What's the matter, old chap?" he asked innocently.

"Could you be a little more precise?" asked Rattray through clenched teeth.

"Oh, nothing significant," said Webb airily, moving with confidence on the familiar ground of manipulating staff rivalries, and beginning to walk on again. "It's just that Bernard had the bright idea of asking Thickett to check his sheds, make sure that no chemicals were missing. You can make bombs from weedkillers, apparently."

Rattray hung back on the path, his expression sullen and importunate. Webb stopped again, impatiently.

"Really, Ratters," he said. "You may resemble the Ancient Mariner, but I'm not the one of three. Don't take it so personally. It was just one idea among many that will probably come to nothing. The police don't seem very interested."

Ratters was not mollified, but began walking again.

"Do complete the story, old chap," said Webb, almost jocular again now. The whole episode, crowned with the little literary allusion – a rare thing for him – had perked him up no end. "We're nearly there and it's grace in about two minutes."

"Ah, yes. Well, to be brief: I open the door to challenge the miscreant, and as he turns to face me he is transformed into a dragon, slavering and breathing fire."

"Really." Webb's comment was flat and perfunctory: he had heard all this sort of thing before. Scenes from mediaeval courtly allegory were another of Rattray's familiar stocks-in-trade. The pace of the narration now took a more dramatic urgency.

"I flee, I am pursued. But as I leap over the rose-garden wall, I acquire all the accoutrements of the jousting knight, and am able to turn and do battle with the dragon. I am closing with him at a thunderous speed, mounted upon a splendid charger, when, most unfortunately, I am disturbed by the rising bell."

The two men passed through the cloister and turned into the dining hall, where the hubbub was higher than on a normal morning. Webb noticed that several of the masters looked quite haggard, and as he stood behind his chair while the grace was read by one of the senior boys, he spoke to Briggs out of the corner of his mouth.

"This top table looks like none of them has had a wink of sleep," he stage-whispered.

Through the mumbled tributes to God, the sovereign, and various glorious benefactors, Briggs whispered back.

"They've been up all night investigating bomb scares. Some delinquent left some sticks of rock in a plastic bag outside Harrington's study. Bought it in the tuck shop, taped it together to look like sticks of dynamite, you know, like B-movie Westerns on TV."

Webb groaned.

"I thought something like that – Amen! – might happen. Every clever dick in the school is going to be trying his hand."

Rattray leaned over Webb's shoulder as the school sat down with a cacophonic squeal of dragged benches and the servers rushed at the steaming porridge pots.

"I do urge you, headmaster, to pass on my insight to the police," he said. "And I shall keep you posted on any further communications."

"Certainly, Ratters," said Webb, courteously but dismissively, and the older man went off to his seat wearing the expression of a hen sitting on an egg. Webb looked gloomily at the watery gruel placed before him and wished he was still in bed with his head under the pillows.

* * * * * *

"Here, Mr Slicer, look at this."

"Ron, please," cajoled Slicer. "Call me Ron, Bert."

Crump ignored him and stabbed a chubby finger at the document he held in front of him.

"Just as I suspected," he said, grimly satisfied. "There's a fair amount of traffic through that door, and a high proportion of it by one particular individual."

Slicer sighed theatrically.

"I don't know," he told the rest of the office, which was empty. "Here we are, working shoulder to shoulder on this important, this *crucial* investigation, and he can't even let his hair down far enough to call me by my first name. What's the matter with me? Is he a superior being? Don't I wash?"

He ducked his head in pantomime down towards his armpit, sniffing in mock experiment.

"Come here, Mr Slicer," hissed Crump, purpling from the collar up. He was in no mood to take any more lip from this cocky young sergeant. One of his hunches had been confirmed, he had a small coup to announce, and he was determined that Slicer, with his shiny little suit, his shiny little motor and, no doubt, his shiny little prick, was going to sit up and take notice, for once. He, Slicer, was going to give recognition to the policemanly talents of Albert Crump, just for a change. Slicer had been getting too clever by half of late, and here was an opportunity to take him down a peg. The younger officer ambled over and put an infuriatingly matey arm along the back of Crump's chair.

"Here I am, Sherlock," he announced jauntily. "What have we got here, then, a set of Cluedo cards?"

"This, Mr Slicer," ground out Crump in hard, frozen syllables, "is the fingerprint report from the forensic laboratory, rushed through in double-quick time at my special request. You may find it amazing that they have produced results so quickly. The speed alarmed me somewhat as well. We don't want them to burn themselves out at an early age, do we? Nevertheless, here it is. I asked them to concentrate on one particular set of prints, which I personally took up to them last night, and to compare them with the marks on one particular door. They have come up with a confirmation of a little theory of mine, Slicer, which just might take us a good way forward in this investigation. A result, quite possibly, as you would say in this part of the world. So pay attention, please, if it's not too much trouble."

Slicer, to Crump's intense gratification, seemed slightly rattled, and stepped away from the chair.

"Give us a break, guv'nor," he complained. "I know this investigation's taking place in a bleeding school, but I'm not one of the fourth formers, know what I mean?"

Crump stared at him with deliberate blankness for two steady seconds.

"Forgive my mistake, Mr Slicer," he then replied. "But let's not get bogged down in these minor clashes of personality, eh? Shall we just get on with considering this report – if you don't mind, that is? If you can spare the time?"

Slicer held up his hands to simulate surrender and put on an expression of bearing slights patiently. Crump went on, half-musingly, as if thinking aloud for Slicer's edification.

"A fairly good crop of prints, as I was saying. One set is as yet unidentified, will almost certainly prove to be the housemaster's. I gather he's coming out of hospital later today, incidentally. But the other prominent set, as I suspected, belongs to young Charles Melfort. Took the prints of all the prefects who have the right to use it, you see, and none of them seem to be there. Melfort's our boy."

Crump pushed his chair back and looked up smugly at Slicer, who had stopped his clowning and now wore a tight little frown of concentration.

"Ah, yes, Melfort," he said, seriously. "You did mention his being a likely candidate. Couldn't, er, give me a quick run-down, could you, guv, put me in the picture with what you picked up on him yesterday?"

"I most certainly will, Mr Slicer, seeing how this young whippersnapper" – at last! he could use without scruple the word that had turned longingly in his mind all night – "is a hair's breadth away from being seriously implicated in this offence. All we need is something more from forensic, something good, and we're home and dry."

He put his feet up on the desk, lit a cigarette, and, savouring this rare moment of feeling good about himself, studied his brown suede brogues, rather small in size for such a large man above them, with satisfaction. The shoes, though battered, were tidily kept. They seemed to represent everything about himself that was solid, that he approved of, that was reliable, despite the sags and strains he was increasingly aware of in his vulnerable, ageing personality. They seemed to speak of the methodical yet astute, solid but intelligent police work of which he liked to consider himself an exponent. They seemed to refute the slick, corner-cutting methods of the likes of Slicer. He could not resist a quick glance down at Slicer's shoes: yes, sure enough, just as he had expected – thin, shiny, patent leather efforts, Italian as like as not, with cheap and spivvy little gold buckles on the side. Flashy, but unreliable. Not solid.

Puffing casually on his cigarette, he gave Slicer the 'run-down' he asked for, unconsciously embellishing the details to support the theory now firmly rooted in his mind. He mentioned the drugs, the stitch-up to keep Melfort at the school, the highly developed grudge against Rhage. He then stubbed out his cigarette with self-important delibera-tion and fiddled with a pen instead, twirling it with unlikely agility in his fat fingers. And what he entirely failed to notice was the effect of his narrative on Slicer: the flush had kept on rising in the sergeant's neck and a glitter was hardening in his eyes.

"You and I may wonder," concluded Crump, "that the young pup was not thrown out on his ear with none of this pratting around. But such mysteries are not for us to contemplate, Slicer. Our job is to pin the blighter down, and that's precisely what I intend to do."

His eyes slid off sideways and he gazed through the window. Beyond it was a misty vision of the Chief offering his smiling congratulations; then his mind moved in lateral sentimentality to his daughter Amanda, and his emotions softened with parental affection and regret.

"I don't know, Mr Slicer," he went on with a heaving sigh, quite unaware that Mr Slicer, who had started viciously straightening and then grotesquely twisting paper-clips from a tin on the table, was looking fiercely out of the window and listening to not a word. "They must be a terrible disappointment to their parents, kids like that. The top families aren't what they were in this country, you know, not like they were when I was a lad. It's these get-rich-quick merchants – all sorts of vermin climbing the ladder, giving themselves airs and graces. It's all wrong – they don't keep up the same standards, don't set a proper example."

Crump's misting gaze shifted to the distracted Slicer again and focused, as did his voice.

"Mind you," he added. "Look what they have to contend with. Social standards generally slipping right down the pan. Drugs, immorality, corruption, sex before marriage, pornography."

The excitement in Crump's voice now betrayed that his real feelings about such phenomena were not entirely contained by the disapproval he professed. He eyed Slicer nastily up and down, and added a little drop of poison.

"Standards in the police force have been dropping, too, don't you think, Mr Slicer?"

Crump's clumsy irony was lost on his colleague, who seemed for the moment to be in another world entirely; it was as if his attention was turned inwards on private new reflections flashing through his brain, new and irresistible emotions pumping through his heart. An unusual scarlet flush was playing up and down his neck like wind on flat water, as if some violent vascular event was about to take place inside.

"Mr Slicer?"

Crump leant forward in mock concern, waving a hand hesitantly before the other man's blank but button-bright eyes.

"Attack of the vapours, is it, Mr Slicer?"

Slicer's face suddenly came alive again, as if he had come to a momentous decision.

"Good-looking kid, this, eh?" he asked sharply, his eyes piercing his fat superior. "Popular with the young ladies, would you say?"

Crump looked back suspiciously, uncomprehending.

"I fail to see the relevance of the question, Mr Slicer," he said guardedly. He was always worried that Slicer was several jumps ahead.

"The relevance is, guv'nor," blurted Slicer in brutal impatience, "that he just might be getting his leg over the au pair."

Not only did Crump not salute this one, but he seemed extremely irritated that Slicer had run it up the flagpole at all. It destroyed his theory and was outside his particular range of prejudices about the behaviour of modern youth in

71

general and public schoolboys in particular. He eyed Slicer slowly and coldly.

"Are you feeling quite well, sergeant?" he enquired. "A schoolboy, and one that's meant to be a gentleman, at that, seducing a sophisticated young foreign lady like that – bit unlikely, isn't it? He's probably more interested in having it off with his hand."

"I'm quite serious, guv. Perfect way of lifting two fingers to the housemaster, snoring away like a regular citizen only a couple of yards away from the dirty deed. And you said yourself they go in for sex before marriage these days. It's all the rage – not like in your time, you know, they've got the pill now. And it would explain the prints on the door."

Crump glowered defiantly at Slicer, like a dog determined not to have this particular bone wrested from him. If the sergeant was one jump ahead, he was definitely bounding off down the wrong road, he decided.

"Yes, well, I wasn't referring to the inmates of distinguished public schools, sergeant. Sexual immorality may be rife in the world outside – as I'm sure you know from intimate personal experience – but I really think it's a bit far-fetched. From what you tell me, she's a mature and beautiful young lady. I hardly think it's likely she's going to consider being po . . ., er, having relations, with a seventeen-year-old."

Slicer opened his mouth to reply, but changed his mind and shrugged his shoulders. His agitation seemed to be receding.

"Whatever you say, then, sir," he conceded with quite untypical and no doubt temporary humility in his voice. "Are you going to interview him again, now, sir, do you think, see if he'll let on, come clean?"

Slicer studied Crump with secret and renewed contempt. The silly old fart couldn't see beyond the end of his marshmallow of a nose; he seriously believed that some schoolkid was going to knock up some TNT in a chemistry lab and blow up his housemaster for giving him a beating? These toffs probably loved being beaten, for Christ's sake! The kid had even blushed when it was pointed out he had access to the key to the landing just outside the bedroom of – what was the little tart's name again? Elkie? – and still poor old Crump put two and two together and came up with a lemon. He couldn't resist ploughing on with the first thought that came into his head. He could imagine drugs and bombs in a public school, but not sex. Probably thought the upper classes didn't do it, like the Queen. It was too strong for him. Someone was going to have to rip the old idiot's blinkers off.

Crump's faint inner glow, meanwhile, had not only survived the logic of Slicer's alternative theory about the prints – it had been further fanned by the 'sir' which had passed, albeit insincerely, over Slicer's lips. He casually twirled the pen again and pursed his lips, portraying himself in his imagination as the cat playing with the mouse, choosing his moment casually.

"Noooo," he tried to drawl. "I think we'll let this young man sit it out while we wait for forensic to come up with the clincher. After all, I can't see him skipping the country, can you, eh? Doing a Lord Lucan?"

Slicer gave a nasty little grimace at Crump's half-joke.

"I shouldn't be too sure, chief," he warned mockingly. "Way you've described him – international drugs syndicate, millionaire background – he probably has a private executive helicopter waiting out on the cricket ground."

Crump smiled pityingly, and turned away to bend again over the initial report he was preparing for the Chief Constable.

"Give forensic a bell and find out how they're getting on, will you, Mr Slicer?" he murmured dismissively.

Slicer's eyes bored venomously into Crump's back as he held the receiver, waiting for an answer; he noticed with revulsion how Crump's thick neck sat fatly on his shoulders, how tightly the thin blue suit was stretched over the beefy back. Like a bloody hippopotamus, he thought, basking in a muddy river making self-satisfied blowing noises through his nose. He'd bring the old idiot to his senses soon enough, he thought. All that was needed was proof positive about that little bastard Melfort screwing young Elkie, and Crump's whole half-inflated balloon of a theory would blow out all its air in one of those long, wriggling raspberries. And proof there would duly be, he thought gleefully; he would see to that. He wasn't going to be made a monkey of in matters sexual by some teenage toff.

"Frensic?" said an irritable female voice.

"Ah," said Slicer cheerfully, all his customary self-pleasure restored in the anticipation of his newly forming plans. "Detective Sergeant Slicer speaking, but you can call me Ron, darling. Any joy yet on the Upperdown bang?"

11

It was a hero's welcome, and Rhage played it like VE day all over again. Webb had thought it would be a nice gesture of moral support for the boys of Paine House to be assembled on the avenue to welcome their master back. The rest of the school, however, would continue diligently about its business, in order to emphasise that the daily life of a great institution could not be disrupted by the actions of mindless fanatics. Paine was duly briefed on how the victims would still be 'a bit groggy' and told there should be no noisy demonstrations or cheering – maybe a little discreet clapping if their feelings overwhelmed them. One of the junior housemasters, a forgetful man who looked like a smiling, round-headed robot and rejoiced in the name of Nogge, and to whom the boys had therefore never felt the need to give a nickname, organised the modest parade for three thirty, when Rhage and the others were due to arrive. The house would then proceed in an orderly fashion to afternoon lessons.

The returning victims rolled up slowly and grandly in a large black Ford, the most impressive vehicle in the fleet of the Get-U-There Taxi Service (Weddings and Ceremonial Occasions a Speciality) – "and if this isn't a ceremonial occasion I don't know what is," Nogge had murmured fervently to himself while plying the yellow pages and carefully organising everything over the telephone. The car glided to a halt and the driver, who for some reason wore a glittering brand-new blue peaked cap above his sweater and dirty jeans, jumped out smartly, tripped over the kerb, and recovered swiftly to open the rear door with a flourish.

A large foot appeared and groped slowly for the ground, a stretch of white bandage showing between the cavalry twill and the Hush Puppy. It was followed first by a hospital-issue walking-stick which ended in a large, black rubber shoe, and then by the rest of Rhage. He drew himself unsteadily to his full height, settled and shrugged himself into a statuesque position – almost Churchillian, only Rhage was not so squat and lumpy – and cast a glance of fierce inquiry about himself as he leant down on the stick. Despite the recent trauma, Rhage looked very much his usual rugged self, although thirty-six hours on a hospital pillow had left the pepper-and-salt hair round the back of his head sticking out disjointedly like the neck feathers of a scruffy sparrow. One side of his face was also lightly scorched to the rosy pink colour of a piglet. He was a little battered, certainly, but for the most part unbowed; and sure enough, a little ripple of hesitant clapping flowed through the awe-struck boys. It was started impulsively by Smithson A. J., whose sturdy, simple feelings were suddenly pierced at the sight of this iron man. Only the previous morning he had been tottering around his blasted bedroom, and here he was again, undefeated. It mattered not that the shadow of Rhage's cane still lay over Smithson for his offence of early rising – he had been at Upperdown long enough to know how to respect, perhaps even love might not be too strong a word, the arm that beat him. Melfort's pale and handsome face, meanwhile, wore a worried smile as he refrained from joining the applause. The matron, portly Miss Dearsley, sobbed gratefully into her hanky. She loved humiliating adolescent boys, but she had always had a soft spot for Killer Rhage.

Rhage stood for a moment while his eye played critically over his charges like that of a general reviewing the troops. Then, almost reluctantly, he raised his hand in modest acknowledgment of their welcome, and a small grin cracked his stern features. He moved a few steps forward to allow his wife and Elkie out of the car. Mrs Rhage looked shaken, but the line of her chin was as plucky as ever and she looked every bit the stout-spirited mate that Killer, by common consent, deserved. Elkie was pale, with downcast eyes, and wore a heavy cardigan despite the warm afternoon. Only briefly did she glance up, scanning the ranks of the boys as if searching someone out.

With the two faithful women standing a pace behind him, Killer's uplifted hand moved into an open-palmed interdictory position, and the appreciative noises stopped instantly. It was one of those times when an Englishman recognises that A Few Words are in order. When he tried to speak, however, some obstruction around the vocal cords, doubtless lodged as a result of more than a day of giving no loud orders, prevented anything more than a thin squeak from emerging from his mouth. The driver looked startled, and hurriedly got back into his car to drive away. By the time the strong hum of the engine had died, Rhage had nudged the phlegm out of the way with a series of skilful and judiciously pitched little coughs, and his voice rang out strongly.

"Well," he said in buck-you-up tones, eyes running up and down the ranks again. "It's good to be back with you all. As you can see, we're none of us too much the worse for wear, despite the attempts of our friends – whoever they may be – who arranged that rather original little alarm-call yesterday morning."

He paused for the appreciative laughter to die down, gazing reflectively at the damaged front of his home, which stuck out like a shattered limb from the side of the main body of Paine House. The men putting up scaffolding to start rebuilding the top floor had also paused respectfully to observe the ritual homecoming below them.

"Unfortunately we can't move back into our own house just yet because a few improvements and modernisations are in hand" – more sycophantic titters – "but the children are already being looked after by Mr and Mrs Connolly, and we'll be moving into Pavilion House for a while with them too. It was fortunate that another master had so much space available in a house so near to Paine – it means I'll be close enough to keep an eye on you and prevent you getting up to any tricks."

Smithson A. J. and Nimmo Senior glanced at each other; Nimmo, who forgot his fear of Rhage less easily than his comrade-in-crime, grimaced uncomfortably at what was probably in store for them. The Connollys' house, whose name derived from its view over the first and second elevens' cricket pitches, was a large, rambling Edwardian structure with ornate multiple chimneys, fretworked balconies and curlicued barge-boards. It stood near Century Copse only a couple of hundred yards from Paine. Rhage, even though in convalescence, was indeed going to be close enough to keep his customary iron grip on things. Even now, his eye took on a sudden glitter as he cleared his throat to deliver the final back-stiffener.

"In a word, life goes on as normal," he commanded, lifting the heavy hospital walking-stick and jabbing its surgical, rubber-booted end at them for emphasis. "We're not the sort of people who get flustered and run round in circles like headless chickens when somebody starts getting ideas above their station and trying to make trouble. We don't take any notice of naughty children – we give them a firm smacking and ignore them, and that's very much the attitude that applies to these johnnies, whoever they are. You boys don't remember the war, of course, and the spirit that got us through that; you're all far too young. But I remember it, and by Monty, I'm going to see to it that the spirit lives on at Upperdown. So let's rise to the occasion and – on with the show."

The blood had risen warmly to his face, and his nostrils, the most delicate part of a physiognomy which generally resembled nothing so much as an outcrop of rock, were flared in defiance and determination. As he lowered the stick to the ground again and stared fiercely about him, Nogge, radiant with naive admiration, lost control of his feelings and called out excitedly.

"Three cheers for Mr Rhage and his family!"

The boys responded raggedly; an astute observer, though, would have noticed Melfort's sulkily clamped lips. The cheer was a warm movement of affection for the warrior who had returned from doing battle with the barbarian to assure them that things would not be changing and that their safe, if not always comfortable life was going to go on as before. Nogge, of course, had entirely forgotten that the headmaster had specifically warned against overexciting the bomb victims with anything as effusive as cheering. In the event, the three ex-patients seemed to quite enjoy it; Mrs Rhage bridled sweetly with a gesture of the head she had learnt at the age of six and never felt the need to change, and Elkie was projecting a coy smile in the direction of the cheering boys.

Webb, meanwhile, was watching the scene from his study window further up the avenue and experiencing little internal twitches of envy; you could earn an awful lot of popularity by getting yourself blown up, he thought. Only trouble was, there was no guarantee you wouldn't end up in a wheelchair or worse. His slight shudder as visions of amputation and mutilation shot through his mind turned suddenly to annoyance when he heard the cheering he had so deliberately forbidden; this sort of lapse was why Nogge had remained a junior housemaster teaching O Level geography for the last twenty years. Chap simply couldn't be relied upon to follow the simplest of instructions.

12

Crump pushed the pile of papers heavily away from him and began rubbing his weary eyes, moaning at the near-painful satisfaction it gave him and watching the familiar kaleidoscope of fireworks and scrambled egg whirling up inside his lids again. Then he remembered the row last night when he had been forced to agree with his wife that he should stop doing it before he made himself blind, in which case, she had said, they would have to live in poverty. Grudgingly he extracted his knuckles from the folds of dark skin in his eye sockets. But when he stopped rubbing he began to think about his interview with the Chief Constable earlier that day, and decided defiantly that he wouldn't actually mind being blind; at least he would be able to sit quietly in a corner all day, avoiding all responsibility for everything and having things done for him. The Chief had ranted and raved about 'political consequences', poured scorn on Crump's pet theory – just like bloody Slicer – made a few snide references to his recent clear-up record, and generally been unpleasant. So Crump began rubbing his eyes again, like a child returning to its thumb-sucking despite dire warning of poisoning or malformation, and continued to his heart's content. All unwanted thoughts were pushed out of his mind by some spectacular new visual effects he managed to stimulate – shooting-stars and flashes of lightning, no less.

He was slumped back in his chair five minutes later, panting lightly in rotund consummation, his arms hanging limply down like an ape's, when the telephone on the desk rang. The noise crashed in violently upon his new-found feelings of peace. For a moment only his eyes moved, snapping on to the black instrument with waves of hatred. Who the hell could that be? It was gone seven; he deserved a few moments to himself after the torture he had been through today. If it was the Chief Constable again, he thought, he would pretend to be someone else – hold his nose and imitate the adenoidal cleaning lady whose vacuum cleaner was already whirring several offices down the corridor. Heaving a gross, fatalistic sigh, he stretched his pudgy hand out to lift the receiver and bring it slowly up to his ear. The voice at the other end did not even wait for him to speak.

"Mr Crump? DCS Crump?" it asked hurriedly, and then, for no clear reason, giggled.

"Yes, Crump speaking," said Crump cautiously. Not a ruddy nutter, surely, he thought. He almost wanted it to be one, though, so he could bawl out the switchboard operator afterwards for putting a madman on the line.

"You don't know me, Mr Crump, but I'm a friend. Got your interests at 'eart, you might say." Again the giggle followed the words, which had a definite rustic, ooh-aar sort of accent to them. A memory stirred sluggishly in Crump's somnolent brain.

"Could you tell me your name, where you're calling from, and what it's about?" he said, forcing briskness into his voice. "Then we can have a sensible conversation."

He began fiddling in the drawer for a tape-recorder to connect to the phone, and wondered frantically if there was still someone in the next office he could get to call the switchboard and have the exchange trace the call.

"Oooh, I don't want to worry about that sort of thing," said the voice airily, with another unnerving giggle. "All that formality, and that. I just want a bit of a chat about the man in the little black car."

Little black car? What little black car? There was one little black car that he loathed and despised passionately, and which therefore sprang into his mind – Slicer's Alfasud. But that couldn't be it. What the hell was this lunatic on about? Crump's mind lurched about in a semi-panic. Good solid coppering, he tried to remind himself – cool, methodical. He reached over the desk, lifted another phone, dropped it noisily, cursed quietly, and dialled the switchboard.

"Do I understand that you wish to offer anonymous information on a subject of interest to the police?" he asked with a stilted slowness which made his northern accent a

parody of itself; then he covered the mouthpiece, and hissed
into the other phone.

"Get this call traced, will you? The one on 617."

"I 'eard that, Mr Crump," giggled the voice as he put the
other phone down. "It's not necessary, you know – this is
just a short private conversation, like, for your own benefit
as I said."

The rustic accent was still setting off little bells as Crump
pushed his weary mind into a higher gear. Where had he
heard this voice before? Or was the caller putting the voice
on, disguising himself? The giggle didn't quite go with the
voice. It came back again, slightly more harshly, as he
finally managed to push a cassette into the machine, pressed
the sucker on the side of the phone, and pushed down the
'record' button.

"Are you there, Mr Crump? This is important, you
know. Do you want my information or don't you?"

"Yes, yes, go ahead."

"You sound a bit flustered, Mr Crump. Getting a bit on
top of you, is it? As I say, the man with the little black car –
bit flashy, foreign sort of thing. Driven by fellahs like carpet
salesmen to prove they've got big cocks, eh?" The giggle.

Crump quite liked that one, and tried to file it away in his
mind for future use; he could try it on Slicer sometime. He
warmed a little to the caller.

"Go on, get on with it," he said encouragingly, more
relaxed now.

The giggle came again, high-pitched and hyaena–like.

"Certainly, Mr Crump. May the third this year, a Friday
night. Only two or three weeks ago, wasn't it? This chappie
parks in the lay-by just outside Upperdown School, and I
'appen to be passing by at the time. Now I recognise the
young lady at 'is side, see? Mr Rhage's au pair girl, I 'appen
to know, whose name in the *Daily Comet* today is given
as Elkie van 'Orning. I observe what passes between them,
Mr Crump, and it's obvious to me that she refuses" – the
giggle – "to bend to 'is desires, you might say. Saw it all,
Mr Crump, I did. Anyway, in the end, she fights 'im off and
gives 'im the slip. 'E gets left standing with a loaded pistol,
so to speak. But what I'm trying to say, Mr Crump, is, it's
a bit of a blow to 'is pride, see?"

There was a pause. Crump sucked at his cigarette; his mind raced blindly ahead to a spectacular success and the Chief again, this time with a smile of pleasure and congratulation on his face.

"So?"

"You're the detective, Mr Crump." The giggle. "Or so I'm led to believe."

"Don't you start getting clever . . ." The aggression welled cleanly and smoothly up its well-worn channels in Crump's simple system.

"Sorry, Mr Crump. 'Cept I should've thought it was obvious. You're looking for a motive for the explosion, which 'appens, according once again to my zoomaway *Daily Comet* of this morning, just outside the bedroom door of the young lady concerned. Nobody likes to get turned down, now, do they, let alone kicked in the goolies like that? Quite enough to make a man turn nasty, I shouldn't be surprised. Looked the nasty sort, too, this one, dark hair, little moustache. Sort of foreign, almost, like a wop."

A strange, heavy pulse had began building up in the back of Crump's neck: the black car, the dark man with the little moustache. Experience had taught him to be highly sceptical of the information of snouts and grasses, especially the anonymous ones, but the alternative theory sparked off by this giggling telephone caller had blown such simple rules out of his head and taken a sudden hold on his heart. Some large and unruly emotions, normally kept more or less trussed up and dumped in an obscure corner emitting no more than constricted squeaks and snarls, were suddenly running free, lumbering along with great strides, raised arms and open mouths, screaming in perfectly pitched unison.

"Yes!" they caterwauled, full-throated. "Slicer! Get him! Have him! Finish him off!"

"Very interesting," said his own voice, with enthusiasm held painfully down and scepticism artificially emphasised. "And did you take the precaution of noting the number of the vehicle?"

As he asked the question, Crump edged nearer to the window, at the risk of pulling the phone on to the floor, and peered down into the carpark. Yes, Slicer's car was still there, next to his own battered Morris Marina. No doubt the little blighter was still round in the Jailer's Arms exchanging drink and bullshit with other fatheads. RON 916 was still visible in the fading light – Slicer had been the butt of many jokes when he had bought his personalised number plate off an eighty-year-old widow's rusty Riley in Hastings.

"I'm afraid not, Mr Crump. I must 'ave been too upset at the sight of an innocent young girl being assaulted like that, and I wasn't going to stay around afterwards and let 'im 'ave a go at me, now, was I?" – the giggle – "And besides, it was quite a dark night. Anyway, I've told you all I know, Mr Crump, and I'd better be off before your mates start tracing this call. I don't know why you're botherin' with all that, really I don't. I'm just a local well-wisher, as I said, and I'd better be off. 'Bye for now, Mr Crump. Take care of your magnifying glass."

As soon as the final thin giggle had been cut short by the dialling tone, Crump feverishly banged the button to summon the switchboard. The voice of a bored, weary woman came on after twenty seconds of agitation.

"Did you trace that call?"

"Sorry, love," came the voice, and yawned. "The operator was just closing in on him when he hung up."

Crump banged down the phone with such violence that its protesting bell reverberated loudly round the empty, untidy office. He stood there staring at the wastepaper-basket, and then it dawned on him: the voice was that of Thickett, the giant groundsman who had dragged that runt of a reporter in the other night. The only difference was, though, that Thickett had never giggled like that. He had looked as though he had never giggled in his life. Another estate worker, perhaps, given to wandering around at night leering at the antics of courting couples in parked cars? You never knew with these bloody yokels – some of them were cavemen. Perhaps Thickett was disguising his voice, deliberately introducing an unusual mannerism because he felt ashamed at the possibility of being recognised? Wanted to give the information, but didn't want anyone to know he went round spying on people like that?

As he thought about it, however, Crump's mind persisted in slipping off the problematic subject of the caller's identity and on to the exciting sledge-run of the new theory. It fitted, oh! it fitted so well. And it was especially attractive now that the Melfort theory – under attack by the Chief as well – seemed to be slipping. True, it had been Slicer who had first undermined the Melfort approach by pointing out that the fingerprints would more likely indicate that he was giving the girl a poke rather than that he wanted to blow up the housemaster. But Slicer wasn't to know that his own little tussle with the girl – it must have been him, Crump now felt certain – had been observed and was going to be reported. Slicer had been assuming that no one could be aware of his own motive, given that the girl had evidently decided not to do anything about the assault. And perhaps he thought he was covering his tracks by suggesting it was the boy who was debauching the girl he had had a go at himself. And there was no doubt that Slicer, with his sordid underworld contacts, could have laid his hands on the necessary hardware.

Everything, yes, everything, fitted with the details which he knew and hated about his younger colleague. The smart little car with its loud noises, the casual pick-ups, the readiness to bully people when he didn't immediately get what he wanted. The description fitted, of the car and the man. And yes! Damn and blast him to hell! Slicer's behaviour when he'd come back from the hospital, from seeing his own victim – all that flippant, jolly overcompensation. Not quite his normal style, a bit exaggerated even for him. And then – Crump's chest was thudding with excitement as his mind raced on – then he had blushed and gone all quiet when the prints came through and he realised that she'd preferred to have a schoolboy poking her than him! That would probably incite the murderous little bastard to have another go.

Crump sat suddenly and heavily on a chair and uttered a little moan. He must slow down before he burst a blood-vessel, he thought. He was getting overexcited, assuming guilt where there might be a quite simple explanation – there was bound to be one, in fact. Surely not even a rotten toe-rag like Slicer would try to blow a young girl up just because she rejected him and kicked him in the balls? Perhaps the caller wasn't Thickett at all, nor one of the farm labourers who frequented the secluded, woody area of the lay-by, but some clever villain trying to set Slicer up to settle an old score, to make trouble? God knows there were enough of them with a motive – Slicer, the clever little sod, had fitted up enough of them over the last few years. And anyway, what was he doing, jumping to conclusions on the uncorroborated evidence of a single anonymous caller? He must slow down, take it step by step – good, methodical coppering, he told himself. He took several deep breaths to try to slow the hammering in his chest, but this only provoked a fit of harsh coughing. The voice on the phone, he told himself when the spasm had passed away, leaving him light and faint: he must listen to it again, think more carefully. He reached unsteadily for the tape-machine and pressed the 'rewind' button. As the tape whirred busily backwards, a cloud moved on in the evening sky and a warm beam of sunshine suddenly flooded through the window on to the desk. He pressed the 'play' button.

To his great shock, there was a brassy introduction of night-club stripper music at full volume, and then a sultry female voice with an upper-class accent said: "Darling, I've been wanting you to fuck me all evening. I want to get my lips round that big, pulsating cock of yours . . ."

Crump stared at the little machine in horror and incomprehension. The music faded in and out, and the voice returned, an irritable edge to its matter-of-fact sexiness.

"You're a bit slow, aren't you, darling? I'm getting awfully hot in this tight little dress – you couldn't undo it at the back, could you? That's right – move a bit closer, though. Ooooh! That's nice, darling, I can feel that bulge in your trousers rubbing against my arse. Aaaah! That's better . . ."

The door of the office opened and Detective Chief Inspector Walker, a meaty man carrying a black executive briefcase and a light raincoat slung over his shoulder, put his grinning face around it.

"Night, Mr Crump," he shouted against the background of the brassy music. Crump, his face aghast, jabbed at the machine repeatedly until his finger hit the 'stop' button.

"Didn't know you went in for that sort of home entertainment, old chap," grinned Walker. "Still, whatever you need to get it up. See you."

Crump stared in mortification at the closing door, unable to think of anything to say that would not sound hopelessly feeble. Then he furiously ejected the tape and studied it as it sat in his trembling fat hand. "Sounds to turn you on by," read the ill-printed label. "Mandy will take you home, warm you up, put you through your paces, and finish you off. Satisfaction guaranteed!"

He hurled it into the open drawer. Bloody Slicer again! He must have been using this desk and leaving his bits of filth lying about. That was probably his idea of a laugh, a bit of fun. Typical! Crump was in a frenzy of frustrated hatred, which he relieved by pacing up and down the room with a guilty twitch of titillation in his groin, kicking at furniture, which was fortunately lightweight, and spitting out an imaginative combination of expletives, all linked to that disgusting little animal Slicer. Not only had he gone beyond what was acceptable in abuse of a colleague's desk, he had also prevented an important piece of potential data, evidence even, being recorded.

Suddenly, Crump felt a peculiar event take place somewhere in the cavity of his chest, in an obscure spot deep below the copious ramparts of flesh which enclosed him. It was not a pain, nor an ache, nor a stab, but simply a feeling that something had moved, shifted its position quite significantly. He stopped in front of the window and leant forward with his hands on the sill to support himself in the sudden, calm weakness which invaded him. Sweat broke out on his forehead and he felt a drop course down through the short hair on his temple. There seemed to be a slight reddish tinge to his vision, which put everything out of focus except the black car down below in the carpark. Slicer. That lousy little rodent had pushed it too far now, he told himself with the single-minded, murderous determination of a brain-damaged heavyweight lurching out for the twelfth round. Slicer was going to get nailed good and proper, this time. He, Albert Crump, would see to it, one way or another.

13

Smithson A. J. drew noisily on his Pall Mall cigarette an[d]
the tip glowed fiercely in the pungent, dusty darkness.

"Amazing snout," he said reflectively, in what he fancie[d]
to be the tones of a gourmet admiring a vintage.

"Bloody good," came back the calmer voice of Nimm[o]
Senior, sitting invisible and irritatingly non-committal [a]
couple of feet away. "Where d'you say you got them?"

"Just got them posted in," said Smithson casually[,]
exhaling long and loudly, and grateful that the darknes[s]
hid his furious, painful blinking against the stinging smoke[.]
He held his voice rock-steady against the agony. "It's tha[t]
mate of mine at home, the one I told you about, goes to th[e]
local grammar school. Told him to make sure the parcel fe[lt]
like a book – usual trick."

"Why go to all that bother?" came the considered an[d]
rational reply after a moment's thought. "Why not just g[o]
and buy them yourself in town on a half-hol? I've seen thes[e]
at the kiosk near the station, they're not that hard to get."

"Oh, for God's sake, Nimmo, d'you have to be such [a]
wanker?" snapped Smithson. He recognised immediatel[y]
that Nimmo was right and that he would lose any argumen[t]
if they went into the rights and wrongs of the subject, and s[o]
he instinctively attacked on a broad front rather than pur[-]
suing the particular point.

Why, thought Smithson furiously, did Nimmo have t[o]
be so dry and matter-of-fact about everything? In his ow[n]
chaotic-romantic adolescent scheme of things, there wer[e]
many important reasons why he had decided to have th[e]
parcel sent in – the quasi-martyrdom he could enjoy b[y]
prompting his grammar-school friend at home to believ[e]
that his incarceration at Upperdown was more complet[e]
than it actually was; the excitement of conspiracy; th[e]

pleasurable anticipation of a package in the post, lying there on the table for him after breakfast, and the heightened importance he expected in the eyes of his companions-in-smoking from the telling of the anecdote of the cigarettes' provenance. How demanding he was (they would think) about the quality of his cigarettes – he had the best in the world posted boldly in to him. In fact, they tasted the same and made him feel as sick as all other cigarettes. But he wanted to believe it was like Buckingham Palace having strawberries flown in from Morocco in mid-winter. And so on. If he tried to explain all this to Nimmo, he would deliberately refuse to understand, and would only go on and on about how he could buy them himself a short bike ride away on a Wednesday afternoon.

His annoyance with Nimmo was exacerbated by the effort of suppressing an intense desire to cough; and this might detract from the effect of the wounding barb of 'wanker' which he had just hurled. Being a 'wanker' was a cardinal fault among boys of their age, in the same way that being a 'wet' was the worst sin among squits and being 'boring' was the ultimate crime in the most senior generation of boys. The term 'wanker' was not necessarily a literal one, but a general and conveniently imprecise one, although the connotation of fruitless and self-defeating behaviour was always vaguely there. Smithson commonly used it as an accusation of failing to go along with one of the latest mid-teen fashion crazes and fads – wearing your tie slightly pulled down and off-centre, for example, spitting casually on to the grass, or pretending that you had extensive sexual experience.

"I don't see why I'm a wanker just because I talk sense," came Nimmo's methodical, pedantic voice after the usual pause for consideration. He would always stubbornly and doggedly refuse to suspend his disbelief.

Smithson felt even crosser, and his back was prickling with sweat. It was extremely hot down here in the confined underground tunnel which carried the pipes and cables from one building of Upperdown to another. It was a long subterranean passageway, high and wide enough for two people to stroll comfortably along, lit by the occasional dim bulb and shaft of pale light from glass gratings. The big

cupboard where they sat on piles of old tent-ropes wa
airless and stifling, separated from the main tunnel by
heavy wooden door. It had always puzzled Smithson tha
Nimmo, with his highly sensible outlook on life, eve
bothered to come on such risky expeditions whose actua
rewards were rather obscure. He lost control of his anger.

"If all you want to do is talk sense, Nimmo, why don'
you bugger off and join the bloody debating society wher
you stick your finger up your arse and sound off? Why don'
you go and bore the pants off yourself in Bernard Briggs'
sitting room on a Saturday night, eh? Getting served frill
sandwiches by his ugly old wife? I don't understand wh
you bother to come on things like this; it's not very *sensible*
is it, after all, and if we get caught you're really in the shit
Why don't you go and talk about railway timetables wit
that moron Deuchar?"

These were questions that the other boy, in fact, ha
asked himself and come up with no satisfactory answer.
was probably something to do with a deep adolescent nee
to break rules, a need which moved even in the cool bloo
of Nimmo Senior; a sociologist would have noted that, a
the restrictions and rules at the school had been graduall
relaxed over the previous decade, certain types of boy
always discovered new offences to commit, some of them
so beyond the pale that even the liberal regime of post
'sixties Upperdown could not accommodate them. On
senior had begun a protection racket where juniors paid i
cash or kind to avoid persecution, a crime only discovere
when the matron found over seventy fifty-pence pieces i
socks in the boy's locker. Another, whose father wa
extremely rich, made off with new sports equipment an
sold it to a habitual petty criminal who dealt in stolen good
in a back street of the town. A third, blind drunk, ha
crashed the headmaster's car into a tree on Great Sward a
3 a.m. All these episodes, of course, had been carefully kep
from public or parental knowledge.

Nimmo's continuing silence was not, however, becaus
of his failure to understand the contradictions inherent i
his own Weltanschauung. It was because he had hear
something. He leant forward soundlessly and groped fo
Smithson's arm. As Smithson began to shake off the han

in incipient terror that his companion was going to try to start 'queering about', Nimmo whispered urgently.

"Sssh, you clod, there's footsteps outside. Put your snout out."

Smithson realised it was true. A spurt of horror-laced adrenalin ran through his blood. While he had been banging on so loudly and getting so steamed up, the footfalls must have been gradually drawing closer. In sudden fear and despair, he shrank back into the smells of canvas and dust in the corner of the cupboard: they had been caught by Killer on the day he had been blown up, and now they were going to get caught again on the day he came back from the hospital. Fate was against them.

The approaching steps outside were stealthy, but casual. It was as if the walker was making as little noise as possible, wearing lightweight shoes and placing them carefully, and yet at the same time was used to wandering along these underground passages, confident of his direction, of not bumping his head on projections or tripping on articles lying about the floor. A master? A prefect? They were among the few who were allowed down here and might know their way around so casually. There was no pause in the rhythm as they approached, and the two boys, their cigarettes ground out underfoot and the breath held high in their pounding chests, prayed that he would saunter on past.

The steps became louder, passed outside the door, and had begun to recede again when they suddenly stopped. A little moan of disappointment escaped from Smithson. "Bugger," he whispered to himself. After a moment of silence, the steps came slowly back and halted outside the door. There then came the sound of someone sniggering gently under his breath, as if at some private joke, and making exaggerated sniffing sounds. Oh, come on, Nimmo thought despairingly: get it over with. Why prolong the agony?

Slowly the door opened and in the glimmer of light which played down the tunnel from a dim bulb many yards away, they saw a large, pale and smiling face looking in on them. The face wore round glasses which glinted, and was set on a thick, short body dressed in what looked like dark overalls. As they sat there immobile in fear, confronting this haunting, unrecognised stranger, the two boys could say nothing. The man said nothing either, and after a second or two, nodding and almost giggling under his breath, he slowly closed the door on them again. The light disappeared and the careful, sauntering footfalls slowly disappeared into the distance with the slight, rhythmic squeak of rubber on concrete.

After half a minute's panting, petrified silence, Nimmo switched on the tiny pocket torch he used for reading under the blankets in the dorm. Its light illuminated both their faces from below, turning them into grotesque, gross-nostrilled, eyeless masks as they stared at each other.

"Christ," Smithson's voice trembled untypically. "Who the hell was *that*?"

14

It was Thursday, two days after the explosion. The phone rang even before Crump had finished peeling off his jacket to face what he knew would be another day of purgatory. Please, God, whimpered a little boy inside him, don't let it be the Chief. Please don't let MPs, or old boys of the school, or the Prime Minister, have telephoned him to complain. I'm a sick man, a tired man, an angry man, and I can't take any more just now. Please, God, I'll stop hating my wife and go to church every week, just as long as it's not the Chief.

He lifted the phone.

"Crump," he half-whispered, hoarsely.

"Major Bland."

It was not the Chief. Crump immediately forgot his promise to God and his spirits tilted slightly upwards. It sounded like this was more forensic coming through. Excellent – and very quick work. They often took weeks.

"Ah, morning, Major Bland. Got something for us, have you?"

Bland's voice – formal, flat and unexpressive as usual – gave nothing away.

"Well?" asked Crump, with rising impatience. "Anything of interest?"

"I believe you will find it contributes to your investigation, Mr Crump. If you would care to come over here we can explain it to you fully."

"Can't you tell me over the phone?" asked Crump grumpily.

"No," came the impassive and final answer.

"All right," Crump sighed. "I'll be over in half an hour."

Crump walked out to his car through the cool, pale sunlight of another fine morning, his step lightened by hope. Perhaps they had had the breakthrough that would solve it – with a final piece of solid but astute detective work by himself, of course, to put the lid on it and attract the ultimate credit. He greeted two colleagues with warmth, and they turned and squinted after him suspiciously: it wasn't like Crump to be so full of the milk of human kindness.

When he reached the laboratory, Major Bland's expression was as flat and non-committal as his voice. The contours of his face never moved, leading others to suspect that it was covered not with flesh but with some look-alike synthetic material, and his everyday conversation was the same dull monotone he used in the witness box. Crump had seen his particular brand of immovable dumb insolence incite cross-examining barristers to expressions and suggestions unbecoming of the legal profession: all had bounced harmlessly off Bland's nerveless carapace. He had receding sandy hair, a small moustache surviving from his days in the Royal Army Ordnance Corps, and he always wore a white shirt, his blue-and-red regimental tie, and a sports jacket of nondescript grey-green tweed. His face was as long as a door and the colour of stone. If it wasn't for the movement of his eyes, people might wonder if he was actually alive. The hard green eyes now bored into Crump.

"Ah, take a pew, Mr Crump," said Bland, whose only indulgence was a penchant for religious metaphors.

"What have you got then?" asked Crump rather rudely, staying on his feet. He had no time for the formalities. The major's eyebrows lifted the tiniest fraction – or did they?

Bland settled back into the hard chair behind his metal desk and stared silently at Crump for a moment, as if the detective was a piece of material evidence about to be put under a microscope, tested with chemicals, dissected with scalpels and generally pulled to pieces by his team of white-coated scientists. The stare continued as he began speaking in his flat, automatic tones.

"We sifted the debris collected from the scene of the explosion and attempted to assemble any remnants of the device itself. There appears to be very little trace of the actual explosive material, indicating that it was of high quality and high grade. However, we did find several fragments of a smooth white ceramic material which aroused our interest. We searched the debris a second time and found further fragments."

"Yes?"

Crump's heart had given another of those nasty little bounces and he sat down, trying to keep calm, to discipline his impatience. This gimlet-eyed robot was worse than the bloody headmaster at getting to the point.

"Eventually we hypothesised that the detonator had been triggered by a timing device, and that this device was a watch. The fragments of white ceramic material, we deduced, were quite possibly from the watch face. This, however, we considered to be highly unusual."

"Unusual? Why?"

Bland's eyes sparked fire for a tiny instant.

"When the kind of vermin who make such unholy instruments of murder, Mr Crump, use a timing device, it is usually a cheap watch purchased for the purpose, often with a face made from little more than cardboard. Not much to sacrifice on the altar of the cause, so to speak. But from what we can make out, this was an expensive watch, possibly many years old or possibly with an imitation antique face, made from a devilishly hard ceramic material. We also found one of two small traces of gold which probably came from the casing."

Crump sighed and stared out of the window, feeling the Chief stealing up on his thoughts again. Fat lot of help that was. He sighed and turned back to Bland; he had not moved a muscle.

"So where does that get us?" asked Crump.

"I have not yet finished, Mr Crump," came the flat reply. "The fact which I regard as particularly interesting is that we were able to assemble enough of the face to make a tentative hypothesis as to four of the letters inscribed on it. One of them is a capital letter, the others lower-case, all of them in black and in antique style."

Crump was now sitting bolt upright, suddenly transformed from a weary, overburdened fat man to an alert sleuth.

"Really?" he said tightly, eyes even thinner than their normal fleshed-in obscurity. "And what are they?"

"The capital letter is, we believe, Z, and the lower-case

letters, which we believe were next to each other on th[e] face, are d-a-m. We also believe we have identified anothe[r] letter which could have been on another part of the face, or equally, adjacent to the others – an upper-case A, also blac[k] and in . . ."

"Yes, yes, I know, antique style," Crump cut in testily[.] "Come on, Major Bland, I haven't got all day. Anythin[g] else?"

"No, Mr Crump, not in your terms. We are trained to b[e] thorough in this department."

"Yes, yes, not like us CID men, all blind guesses and daf[t] ideas. Is all this on paper yet?"

"Yes, Mr Crump. A colleague and I stayed up until a[n] ungodly hour late last night to prepare a report. Only a[n] interim report, you appreciate, so you can't take it entirel[y] as gospel. This was a stroke of divine luck, you know, an[d] there's a lot more material to be examined. We'll let yo[u] know if anything more comes out of it."

Bland unlocked a drawer and took out a folder which h[e] handed over the desk with a mild trace of doglike reproac[h] in his eyes. He got no dog biscuit, however, from Crump who snatched the folder and headed for the door with [a] brusque "thank you" tossed over his shoulder. Bland's eye[s] hardened again as he sat staring for a while after the lumpis[h] policeman, toying secretly in his icy mind with the anythin[g] but Godly reflection that he had found an ideal contemporar[y] candidate for the nastiest little device he had come acros[s] in all his professional experience – the efficient little bom[b] strapped round a bound prisoner's midriff by the Algeria[n] nationalists, and timed to go off in a couple of hours.

15

Robbie MacPherson slammed down the receiver with a reptilian grin.

"Cracked it!" he announced triumphantly to the somnolent after-lunch newsroom which was basking in beer fumes amid the grubby desks and overflowing waste-bins. A man at the opposite desk with a neck like a pillar raised his head threateningly from the previous weekend's *News of the World*; he had a small, livid scar on his cheek.

"Knock it off, Robbie," he growled. "I've still got a hangover from last night. Keep it quiet."

"Fuck you, Jimmy!" responded MacPherson instinctively, hackles rising, terrier-like. "Some of us here are working on *real* stories, real scoops, not fart-arsing around rewriting last Sunday's fliers. It's about time you got off that fat arse of yours, Trevor."

Trevor's bloodshot eyes rested with deceptive mildness on MacPherson as he debated with himself whether to do exactly what his diminutive colleague suggested, come round the desk, and give him a good scragging. It had happened before, after all. But MacPherson's aggressiveness was an old story, and Trevor's eyes sank back into tales of pimps and princesses, villains and whores.

"Shut it, Robbie, or I'll ram your typewriter up your bracket," he said with a finality which even MacPherson, beyond throwing up a V-sign and curling a lip, decided to respect. MacPherson had plenty on his mind, anyway, and strutted off excitedly across the scuffed lino to tell the news editor of the latest developments.

The news editor, a balding Australian whose thin white shirt was stretched tightly over the various bags and sags of flesh on his chest, was lounging in his tattered chair dictating the news list to a secretary as MacPherson came and perched on the desk next to him, twitching like an excited bird. It was evident that the news editor was not in the best of tempers about the contents of the list, which he would have to present to the editor when he got back from the Savoy in half an hour's time. It was all heavy stuff today – nothing light, no colour – and the editor liked a few funnies after lunch at the Savoy.

"Er . . . mother of two in shotgun hostage drama," he drawled grumpily at the secretary, who tapped obediently at her typewriter. "Er . . . 'I thought I was going to die,' says Brenda, thirty-eight . . . Now, what the hell else have we got . . . Er . . . Para in death plunge horror . . . Er . . . Chute fails to open, says Army . . . What is it, Robbie, can't you see I'm busy?"

MacPherson grinned sycophantically and slid closer along the desk.

"You'll like this one, Dave," he promised, his voice oily and confidential now. "Great tale. I've cracked this Upper-down story. I'm going to blow it apart, I tell you. I got their cricket fixture list from the sports desk, and contacted the firm which . . ."

As he was speaking the news editor had been briskly rolling up a government press release into a tight rod of paper which he now used to interrupt MacPherson by poking him imperiously on the chest.

"Now look here, mate," he said. "This is something of a no–no now, you know what I mean? A hot number. I'm not sure I want to know what tricks you're getting up to. Sir Bruce doesn't like getting these letters of complaint from toffee-nosed Pommie schoolteachers. It's a weakness of his, and you know very well I got a memo telling us to go easy. Now, I'm not sure I want to take this any further . . ."

"Fuck me, Jimmy, are you a newspaperman or a mouse?" blurted MacPherson, a little gob of excited spittle flying from his lip and landing on the black-stockinged knee of the secretary, who demurely brushed it off, looking away. "I've got one of the best exposés of the year lined up, and you start wittering on like an old woman about fucking superannuated schoolmasters. That guy will be *finished* when I've sorted him out, I tell you. Come on, Dave, give us a break, eh?"

The news editor stared at MacPherson for a few seconds, like a gang boss at one of his mobsters, tapping the rolled-up paper on his sharp slip-on shoe to aid his thought.

"OK, Robbie," he said eventually, jabbing the paper again to emphasise his points. "Go ahead, but I don't want to know all the gory details, right? If you get it, you get it, and if you don't, you don't. You're on your own on this one, mate, and if the shit hits the fan I don't know anything about it. No back-up. Right?"

He turned dismissively back to his dictation. "Labour in new split row," he began. MacPherson sat for a few seconds longer, breathing heavily and staring in bright-eyed resentment at his boss's meaty form. Then he slid off the desk and prowled back to his own part of the room.

"Fucking kangaroo bureaucrat," he spat under his breath. "You'll fuckin' take notice by the time I've finished with you, Jimmy."

16

Crump swigged the last of his tea, gave a semi-belch of tired satisfaction, loosened his belt to match his pulled-down tie, sat down in his swivel chair and put his feet up on the desk. He looked out unseeingly at the pale, light clouds drifting over the sky, and reviewed developments in his mind: not a bad day, not a bad day at all. The Chief somehow stole into the edge of his reflections and presided over them, but this time looking more like a smiling and benevolent Buddha than the vengeful totem of the last couple of days. For the first time, today, he felt he was on top of this investigation. He could definitely see a result, as they insisted on calling it in these southern parts: his picture in the papers, a few words from the judge, promotion, decoration – that sort of thing.

He was especially pleased with his intuition and powers of deduction today – his good, old-fashioned coppering skills, as he liked to call them. It was obvious to him the watch used for the timing device had been made in Amsterdam and he'd set one detective on trying to work out the actual manufacturer and get to talk to them. So, who came from Amsterdam and was a party to the present case? The city of Rembrandt and vice, as Crump liked to think of it – he'd been there ten years before on an inspectors' outing from Grimsby and spent half an hour in the museum and the rest of the weekend in exhausting and unusual forms of debauchery. A quick phone call to the housemaster, Rhage, had confirmed that, yes, Miss van Horning's home town was indeed Amsterdam itself. He would have to wait until the following day to interview her, however – medical advice, apparently. No matter – there was still progress to be made in the meantime.

Crump sighed and settled further back in his chair to

confirm his self-satisfaction. He saw himself as moving forward on three fronts. There was still Melfort – he had the motive against Rhage, he'd left the prints, he could still be the culprit, and Crump was reluctant to abandon his original hunch too easily. Granted, Melfort wouldn't have wanted to blow up his own girlfriend – assuming, for the moment, that Slicer was right and he *was* getting his leg over – but there could have been a mistake; maybe she should have been out of her room at the time of the explosion. And even if Melfort hadn't done it, he was still a cocky little bugger who needed taking down a peg and deserved to sweat it out for a bit.

Secondly, of course, there was Slicer. Crump lit another cigarette, and his eyes narrowed vindictively: yes, Slicer. He was a strong, perhaps the currently preferred, candidate. Crump badly wanted to see him hanging up by his horrible, overactive, adulterous little testicles. Thinking back to the anonymous call, Crump felt increasingly certain that the voice had mentioned the dark man picking items from the lay-by which could easily have included the watch, perhaps detached from the girl's wrist in the violent sexual struggle. And the fact that there was no tape-recording to check this out gave him just another grudge against Slicer. Crump felt sentimentally sorry for Slicer's young wife Brenda, forgetting all the times he had abused and deceived his own wife in deed as well as in thought. But he fervently hoped Slicer's come-uppance was in the making.

And thirdly, there was the Voice. It followed that if Slicer could have picked up the watch, so also could this other unidentified witness. Thickett, or one of the estate workers, could conceivably have a grudge against Rhage, or indeed against the tantalisingly sexy young Elkie. They might have taken against her for allowing herself to be fondled in cars – there was no accounting for the bizarre puritanism which popped up amongst all the incest and sheep-shagging of country life, as he'd discovered in his first policing job in a partly rural area of Yorkshire. And the phone call, according to this theory, would be a cunning attempt to divert him on to Slicer's scent.

This was why he'd given Slicer, earlier that day, the tiresome task of going round all the estate staff interviewing

them on a general trawl, to see if he could get a lead, an ide
a confession even. Deliberately, though, he'd sent Slicer o
without telling him of the call and its contents, or of th
forensic news about the watch. That would have showe
too much of his hand to his hated colleague. And wh
knows, thought Crump dreamily, one of the yokels mig
even take offence and push a pitchfork into Slicer's guts.
would do the trick perfectly, and the new murder invest
gation thus created would be gratifyingly simple.

The telephone crashed violently into his reverie, in whic
he kept his three balls moving simultaneously, blurrin
through the air, like a skilled juggler. He waited a secon
before lifting the receiver. With any luck it would be th
giggling informant again. This time he had a new blank ta
in the recorder in the drawer by his right hand.

"Wotcha, guv'nor."

Crump grimaced as if a wet flannel had been thrust cold
and unpleasantly against his ear. Slicer was sounding horribl
uppity. He rummaged round in his mind for a few choi
put-downs, and remembered the jibe about the carpet sale
man's penis extension.

"Yes, Mr Slicer?" The icy weariness was consummate.

"Thought I'd knock off for the night, guv'nor, if that's a
right with you."

"Being a policeman is a twenty-four-hour job when there
something important on, you know that, Mr Slicer. Wh
have you done today, exactly?"

"Got the staff list from the school, guv, working my wa
through it. Dead boring. Half these old codgers are dea
blind or daft, and the younger ones are downright weird
bunch of real headbangers. One of the buggers starte
following me round – stuck to me all day like shit to
blanket, kept popping up behind hedges and grinning
me like the village idiot. Threatened to arrest him, but h
wasn't impressed. Didn't seem to know what it meant."

Crump smiled. It was gratifying to know that Slicer wa
having such an unpleasant time. Long may it continue.

"I see," he said. "I expect he took a fancy to you becaus
you look like a bloody gigolo. And now, I suppose, yo
propose to climb into that carpet salesman's penis extensio
of yours and retire to the Dog and Arsehole for a few pin

102

on the way home. Very well. I can't be responsible for your lack of dedication, I suppose, Mr Slicer. But before you swan off, do you mind telling me if you actually achieved anything today, if it's not too much trouble?"

"What was that about the carpet salesman? We've got a bad line here."

"Never you mind, Mr Slicer. Any news on the investigation?"

"Not so much as a cough, splutter or fart, guv. They all grin and shake their heads and pretend they don't even know what you're talking about."

"And what about Thickett?"

"He's a deep bugger, that one. I got the feeling he'd pick me up and snap me over his knee if I stepped out of line – no sense of humour, at all, I'm afraid. Didn't give away a dicky-bird. Didn't like being asked questions, either – went red in the face and carried on about how he'd helped the investigation by catching some reporter sneaking around, said was this his reward, having coppers coming round asking him personal questions. I scarpered soon as I could."

"Hm. All right, Mr Slicer. You slide off to your disgusting nocturnal pleasures. Report here first thing tomorrow."

Crump pursed his little purple lips in renewed thought as he replaced the receiver with unusual slowness and gentleness. When it was lying in its cradle, he continued to stare at it, an intense light spreading in his small eyes. His intuition was at work again, stirring at gut level. Gradually, the lips relaxed and took on a slight, wry grin. He sat there immobile for fully five minutes, the evening shadows deepening slightly in the unlit office. Then, slowly, he pulled a leaf from his desk, ran his finger down a paper list that was taped to it, and began mouthing a number silently, like a child unfamiliar with figures. He lifted the receiver again and dialled.

"Hello?"

"Mrs Slicer? Evening, it's DCS Crump here – your husband's boss. Sorry to bother you – is he there?"

"I'm afraid not, Mr Crump." The voice was timorous, beaten. "In fact, he rang about two minutes ago to say he'd be working very late on the explosion case and might not be back until after eleven. Isn't he with you?"

"No, we've been out of touch all afternoon, working in different places. He should have rung me. I just assumed he'd be home by now – shows how wrong you can be when you've got a conscientious fellow like your Ron on the strength."

Crump entertained himself cruelly with a few more sly pleasantries, all the more amusing to him for their insincerity and the fact that Brenda Slicer was unaware of his irony. When he put the phone down, the hunches were running fast and furious through his skull, and the smooth, fat features took on a hard and determined sheen. He took his feet off the desk, stood up, tightened his belt, pushed his tie up to his chin, patted himself reassuringly here and there, and reached for his raincoat. He was sure he was on to something; that bastard Slicer was about to be nailed to the floor, one foot at a time.

* * * * * *

The summer dusk was falling softly around Upperdown as the dark car stopped in the lay-by under the big-leaved chestnut trees, and its sidelights were silently switched off. The languorous sounds and smells of the past day still lingered in the warm air, and the swelling darkness seemed to pass the lush green of the countryside into the mysterious possession of nature. The world seemed now to belong to the invisible whirring insects, the sudden passionate bursts of birdsong, the lowing and trampling of cattle being driven home to the school farm, the unknown rustlings and ploppings around the edge of the nearby lake. There was the sweet, lazy scent of mown hay.

The trance of this rustic quietness did not extend into the heart of Ron Slicer, however, as he sat in his imitation velvet driver's seat waiting for darkness to be complete. He fiddled again with the camera on the passenger seat beside him, making obsessively sure it was properly set up, the flash unit tightly connected, the film wound on. He had casually checked during the course of the day exactly where the Rhage family were now staying after their homecoming from hospital. He had gone over the geography repeatedly on the little map he had made, and checked his notes about the school's evening routine of bedtimes and lights-out. Anxiety and glee vied for control of his stomach, and the excitement was building up in his veins: he was sure, deeply sure, that his instinct was correct and tonight would be the night. His familiarity with a certain area of human nature told him they would not be able to wait.

A quarter of a mile away, in the senior dormitory of Paine House, something stirred. Such nocturnal rustlings of bed-clothes, discreet changes of position, and carefully disguised secret movements were not unusual; they were part of the perennial life of schools such as Upperdown. Boys, lying studiously in the attitudes of sleep, but with eyes staring widely at the high, dark ceiling, were at such moments conducting their first lonely experiments with sex – without the complementary presence of a female body and within a few feet of suspicious contemporaries in a dormitory the size of a football pitch. Those who were doing it pretended they weren't; and those who weren't doing it tried to escape guilt about their own past episodes by plotting to catch others doing it.

"Don't wank so hard, Davies, you'll break your pyjamas." Smithson A. J. broke the unquiet silence of that first hour after lights-out. It was an old joke, but one which unfailingly struck a chord. A little wave of uneasy sniggers broke around the dormitory.

"Fuck off, Smithson," replied Davies. His attempts to make his voice sound drowsy, as if he had been rudely dragged back from the edge of sleep, failed to banish a tone of nervous wakefulness. "Just 'cos you're always pulling away doesn't mean everyone else is."

Charles Melfort, who was lying fully clothed except for his shoes in his bed at the top end of the dormitory, heaved a sigh of impatience and boredom. He really did consider himself a cut above all this rather low and juvenile nonsense. He, after all, had graduated into a different world, the world of the Real Thing, at the end of the previous term, when the ravishing Elkie had taken the awkward and painful little bud of his virginity into her experienced care and coaxed it with her uninhibited little body into a raw, red flower of constant sexual excitement. Melfort was now addicted to the powerful opiates of eroticism – the sighing, sucking whispering sounds, the electrifying female smells and secrets, the abandoned jerking and undulating of naked limbs. These things had taken over his mind and body like an invading army, intruding upon and interfering with all his deeds and thoughts. His arrogant sense of superiority, growing with age, was reinforced by this relationship with Elkie; although his passion for her threatened to undermine his languid pose in life, the most significant effect was that he felt chosen, still further set apart from his contemporaries and other mortals. She, after all, had been the object of everyone's lust ever since her arrival at the beginning of the school year, and had even rejected the advances of masters, including Bernard Briggs, it was believed; she had chosen him instead from among 500 other males. And now, as he lay and followed with his eyes the final traces of shadow cast on the ceiling by the ebbing of the long daylight, he was in the throes of an immediate hunger, to see her, now that she was back from hospital, to reassure himself that her blonde limbs were whole and undamaged and still at his service. He glanced at his watch: still only half past ten.

Down at the other end of the dormitory, the stirring had grown suddenly into a little gust of activity. Smithson, on edge and unusually vindictive because of the interview with Killer due the following morning, had taken extreme offence at Davies's reply and reacted with violence. He had sprung out of bed and pushed the other boy's mattress off the wooden boards of the bed-frame, and on to the floor Davies, lying on his face frantically trying to tie up his pyjama cord while ensnared in a tangle of bedclothes, cursed Smithson with wild and fluid abandon. Smithson, incensed returned to the scene and kicked at the writhing heap with his bare feet. A serious fight was threatened, until one of the more senior boys imposed his authority and threatened Smithson with Nogge.

"Can't you leave a chap to wank in peace, Smithson?' asked the senior ironically, as Davies shuffled round remaking his bed and uttering incoherent little snuffling sounds of humiliation and distress.

Console yourself, Davies, with the thought that, although things are bad now, they used to be a good deal worse

Consider the case of the boy in the not-too-distant past, when two call-girls were putting the post-war years – and government ministers – to bed, and exposing a new era; a time when Carnaby Street was beginning to be talked about, but not yet, quite, at Upperdown: the time, again, of the seminal and turbulent 'sixties. He had been put through an altogether harder discipline. He had fought his impulses harder than most, that serious, round-faced boy who wanted so much to learn the rules and play the game. He had inwardly digested *Scouting for Boys* well before coming to Upperdown, and prayed to God to quell the unpredictable stirrings of his newly tumescent penis. And on only the second occasion when he had given way to temptation, when he had waited until he was certain that the rest of the dormitory was soundly asleep before quietly lowering his pyjamas to his ankles, he had been caught. With a pagan whooping and jeering the Wank Brigade, a self-appointed ad hoc group of sadistic seniors, had burst into the junior dormitory, whipped the bedclothes off him, and pinioned him there, half-naked and spreadeagled like a laboratory frog, while the other occupants of the dormitory were required to file past and snigger at their colleague's humiliation, silently thanking their guardian angels that they were not in his sobbing, struggling position this time. For months afterwards, the round-faced boy felt that even the matron seemed to smirk with secret knowledge whenever she laid eyes upon him. Console yourself, Davies, that times have at least moved on a little.

Crump parted the bushes again and stared through at the small black car; Slicer was still there, sitting immobile as he had done for half an hour. It was quite dark now, with a chill in the air and some sinister little splashes and cries coming from the lake a few yards away. Crump felt vulnerable and ridiculous, lurking here on his knees in this roadside copse: how would he explain it to the Chief, still looming large in his thoughts at the moment, like the fierce tribal totem pole once again. He was also slightly frightened, hungry, worried about his health, beginning to feel cold, and in aching need of a crap. It had occurred to him that he could easily relieve himself here, in this dark and secluded

spot, but he had become convinced in this moist-smellin[g]
rustling gloom that as soon as he lowered his trousers [he]
would either be shockingly assaulted from underneath [by]
some feral creature of the undergrowth, or would sudden[ly]
find Slicer standing over him laughing – or doing wh[at]
passed for laughter in that odious reptile – and making t[he]
usual unfunny jokes.

All this contributed to an almost complete loss of co[n]
fidence in the enterprise. It had already begun to ebb in t[he]
journey over here in the car, when the heat of the fi[rst]
impulse had passed away and his speed of driving slow[ly]
decreased, and now he could no longer give himself a cle[ar]
and convincing answer to the only question which ca[me]
into his mind at the moment – why the hell was he here? H[e]
tried to forget his burning sphincter, his aching legs and h[is]
growling stomach, and to force his blurring thoughts aw[ay]
from another rehearsal of his increasingly tangled positi[on]
in this case. It was his duty to follow the promptings of h[is]
professional instincts, he told himself, to pursue his natur[al]
flair for detection – especially if, in doing so, he could n[ab]
the little swine, Slicer, in the very act. Oh, yes!

But as he sank for temporary relief in this warm a[nd]
reassuring fantasy of Slicer with his trousers down at t[he]
very least, another cold little voice would rise in Crump['s]
mind. A member of the police force, whatever his nas[ty]
foibles, would hardly get involved in such blatant crimin[al]
acts in the first place, let alone return to the scene of t[he]
crime so soon. And a man who took such a casual attitu[de]
towards women would hardly be moved to such extrem[es]
as explosives exploits in order to have his revenge on o[ne]
who humiliated him. So – well, perhaps the most like[ly]
explanation was a professional one, that Slicer was w[ay]
ahead of him, and had himself returned to follow up som[e]
brilliant hunch arising from the fingerprint evidence whi[ch]
would solve the crime at a stroke, eclipsing his superi[or]
officer for ever. Perhaps he, Crump, was inadvertent[ly]
about to put his foot in Slicer's planned coup, attracting st[ill]
more execration on his head. The totem glowered abo[ve]
him again. He tried desperately to think in new directions[:]
who had really made that phone call, for example? But t[he]
anxious speculation fogged and slipped in his mind and [he]

could make no progress. He rubbed his face despairingly, and was about to start on his eyes when the unmistakable click of a car door being discreetly closed brought him instantly back to a heart-fluttering state of nervous alertness. He parted the bushes; yes, Slicer was moving off, carrying some sort of shoulder-bag. Crump took a deep breath and stood up, clouting his head on a low branch and half-uttering a cry of pain and frustration. His knees were numb and weak, and he limped off heavily after his brisker colleague.

He kept Slicer's dark, sleekly moving figure in view, forty yards ahead of him, until they reached the little copse near the back of Paine House where Smithson A. J. and Nimmo Senior had paused before making their unsuccessful dash for home on the morning of the explosion. There was an ideal amount of discreet light from a low, thin moon, and Crump began to forget the pain of his bashed cranium and bulging bowels and to feel like a boy scout again. He moved from one piece of cover to the other, taking elaborate care not to step on pieces of twig and branch, until, entering the edge of the copse with his attention on the ground, he badly startled himself by almost colliding with a large tree, stopping with his nose only a sudden inch away from the black, gnarled bark.

All he had to do for a moment was stand quietly, look and listen, he told himself, panting nervously. He noticed how close they were to Paine House, standing in darkness twenty yards away beyond the dark, flat asphalt. Then, just as his mind began to slip once more into confused and inconclusive speculation, things suddenly began to move. A figure had silently appeared by the back door of the house and was standing there immobile, as if checking that the coast was clear. It wore dark clothes, with a glint of white shirt between the lapels of a jacket or blazer, and as it moved stealthily away, across the back of Rhage's now-deserted house, Crump recognised it – the young whippersnapper! Charles Melfort! His excitement rose so high that he felt faint and put one hand out to the harsh, cold tree-trunk to steady himself, the other to his thumping heart. He shut his eyes for a moment.

When he opened them again the sidling figure had disappeared round the side of the Rhages's deathly quiet house.

Crump began to panic, thinking he'd lost track of both of them; but almost immediately, another figure detached itself from the shadow of the copse twenty yards away from him, and moved off to follow the first. The bag of equipment was now swinging low from Slicer's hand. When he had also disappeared from view, Crump followed, lurching slightly, the noise of his heart beating loudly in his ears, his tobacco–damaged breathing rasping loudly through his throat.

Round to the front of the house they went, along the shadow of the beech hedge, Lust, Envy and Wrath pursuing each other stealthily, bound together by a chain of passions across the main avenue in a quick, shuffling dash to a large lime tree, and from there via the cover of the music school hedge to Century Copse, a collection of huge beech and sycamore trees standing grandly on a little knoll overlooking the palely moonlit expanse of Great Sward. The schoolboy disappeared into the copse; the sleek young detective crouched at the end of the hedge, waiting; and the older wheezing policeman waited at the other end of the same hedge: Crump was certain now that he would be discovered but felt so deeply and hopelessly involved that he had no choice but to continue, to plunge on with the whole desperate business.

Melfort moved from the copse towards Pavilion House whose main windows and balconies also looked out over the moon–blanched cricket fields. Slicer now stepped from the hedge into the copse; Crump, trotting forward in painful, lumbering crouch, took his place at the far end of the hedge. Suddenly he realised – this must be the house where Rhage and his family were staying after coming out of hospital, the house the head had mentioned to him. He felt that a spring had been wound up so tightly in his chest that it was going to burst apart, spill all his insides in a wet pile on the slightly dewy grass. Was it Melfort returning for another bombing attempt, to do the job properly, or just to get his leg over again? Maybe Slicer was on to Melfort's crime, had rumbled him, was going to stop him; or was Slicer the one about to have another go – he was carrying the equipment, after all, that menacing little black bag; the first time he'd only had the motive of rejection, but the

110

time it was doubled by the knowledge that Melfort had been screwing her instead. Or were they in league, maybe? Or . . . His mind fuzzed helplessly. He longed pathetically for a nice simple explanation.

Just then a slight, female figure in white appeared, glimmering like a ghost, on one of the little balconies cut in below the ornamental eaves of the house, and leant down over the rail. Twenty feet below her was the dark figure of Melfort, who signalled up at her with his hand; she waved discreetly back. Melfort began to climb lightly up a drainpipe, eagerness discernible in his movements even at this distance: Crump sat down heavily, careless of the damp ground, and his back sagged nervelessly against the spiky branches of the hedge. It was all beyond him now: he would not have been surprised if a unicorn had trotted into the picture out of the milky light of the cricket pitches.

When Romeo reached his Juliet, they embraced hotly under the soft moonbeams and disappeared from the balcony into her bedroom. Almost immediately Slicer had also glided over to the bottom of the drainpipe. Crump watched exhaustedly, as if through a haze, as he arranged his equipment round his neck for the climb. That must be it, he thought listlessly: Slicer's going to get both of them, blow them up, because the girl wouldn't drop them for him. The thought made him rally a little this time – perhaps it was going to turn out his way, after all, in that he would soon be grimly marching his junior officer away in handcuffs. But he still had no strength or energy to move. Slicer began swarming up the drainpipe. Do something! Act! nagged an irritable voice in Crump's mind, which reminded him uncomfortably of his wife. But he was unable to move from his collapsed position, and he remained a spectator while events suddenly accelerated through a remarkable dramatic sequence.

Shortly after Slicer reached the top of the drainpipe, there was a quick sequence of bright, soundless flashes from the balcony. My God, thought Crump, a silenced pistol; he's done it, he's killed them. He made another fruitless attempt to stir his collapsed limbs into action. Almost immediately, Slicer slung himself back over the balcony rail and half-climbed, half-tumbled back down the pipe. Arrest that man! screeched Crump's inner voice: and as if in response to

this cry, a bulky figure carrying a long object, which could
have been a stick but turned out to be a twelve-bore shotgun,
appeared round the side of the house and confronted Slicer
as he hit the ground.

"Get your hands up or I'll blow your brains out!"

The growling military tones of Killer Rhage echoed firmly
into the copse from the side of the house.

As Slicer stopped with a jerk in his tracks and obediently
put his hands on his head like a prisoner of war, the figures
of Melfort and Elkie appeared above, very much alive, and
leant down curiously over the balcony. Elkie no longer wore
the white garment, and the strengthening moon gleamed
on her pale, naked shoulders. Rhage's head and gun snapped
up towards them.

"And you two stay where you are!" he barked. "I'll come
and sort out your little game later!"

Crump struggled weakly to his feet and half-walked,
half-tottered into the deeper cover of the copse. A single
thought was forming in his mind and overwhelming the
swimming confusion there: whatever was going on, he
must stop it. The way things were heading, bombs, guns,
someone was going to get killed. And if someone got killed
now, in this dangerous and absurd night-time adventure,
he, Crump, would get blamed for it. It must therefore,
absolutely, be stopped. He took his warrant card out of his
inside pocket, stared at it for a moment as if to draw strength
from it, cleared his throat and straightened his tie, forgetting
the darkness, and stepped to the edge of the trees.

There was another burst of powerful light, this time from
a torch in Killer Rhage's hand which he switched on and
directed mercilessly into Slicer's face. The sergeant, dazzled,
blinked and winced, the camera hanging loosely and not
clearly identifiable from his shoulder. Rhage peered forward
to study his bag, shotgun still crooked cautiously in his
chunkily dressing-gowned arm.

"Hang on a minute," he said in surprise. "I've seen you
somewhere before."

"That's right, sir, indeed you have." Slicer's smarming
tones slipped smoothly into the warm air of the summer
night like a crocodile into a river. There was a slight trembling of fear behind the ingratiation, however.

"I'm the police officer who came to interview you in hospital. I'd be glad if you'd lower that gun so we can have a bit of a chat about this, sir."

"A bit of a chat?" came Rhage's ringing and indignant reply. "You've got some explaining to do, my boy, police officer or no police officer. Even policemen can't go around trespassing and breaking into people's houses in the dead of night. What *is* this all about? Identify yourself."

The long barrel of the gun jabbed towards Slicer's midriff. While Slicer reached into an inside pocket with the gun virtually up his nose, Crump agonised rapidly about how he could announce himself to the assembled company without being shot out of hand by this trigger-happy housemaster. He decided on the cautious method, and arranged himself carefully behind a large tree-trunk, making sure his every extremity and rotundity was protected from scatter-shot, before calling out in his best megaphone voice.

"Mr Rhage, sir," he shouted slowly but clearly, trying to keep his voice firm. He saw the beam of the torch swing unerringly across the darkness and fasten itself like an arrow on the other side of the tree which hid him. "This is DCS Albert Crump speaking, the police officer in charge of this investigation. That is one of my officers you are talking to. When you have given me an assurance that you have put down your weapon, I will step forward and explain the situation to you."

The torch beam did not move a centimetre. There was no sound at all for several seconds. Then came Rhage's cautious reply.

"I refuse to put down my weapon until you have both satisfactorily identified yourselves," he said, suspicion and caution slowing his military drawl still further. "However, I will point it at the ground while you advance and be recognised."

Crump decided to take the risk. He was already looking forward, despite his fear, to liberating Slicer with condescending tolerance and then giving him the bollocking of a lifetime later on. A camera! The little pervert! First filthy tapes, now do-it-yourself pornography! It was almost certainly a police camera as well, and that was against regulations. He stepped forward and walked along

the blinding flashlight beam, his arm before his face, [to]
join the other two men. The balcony above was desert[ed]
now. Face to face with Rhage, he did not like the grim s[et]
of the other man's jawline. Both he and Slicer display[ed]
their warrant cards like guilty children forced to sho[w]
how dirty they'd got their hands while out playing in t[he]
street.

"I see," said Killer grudgingly. "They seem genui[ne]
enough to me. I suppose you must have your reasons f[or]
this rather cloak-and-dagger behaviour, although I m[ust]
say I find it quite extraordinary. Why is this officer taki[ng]
photographs?"

Crump hesitated, realising that he did not really kno[w.]
He summoned his most formal tones, usually reserved f[or]
the Chief and chairmen of magistrates' benches.

"I would rather give you a full account of events tom[or]-
row, in the clear light of day, if you don't mind, sir. I wou[ld]
merely ask you at this point to take it on trust that o[ur]
activities tonight were essential to the furtherance of o[ur]
investigation and the discounting of certain individuals fro[m]
our inquiries."

Rhage grunted sceptically, like a guard dog ordered to [let]
go of its victim's arm.

"Very well. But I insist that you accept on your p[art]
that I have already been blown up once and am natural[ly]
taking all possible precautions to avoid being blown [up]
again."

"Of course, sir. Not an experience that anyone wou[ld]
want to repeat, naturally. We're sorry for the inco[n]-
venience."

Rhage stared grimly from one to the other, his ey[es]
inscrutable in the near-darkness.

"All right, gentlemen. I look forward to seeing y[ou]
tomorrow. I will relate these quite astonishing events to t[he]
headmaster, and I feel I must insist that the explanation w[ill]
be in his presence. And if you do not appear in his study [at]
o-nine thirty sharp, we will telephone the Chief Consta[ble]
to require an explanation from him. Meanwhile" – [he]
glanced up towards the now empty balcony – "I have a lit[tle]
domestic business to sort out. Good night, gentlemen."

*   *   *   *   *   *

114

The two detectives argued furiously as they stamped back towards their cars through the low white mist gathering like a lake on the sports pitches of Little Sward. It moved eerily round their ankles in the moonlight.

"You'll have to come off this investigation, Slicer," snapped Crump.

"Ah, come on, guv, I was only trying to help you out, show you what a simple explanation there was for those prints on the door."

"Thank you very much, Mr Slicer, I accepted your hypothesis when you first mentioned it and was considering it alongside the other possibilities. So why this perverted desire to take photographs to prove the liaison between Melfort and the young lady? No, Mr Slicer, there's more to it than that; don't you think you'd better make a clean breast of it?"

"Look, give us a break, guv, I thought you wouldn't believe it unless I got concrete proof. You seemed so stuck on your daft bloody idea about a schoolkid blowing up his housemaster that I thought nothing else would budge you. Camera cannot lie, know what I mean?"

Crump stopped and stared with cold aggression at Slicer, whose face was creased in unaccustomed contrition.

"You expect me to believe that, Slicer? That you would take police equipment, unofficially, and sneak round like a cat-burglar taking pornographic bloody photos and risking being caught in the act – which you were – just to convince me of a single point which you thought I had overlooked? Pull the other one, I wasn't born yesterday. What was in it for you, eh? A personal motive in all this? Some kind of a drink? Revenge? Something which seems certain to result in disciplinary action, I can see that."

Slicer raised his hands in surrender for the second time that night.

"Nothing, guv'nor – honest. Straight up."

Crump paused to savour the moment and gather his forces for the lethal pounce. His voice came taut and low.

"I happen to have received information, Slicer, in the form of a telephone call, that you yourself may have been involved with this so-called au pair girl. It strikes me she's running more like a one-horse knocking shop rather than taking care of the welfare of innocent children. I was working upon that information when I followed you tonight. Now what do you say to that?"

"Ah," said Slicer, staccato, as if he had just been punched in the solar plexus. "That."

He began walking again, trying to stroll casually. Crump followed him, tasting sweet victory, some warmth in his veins again.

"You are also probably not aware, Slicer," he persisted fluently, "that an unusually swift forensic breakthrough has indicated that a timing device used on the bomb was a watch which almost certainly belonged to Miss Elkie van Horning – if I have her name correctly – which makes you, as an associate of hers, a prime suspect in your own right, young man. Now, what have you got to say to that?"

Slicer stopped with a jerk and stared with wide, shocked eyes at the fat contours of Crump's face, gleaming with triumph in the ever growing light of the still-rising moon. He coughed, and turned away again before beginning to speak, carefully and hesitantly.

"It's certainly true that I had a drink with the young lady one night," he said.

"That's not my information, Slicer," cut in Crump relentlessly. "My information is that you ended the evening parked up in that bloody tart cart of yours, not far from this very spot, wrestling with her knickers until she finally gives you a good kick in the cods, which is just about what you deserve in my opinion. And I am also told that as she escaped, she left a trail of possessions scattered behind her."

"Oh, come off it, chief," Slicer replied, beginning to get heated too. "She spilled a couple of things out of her handbag, that's all; I meant to send them back to her but they didn't seem worth it. Only a comb and a few paper snot-rags. And I didn't see any watch – she'd have been wearing it on her wrist, anyhow. Those things don't drop off so easily, you know."

"Oh, yes, very neat, Slicer. Don't you think, though, that you should have mentioned all that at the outset, when you went to interview her in hospital?"

Slicer shrugged.

"Maybe. Didn't seem particularly relevant. You're barking up the wrong tree, guv, honest. All that happened tonight was, it sort of struck me I might sort of kill two birds with one stone – give you the final proof about her carrying on with this toffee-nosed teenager, and, well, teach them a lesson at the same time. I mean, it's not right, is it, them carrying on like that right under the housemaster's nose? It's obscene, isn't it – there's young children in that house."

Crump snorted like a horse.

"Come off it, Slicer, when did you ever worry about what's right and what's wrong? And as for obscenity, it's oozing from every orifice in your body. I found that revolting tape of yours, you know – oh yes! Is that how you spend your spare time, eh? Oooh, aaah, I'm Mandy, give it to me now, big boy? Can't you get real women to talk to you like that, eh, is that the problem? I feel sorry for your wife, Slicer. You left that bloody tape in my drawer, you know, and by so doing may have seriously hindered this investigation. But that's another matter."

Slicer had had enough. He had not been to Upperdown and did not have the conditioning to receive this kind of punishment without fighting back. He was an offspring of the East End of London. He decided to go on the offensive to save himself any more of a pasting.

"This investigation?" His voice rose and fell in heavy sarcasm. "What investigation? Are you calling this prize cock-up an investigation? What progress have you made in this investigation, *Mr* Crump? Fuck all, I would suggest, except follow up your bloody daft obsessions about schoolboy assassins and sneak round the countryside trying to nick other coppers. What kind of a game of soldiers is *that*? Trouble is, you can't imagine an eighteen-year-old poking this bird because you never had it up till you bloody well got married, and probably not too often since then, by the looks of your old lady. You just keep your blinkers on and stick to your Dixon-of-Dock-Green-type villains, Crump. Fuck me rigid. The only important leads, this phone call you say you've had and the forensic, you don't even pass on to your fellow-officers on the investigation. You don't seem to have tried very hard to investigate who might have made this call, do you? No wonder the Chief thinks you're a dud – *sir*. You've been deliberately concealing information from me, haven't you, you bastard? You couldn't organise a piss-up in a brewery. Face it, this investigation has got fucking *nowhere*."

He stopped and shoved his face against Crump's, their breath, sour with nerves, mingling, and their eyes locked together like exhausted wrestlers.

"Nowhere," Slicer repeated with quiet finality.

Crump stared back in silent hatred as they stood there together in a great luminous pond of mist. He could think of no reply. His sausagey hand moved with an unusually delicate touch up to his chest, feeling it tenderly: he wished he had gone quietly home for a cup of Ovaltine and an early night.

17

"Come in."

Killer's voice was even, measured, polite. He was standing looking out of the window of his study attached to Paine House – the study was still serviceable despite the devastation in the house overhead – and musing calmly about the weather and the prospects for the next day's match. It was when he was calm like this, almost serene, that he was also at his most dangerous, his most remorseless; it was like the utter immobility of the tiger before the lethal spring. Melfort recognised this terrible courtesy as he entered, and his heart sank still further.

"Ah, Melfort, do sit down, old boy."

Melfort sat down silently and waited, pale and impassive, for his sentence. He was worried that when it came, his impassivity would not last long. He had felt the sting of Rhage's cane only once, the previous term, and found it impossible to stay strong and silent. He had yelped like a puppy.

Rhage strolled over and sat down behind his desk. The scorch mark on his face was almost brown now, and beginning to blend in with the light tan his skin always seemed to maintain even in winter. He looked very much his usual robust, forceful, uncompromising self – he knew what was right and wrong, and was going to enforce the right. He studied Melfort with an expression of perplexed benevolence.

"Y'know, Melfort," he said eventually, chatty and friendly. "I had great hopes of you – still have, in a way. Chairman of one of the big companies, maybe, cabinet minister, even. You put your talents to the correct use, you could go far."

Melfort looked at the carpet wondering why his house-master needed to praise people before grinding them under his heel; the same kind of thing had happened over the cannabis incident. Hoping to accelerate the whole process, he looked up for a moment and said quietly: "Thank you, sir."

"Don't thank me, boy — it's not a compliment, it's a statement of fact. However" — he pushed back his chair and strolled back to the window, hands in his pockets — "I'm afraid your career's over as far as Upperdown is concerned, young man. You realise that, don't you?"

He turned as he put the question and fixed Melfort with a gaze designed to be harsh, but not without compassion. Melfort felt confused: instead of erupting furiously, the tiger seemed to be settling down for a nap.

"You mean, I'm being sacked?" Melfort asked dully. It was what he had expected, but he also expected dire retribution.

"I'm afraid there's no getting round it this time," replied Rhage in tones of sad duty. "I'm not entirely happy about it, I dare say you're not happy about it, and I'm damned sure the eleven isn't happy about it; but in the circumstances there's nothing else we can do. The head agrees it's the only course of action, and he wants to see you immediately after this to pronounce the formal sentence, as it were."

"I see, sir. What about my exams?"

"You'll be allowed to come in and sit them at the end of term, but I'm afraid your family will have to organise any teaching for you between now and then."

Melfort's eyes were on the carpet still.

"I see, sir. Thank you, sir."

There was a few seconds' pause while Rhage wandered with an amiable gait back to his chair, looking with narrowed eyes at the ceiling with his head on one side, as if debating with himself whether or not to go ahead and say what was on his mind.

"Y'know, Melfort, I had a good mind to thrash you then and then — in front of Miss van Horning, even. I think might have done you some good."

This announcement caused Melfort to become tense again and his eyes returned to the carpet. Yes, he thought, you have loved that, you raging pervert. And you can't quite resist it now, after all. His buttocks tingled nastily; then h

120

whole body jumped involuntarily in the air as Killer's open hand hit the desk with a report like splintering bone.

"Well, dammit all, boy, it's beyond the pale! It's simply not acceptable behaviour, not by any standards. And certainly not by the standards of a public schoolboy and a gentleman."

Rhage's face was darkening and Melfort set his teeth and leant into the tempest.

"Miss van Horning's a very attractive young lady, I grant you that. And you're at an age where it's quite natural that you might have strong feelings about her. But it's simply not the way to go about things – to take advantage of a girl in somebody else's house. How long has all this been going on, anyway?"

Melfort had worked out that his best chance of the lightest punishment lay in meek white lies. He was not going to provoke Killer into a truly volcanic eruption by trying to convince him of the truth, namely that Elkie van Horning was not the kind of girl who would only be found in bed with a man if she had been 'taken advantage of' with drink, drugs, violence or beguiling lies. Nor was he going to tell him of the frequency of their couplings – their liaison had begun during the last half of the previous term, continued with regular meetings in London during the holidays, and lasted all the present term apart from one week when a prolonged tiff was in force. Still less was Melfort going to relate his real and very sweet revenge for the beating Rhage had given him after the cannabis incident – a veritable all-night sexual Olympiad in Rhage's own floral-patterned conjugal bed while he and his wife had been away for a weekend to visit her parents.

"Only a few weeks, sir, since just after the beginning of term."

Rhage shook his head in disapproving incomprehension.

"I simply expected better things of you, Melfort. First that unforgivable episode last term, which I had chosen to forget until this occurred, and now this even more unfortunate event. I know that nowadays people don't have the same moral standards as when I was young. But we really are heading for Sodom and Gomorrah at this rate. Your father's going to be extremely disappointed."

Melfort knew of several aspects of his father's life whi[ch] made it far more likely that Sodom and Gomorrah wou[ld] provide him, on the contrary, with just the right clima[te.] He feigned total humility.

"I know, sir," he said.

Rhage opened a cigarette box on his desk and offered it [to] Melfort. He believed strongly in the officer's morality [of] granting full physical comforts to a condemned man.

"D'you use these, Melfort?" he asked. "Can't be of a[ny] harm if you're no longer a pupil here."

Melfort looked up at him in surprise, then over at the ca[ne] in the corner which he expected to precede anything li[ke] this. He refused the cigarette and Rhage closed the box. [He] had noticed the direction of Melfort's glance. Again [he] walked to the window and studied the roses.

"I'm not going to beat you, Melfort." He spoke to t[he] window and his voice bounced back, slightly distorted, in[to] the room. "It would hurt you, and it would hurt me. I do[n't] like beating boys when it's not necessary. I beat Smiths[on] and Nimmo last night for breaking house rules – that w[as] necessary. But I consider that sacking you is punishm[ent] enough, one that will probably cause you a great deal [of] lasting regret later in life. And besides" – here he turn[ed] round to face Melfort – "besides, I can understand how [it] happened, y'know. I'm a man, too, Melfort – we're b[oth] men – and I understand how a man can fall into temptati[on.] But when he gives in, Melfort, when he succumbs . . ."

"Yes, sir?" Melfort felt obliged to say, to fill the overlo[ng] dramatic pause.

". . . he has to take the consequences. And in your ca[se] I'm afraid it's the final consequence. You were destined [to] be head of school, Melfort, but that was water under t[he] bridge some time ago. Then you were staying on quietly f[or] the exams, to play some cricket, to rehabilitate yourse[lf.] And now you go and do a thing like this. I'm profoun[dly] shocked, Melfort, both at you and Miss van Horning. A[nd] I'm dashed disappointed about the cricket and tomorro[w's] match in particular – you know how much we need you."

"What's going to happen to Elk . . . Miss van Hornin[g,] sir?" Melfort chipped in anxiously.

"My wife has already spoken to her, Melfort. She'll

leaving our employment, immediately, of course – can't have someone with morals like that taking care of young children. And if she was my daughter, I'd tan her hide, I don't mind telling you, even if she is nineteen years old. I sometimes despair of modern youth, Melfort, really I do."

"Yes, sir," said Melfort, shifting impatiently in his seat. Now he knew he was not going to be beaten, he was reluctant to submit to a long homily on Victorian officer-class morality. He had heard it all before in various forms, and had a certain regard for it, but he had long ago abandoned any intention of conforming to it himself – not for a few years yet, at any rate. Killer sensed his impatience.

"Still, you don't want to sit here listening to a chap who isn't even your housemaster any longer going on about standards of behaviour you evidently have no use for," he said with tetchy sentimentality. "But I think you'll find, Melfort, that, in life, the kind of standards we've tried to instil in you here will stand you in good stead. You may not need them now, y'know, sowing your wild oats and so on, but one day – you will."

Melfort met Rhage's eye and held it for the first time of the whole interview. The boy's expression contained defiance, rebellion, scepticism, some affection, and possibly the resolve of further revenge. Rhage stepped resolutely forward to the centre of the room and held out his hand.

"Goodbye, Melfort," he said in clipped chap-to-chap style. "You will leave the school today and your luggage will follow by train. When you have seen the headmaster, he will telephone your family and inform them of our reluctant decision."

Melfort hesitantly put his hand into Rhage's, an experience similar to running your fingers through a mangle.

"Good luck," said Rhage sentimentally. "I'm sorry it had to be like this."

Melfort said nothing, but thought pleasantly to himself: you will be, old boy, you will be. His hand was released. Outside the door he bent over his crushed knuckles, rubbing them painfully back into movement. He'd almost have preferred the beating, he thought; he didn't use his bum quite so much as his right hand.

18

Usually the policy and executive branches of British authority stay separate, the distance between them strengthening the belief and confidence each has in the other. The officers leave the sergeants to keep the rabble in shape, the members of the board rarely meet the foremen, who enforce their policy for them on the factory floor. The policy men believe the executive ranks to be the salt of the earth, utterly loyal and trustworthy in their blind application of the rules; and the sergeants and foremen regard the bosses as mysteriously unchallengeable, divinely appointed, even infallible. Each party respects the other without having to endure the other's company, foibles, manner of speech, eating habits. It is a uniquely powerful and perfectly balanced system of social control, whose only weak point – the fact that, in the end, both sides are equal in their ordinary, messy humanity – only becomes visible in certain moments of crisis. One of those moments took place when DCS Crump tried to explain himself to the headmaster and Rhage. Matters weren't helped by the fact that Crump had slumped into utter dejection after the events of the previous night, and was giving an unusually poor account of himself.

The attitude of Killer Rhage and Spider Webb was one of pained incomprehension. People like them, who helped to set the tone and procedures of society, appointed people like Crump to put them into effect. They then liked to go away and get on with their own lives, secure in the knowledge that everything was being adequately, if not always fairly looked after at the sharp end. Crump had evidently been allowing things to get badly out of hand. Events like the previous night were extremely embarrassing and threatened to bring the whole system into disrepute – what if the press were to get hold of it, for example? Detectives climbing up drainpipes to take dirty pictures? Horrendous. The policy branch was at pains to reassert itself at times like this. And even though Crump did not, strictly speaking, have to answer before this particular panel of judges, his bones told him that he should do so. It was incumbent upon him, would be the kind of phrase he would use. It was part of the mysterious conspiracy, built into the genes after generations of observance.

"It strikes me as a case where the left hand didn't know what the right hand was doing," said Webb bad-temperedly, having listened to Crump's faltering, rather patchy rationalisation. Webb felt he was in enough trouble himself already – with the parents, politicians, his colleagues – without having faux pas of incompetent policemen blamed on him as well, as would, he felt, undoubtedly be the case. He was, after all, the top man, the headmaster, the place where the buck stopped.

"Not a bad way of putting it, sir," said Crump ingratiatingly. "Although I'm ashamed to have to admit it. A lapse in procedure, you might also call it, combined with an excess of zeal on the part of a junior officer. The failure to convey to Mr Slicer the arrival, and the serious implications, of certain forensic evidence meant he was able to pursue his rather hot-headed personal theories. As it happens, he did manage to establish for the first time with any certainty the existence of an important – er – state of affairs in this investigation, complete with photographic evidence. You have to appreciate that such, shall we say, strokes of personal initiative do have their place in police work and occasionally produce the most remarkable successes. What, for example, if Mr Slicer had indeed apprehended Mr Melfort in the act of placing another explosive device? We would all, I suggest, have owed him a debt of gratitude."

It pained Crump to make this suggestion. Webb snorted and exchanged a look of half-amused disbelief with Rhage.

"I really do consider that to be a bit far-fetched, Mr Crump. I must confess to a certain surprise that my brief relation to you of Melfort's disgrace last term appears to have resulted in a highly elaborate and fanciful theory that an eighteen-year-old boy is going about the place blowing

up buildings and trying to kill people. I'd have expected
little more common sense, quite frankly, Mr Crump."

Crump tried to dredge up some offended dignity from
the depths of his sunken spirits. The process was impeded
by his heart going into a distracting and uncomfortable
gymnastic routine again, as it had done several times already
since last night. Each time it happened, it felt as if the
sun had gone in, leaving him in a sudden chilly shadow.
Once upon a time his heart had been a vague, elusive sort
of organ, a concept loosely attached to an ill-defined
part of his chest, but he had now become acutely conscious
of its precarious, thudding, whooshing, pumping function,
of its exact and delicate whereabouts behind his breast
bone. It had taken to having these fits of jumping about
nervously and erratically like a small caged animal. It
worried him.

"You must remember, headmaster, that policemen have
to bear all possibilities in mind, no matter how improbable,"
he managed weakly. "They cannot eliminate any one theory
because of mere prejudice . . ."

"It strikes me that you chose to follow this particular
theory because of prejudice – prejudice against the modern
public schoolboy," cut in Webb, with a rare stroke of
acuity, stuttering in his hurry to express his insight.

"On the contrary, sir." Crump was deathly pale. "You
have to remember that we had his fingerprints all over
the door, as I said. At that stage we were not aware of
the, er, liaison, which was only conclusively established
last evening. Before becoming aware of that, it would
have been irresponsible of us to discount Mr Melfort as a
suspect."

"I can't help feeling that we aren't being told the full
story," said Killer, frowning. "Naturally I accept your
discretion as a police officer not to reveal certain details of
a current investigation. But I can't see why what you've
told us would lead to Mr Slicer following Melfort without
your prior knowledge, and you in turn following Slicer
without his knowledge. Doesn't quite add up, to my way of
thinking."

Blast you, thought Crump weakly. He had decided on
the way over to the school not to relate the encounter

between Slicer and Elkie which had obviously been the sergeant's main reason for acting the way he did the previous night; he had felt, somehow, that people like the head and Rhage should not have to be bothered with such sordid details, especially since they reflected so badly on the police service. He had also decided not to reveal his own suspicions of Slicer, principally because he felt it would make him look ridiculous and destroy his precarious credibility. It was the kind of thing that could easily get reported back to the Chief, with all sorts of unpleasant consequences. And anyway, he wanted to stay in control of the question of whether Slicer was eventually going to face disciplinary action. He dabbed his coldly sweating brow with his handkerchief, deciding grimly to stick to his guns.

"Mr Slicer was, as I say, following a hunch. And I was acting in a precautionary capacity upon information received at the last minute. I hope you will accept, gentlemen, that I am not willing to go into more precise details at this stage, for, er, operational reasons. Suffice it to say we have, one way or the other, eliminated Melfort from our inquiries and are now in the possession of certain forensic evidence which offers every prospect of quick progress in the apprehension of the criminal."

Rhage and Webb looked at each other again and came to an agreement by signs of the eyebrows that perhaps they had pushed him as far as they could. The fellow had been severely spoken to, had clearly taken the warning to heart, and with any luck they could safely leave him now to get on with it without any more unfortunate cock-ups.

"Very well, Mr Crump," said Rhage. "I'm bound to say that we're not entirely happy with things, but that's where we'd better leave it for now. I must say, I would like to know why you need to interview Miss van Horning so urgently, though. She's been through a lot recently, you know, none of it entirely pleasant."

Crump's policemanly confidence rallied a little now that the heat was being turned down, and he reflected for an instant that Rhage himself had no doubt given the young lady her most recent unpleasant experience while reprimanding her for her promiscuity.

"We believe she may have information of vital relevance

to the investigation," he said as self-importantly as possibl
"We can't be sure, however, until we have interview
her more fully — and made certain relevant inquiries
Amsterdam, I might add."

He turned to Rhage for a moment, noting that he seem
suitably impressed by the dropping of a foreign name. Su
things always gave the impression that inquiries were bei
pursued with the maximum vigour, although it usual
meant the police were casting around helplessly in the dark

"When do you think she might . . . ?" Crump ask
tactfully.

"Well, if you insist, I expect this evening would be
right," said Rhage, evidently confident that this would n
have to be checked with the individual concerned. "T
medico gave her quite a powerful shot to get her over t
hysteria and give her some sleep, but it can't last more th
about eight or nine hours. Give me a ring later on and
prepare the ground with her a bit."

"Very well, sir."

There was a silence. The three men eyed each oth
cautiously. A tacit agreement entered the space betwe
them: one or two harsh things had been said, but th
needed saying; Crump had been pointed in the right dire
tion, the air had been cleared, everyone knew where th
stood.

"Well . . ." said Webb, with the tone of the chairm
winding up the meeting. Rhage, however, gave a lit
warning cough and shot a quick embarrassed look at hi
Webb's brows knotted in irritable incomprehension.

"Photographs," Rhage reminded him shortly, and th
looked casually out of the window, his tan and the scor
mark on his cheek looking a little darker than before.

"Ah, yes, the photographs," said Webb, with a heartin
intended to indicate the triviality of the affair, but whi
betrayed that it was in fact something he considered impo
tant. "Of young Melfort, that is, in the company of t
young lady. They must be, er, of a highly compromisi
nature."

Crump suppressed a little surge of amusement and
morale rose further. The tables began infinitesimally
turn. Dirty old men, he thought; just like anyone else.

"I have not yet seen them myself," he said in an un-interested, matter-of-fact voice. "They are strictly for police purposes only, I can assure you, headmaster."

"Quite so, quite so," stuttered Webb. "I wasn't for a moment going to suggest otherwise. It was merely that we wondered, given that they are presumably no longer of, er, central importance to the investigation, whether they might be destroyed, or handed over to us to be destroyed, merely to ensure, you understand, that they do not get into unreli-able hands. People who might make, er, wrongful use of them. We have, you must understand, a responsibility for the moral welfare of both Melfort and Miss van Horning, a duty to protect them."

Naughty, naughty, thought Crump: oh, no, you don't. The table had now moved right round, and it was one of those mysterious moments when the sergeants had firmly to tell the officers what was what, remind them of the rules, keep them in their places. You can't have the boardroom uncovering the secrets of the travelling salesman or rum-maging in the lockers of the other ranks, muscling in on their perks. That was very much out of order.

"Mr Melfort?" replied Crump with feigned incom-prehension. "I understood he had been expelled and was therefore no longer one of your responsibilities?"

Webb shot a desperate glance at Rhage, but he had opted out and was still gazing vaguely out of the window in an unusual demonstration of cowardice.

"Er, yes, that is correct, in a manner of speaking," said Webb, with panic shading the edges of his voice. "However, if we have your assurance that they will be treated respon-sibly and that there is no possibility of them falling into the hands of the press, for example, then I think the matter can be allowed to rest there . . . don't you?"

"Yes, sir," said Crump, his smile tinged with cheek. Rumbled, you mucky bugger, he thought.

"Right, er, that would seem to be it for the time being, until we see you tonight, I believe?"

Crump drove slowly down the avenue of majestic, pale-green trees and back to town, pausing at the Three Balls for a couple of consolatory scotches and a few therapeutic spins of the fruit machine. His feeling of having come through

the ordeal in the headmaster's study reasonably well – w
honour and position reasonably satisfied on both sides – w
gradually dissipated as he reflected on the state of the inves
gation. Neither of his preferred candidates, Melfort a
Slicer, had done it: no one else that he knew of had
obvious motive; he'd failed to get a proper lead on t
anonymous caller; and it was unlikely that Miss van Horni
would know who had pinched her watch – even if it was h
watch at all. As Slicer had so cruelly remarked – fucki
nowhere.

19

Seen through binoculars from a little hide, built skilfully among the bushes down near the lake, Upperdown was a toytown picture of neatness, order and charm. The ivy on the buildings was neatly clipped, the paths and flower-beds were trim and tidy, the windows gleamed in the sun; the bell above Big Hall pealed out its orders at the prescribed and predictable times, and groups of uniformed boys moved in an orderly fashion from one place to another. In the afternoon they changed meekly into games clothes and released their more chaotic feelings in well-ordered rituals of aggression and submission. It was a vision, a world system, which delighted the parents of prospective pupils: here, surely, that brute nature which they had struggled against in their children with great exasperation and doubtful success would be tamed and harnessed and recruited to safe and conventional and productive pursuits. A few years here would surely turn them into upright and privileged citizens: the good name of the school would carry them effortlessly into universities, merchant banks, accountancy partnerships, solicitors' practices, perhaps even 'the media' if they had that sort of slightly worrying bent. The minor violence involved in pressing young people into this tight mould would be a small price to pay for all these future prizes.

The eyes behind the binoculars, however, saw through this seductive surface now to a harder version of things. If the system took you in and welcomed you, and rewarded you after all the pain and sacrifice and humiliation, that was all very well: you could no doubt look back and laugh at jokes about how you'd come through it all right and it hadn't done you any harm – in fact, all in all, it had probably done you some good. But if the rewards were denied you, despite all your pain and efforts to fit in, and you were not now, against all expectation, being offered the chance to get

your own back; if you felt that the world had never allowe
you to graduate beyond the status of a ridiculous squit; the
your perspective was rather different. You looked back a
saw only, writ large, the suffering and crushing and humi
ation, and you had now begun to think about the system
the only terms it dealt in: compulsion, force, arm-twistir
discipline – and revenge. Revenge against the prefects wh
clouted you round the ear and kicked you in the arse, reven
against the contemporaries who pulled the bedclothes
you while you were wanking and threw mud at you an
called you 'spotty Muldoon' and 'football-face'; reven
against the masters, those surrogate parents who turn
blind eyes and deaf ears to your distress. You wanted, wi
that obsessive combination of passionate feeling and col
deliberate calculation, to claim through retaliation th
recognition which had been offered, promised, by paren
and school, but denied by the vindictive workings of
system which always demanded its scapegoats, its losers,
out-groups. It had been denied because, in this instance, yo
had wanted it all too much, had tried too hard, had been to
keen, and anyway had had a funny accent tailor-made f
ridicule and a large, round head on a short, thick body. An
yet you had still put up with being a figure of fun, smilir
through suppressed tears and clutching to your heart t
belief that one day you would become what your parents
much, so cruelly wanted you to be, that approval wou
finally come and the rewards would one day be there, pr
viding you stuck to the task, grinning and bearing it. B
now they had vanished and the dream had finally collapse
its base eroded by the accumulated knocks and reverses of t
years. The worm had turned. He lowered the binoculars an
made a note in a neat little red-backed book: 'Killer to stu
5.30 – '. Then he settled back in the silent nest, a glitter in b
eye and a slightly deranged smile playing around his roun
pale face as he turned over and examined yet again the bitt
and indigestible memories of his public school days.

*   *   *   *   *   *

When she entered the room Elkie van Horning looked mo
like a frightened schoolgirl than a vamp. Her face was pa

132

and anxious, her long hair looked dark and unwashed, and she wore a large, lumpy white dressing gown. She sat in a fireside armchair with her slippered feet placed chastely together and waited mutely for Crump's questions with an expression which mingled fear and resentment. Rhage and his wife had evidently given her a hard time already.

Crump cleared his throat and walked heavily up and down the dusty study which had been set aside for the interview. He felt peculiarly disturbed to be alone at this time of the evening with a young woman in her nightclothes – especially a young woman he knew to have so recently indulged in illicit love-making. He could not define his unease as he negotiated a path between piles of books and newspapers, most of them topped by empty whisky glasses and bearing the stains of small alcoholic spills. But then Crump was not used for some years now to recognising, let alone admitting, the symptoms of sexual excitement in himself. The decline in the sense of his own potency also had a lot to do with his contemptuous outrage at the philanderings of Melfort and Slicer. Emphasising instead a feeling he was more familiar with of late, he decided to go for the paternal note.

"Now, then, Miss, er . . . Horning . . ."

"Miss *van* Horning, if you please," interrupted Elkie, flatly and expressionlessly, without looking at him. He stared at her in amazement for a moment: he hoped she wasn't going to be cheeky. He cleared his throat again.

"Miss *van* Horning, then," he said patronisingly. "I do beg your pardon . . ."

"I want to be correct," said Elkie, her eyes still in the fireplace. "I am correct with you, you are correct with me."

"Er, yes, quite so," said Crump, wishing wearily that these foreigners would speak proper English; this kind of thing was most disconcerting. "I know you've been through some very difficult and upsetting experiences recently, but . . ."

"You know all already, I think," said Elkie. Her tone was surly.

"Er, I'm afraid not, Miss van Horning."

"What more?"

Crump sat down, carefully pulling up his trousers at the

knees, as if his baggy blue suit still had creases to preserve.
was an unconscious male recognition of her attractivenes
of his hidden desire to be pleasing to her. He wished
passing that she was right, that they did know everythin
that the whole ghastly business was over, with the crimin
tidily in the cells, preferably signing a full confession.

"Do you have a watch, Miss van Horning?"

She looked at him for the first time, out of the corner
her eye. Crump thought the glance was furtive, suspiciou
but that might have had more to do with his need to solve
crime than with Elkie's actual behaviour. A frown grew
her blonde face during the pause, then she lifted her le
hand and pointed at the empty wrist with her right for
finger.

"A watch? No, you see I have no watch. But I do know
is late and I want to sleep."

"I realise that and I apologise again for disturbing you
this time of night, but I assure you that it is an urgent matt
connected with our investigation of the, er, detonation."

Elkie frowned still harder and mouthed the word twice
three times to herself, trying to make sense of it. The wor
was evidently not part of her vocabulary, which was fair
rich in the kind of words and phrases found in scho
textbooks but typically deficient in the clichés and jargon
everyday life.

"Nation?" she asked. "What nation? You say debto
Like if you must give money to people? This is politic
no?"

Crump closed his eyes briefly with a silent prayer fo
strength. You really would think these people would tak
the trouble to learn the lingo, he thought. They come ov
here, they cause no end of trouble, have the authoritie
running about like blue-arsed flies, and then they can
understand a simple sentence. If she was his own daught
he'd . . . He forced his thoughts back to the task in hand.

"No, Miss Horning, you misunderstand me. By detona
tion, I mean the explosion . . . the bang."

"Ah. I understand." Elkie blushed, smiling slightly, an
fiddled with a strand of her hair in an unwittingly flirtatiou
gesture; Crump temporarily lost the track of his thought
again and lit a cigarette to gain time.

"I, er, yes, the watch. Have you never owned a watch of any kind, then, Miss Horning?"

"Please, I said *van* Horning. Yes, once I have a very nice watch."

"And where did you get it from?"

"From my parents. They give it me as a gift when I begin my nurse training."

"You trained as a nurse?"

"For one year only. Then I stop. I do not like old people dying all the time and I start looking after children instead. It is more happy."

"I see . . . And where is it now? The watch, I mean?"

Elkie shrugged and turned down the corners of her mouth sulkily.

"I do not know. It is lost."

"How did you lose it?"

"I am not sure. Why do you ask these questions? It is not about the bang."

Crump eyed her carefully, the headmaster's initial speculation about the perpetrators slipping back into his mind. Even in her little flashes of anger, Elkie did not look like a dangerous terrorist fanatic who had scored an own-goal; but you could never be sure with young people nowadays. Half the women in the Angry Brigade and the Baader-Meinhof gang, he reflected, had looked like Little Bo-Peep. He was glad that the bulky sergeant waiting for him outside had been issued with a firearm before they left the station.

"I must ask you to co-operate, Miss van Horning. The operational basis for these questions will become apparent in due course."

Elkie's face blanked for a few seconds while she worked out the mouthful of jargon, then she shrugged and looked at the fireplace again.

"I think maybe it is stolen."

Crump held back the phrase 'that's what they all say', which came automatically into his mind: the standard sarcasms were no good on foreigners, anyway. He felt his heart jumping around again as he brought out the most important questions of all.

"When and where was it stolen? And who by?"

There was a pause. Then, appearing to make a decision,

Elkie shifted in her seat, pushed her hair back behind her ears with both hands, and looked directly but shyly at Crump.

"If I say you that, I must also tell you a story."

"Er . . . I'm not sure I understand."

"It is a story about the man who came to see us at the hospital. You know him? I think he is also policeman."

Crump's heart was well into its acrobatics again; he really must get to see a doctor. Holding his face as grim and impassive as possible, he replied.

"I believe I know the gentleman you are referring to."

"And I also think you will get angry."

"Why?"

"Because I must say bad things about him."

Crump wished he could impress her by telling her he already knew something of the likely contents of her story from the anonymous giggler on the phone and from Slicer himself. He also wished he could tell her that, far from being angry, he would be delighted to hear all the dirt she could dredge up about his junior colleague. He managed to say nothing.

"I think you will think I only say it because he take the snaps of me and Charlie last night."

Crump suffered a turn of intestinal revulsion. Charlie! That young pup! That whippersnapper! So that would be their baby-talk – Elkie and Charlie! He put a slightly fluttering hand up to his breastbone again. This was just the sort of unexpected bout of stress that could do for him.

"I will judge everything you say on its merits, Miss Horning," he said weakly.

She stared at him suspiciously for a second.

"He is a bad man," she said solemnly. "But I think you don't believe me."

"I believe you," said Crump, not as neutrally as he felt he should have done. "Go on, please."

Elkie looked away and began her story in a flat, strained voice which indicated painfully controlled tears.

"I was angry with Charlie because we have had a row and I go with my friend Lisa to a pub in the town, one where there is disco. This man, your policeman, he looks at me all the time, then he comes and he talks to me. He is very nice

136

he asks me to dancing, we do a little, he buys many drinks for me, perhaps too many, and then" – she paused and heaved a great sigh which seemed to emphasise the frailness of her body underneath the heavy dressing gown: Crump stared intently at her, suddenly reminded again of his own daughter in times of adolescent trouble – "then he says to me that he will bring me home in his car, out here to the school. I do not know if there is any bus any more, my friend Lisa is with another boy and anyway she is living with a family in the town. So I am stupid. And I say yes. We go in his car, a little black car, I think, and he drives very fast. But he is still nice to me, he talks much and says nice things. And then we arrive near the school and he does not go to the Rhage house. He drives instead to the parking place outside the school, near the lake – maybe you know this place?"

Crump nodded, remembering with distaste the hour and a half he had spent crouching there in the bushes like a peeping Tom the previous night. His throat was dry with a strange suspense at this simple, hesitant narrative.

"So he stops the car, and I say, this is not my house, please take me to it. But then he puts his hands on me and begins to say bad things . . ."

"What things?" croaked Crump, leaning forwards towards her. She gave him a doubtful glance, as if something similar was going to happen again, and her eyes measured the distance to the door. Then, eyes demurely down again and choosing words carefully, if not always correctly, she went on.

"He says he likes me very much, and he wants to do things to me. I say no, but it is no good. He quickly moves the seat of the car and the seat falls down . . ."

"He reclines the seat?"

"Ya, and I fall down too, and he, he mounts me and I begin to fight at him. He says he will beat me if I do not do what he wants. So I am frightened and I think, maybe I let him so I do not become wounded.

Crump's ears were singing with some unbearable tension, and her voice seemed to be coming towards him down a fuzzy telephone line. He managed to nod to urge her on, her face now a scarlet fury of embarrassment.

"And then with my hand I open the door and suddenly he cries because I think I have strike him in a soft part with my . . . what is this? . . . ya, elbow. And then I manage to exit the car, on my hands, and I stand up and pull my shorts and I run home. And I do not tell anyone because Mr Rhage does not allow me to go into the town that night and he will be angry."

She had now turned her face away, but Crump noticed her shoulders convulsing slightly and guessed she was sobbing – or pretending to sob. He was torn between his hatred and contempt of Slicer, his half-paternal, half-sexual desire to comfort her, and his upright male citizen's conviction that promiscuous girls like this one deserved anything they got in situations like the one just described. The conflict calmed his twitching impulses and his thoughts slowly returned to the inquiry. Her story fitted with the facts so far, although Slicer's account had been considerably censored, and that of the voice on the phone rather sketchy. He cleared a dry obstruction from his throat after several noisy attempts.

"But Miss van Horning," he said gently, putting it as cunningly as he could. "I understand that you might well wish to make a complaint about this, but what has this got to do with the watch?"

She turned a tear-marked face to him.

"I pull my handbag with me when I run from the car, but it is open and I lose some things. I lose my watch, I lose my small hairbrush, some perfume . . ."

"But why was your watch in your handbag?"

"I always carry it there because it is for a nurse, to put on the dress at the front . . ."

"Ah, yes, I forgot. You were a nurse, of course. And when did you notice that your bag was open and these things had fallen out?"

"As I am running away, over the field. I notice, and I close it."

"And when did you find that the things were missing?"

"Next morning, after I wake up and I want to know the time and it is not there. Also the other things."

"And when did you next see Mr Melfort, er, Charlie, that is?"

138

"Two or three days after."

"And did you tell him of what happened?"

"No, because I am glad we are friendly again and I do not want him to be angry. And also I am frightened to tell my parents because they give me this expensive watch as a gift and it is a very nice, good watch."

"I see."

Crump pondered, staring at the full ashtray beneath the gloomy table lights, reflecting what a sordid business this whole thing was. Unlikely, then, that Melfort took the watch; still quite possible that Slicer had; but now, given the reluctant fading of his suspicions in those two quarters, it was overwhelmingly likely to have been someone else. Someone else? The voice, who must have seen all this? He turned to Elkie, who was not crying any more, but was looking fixedly at her delicate, slippered feet.

"Can you remember, Miss Horning, whether these items fell from your handbag before or after you left the car? Could they have fallen into the car, rather than into the road, or the field?"

Elkie looked at him, forlorn and appealing.

"Why do you ask? The watch is lost, that is the only thing."

"But it is very important that we know *who* took the watch."

"Why is it important?"

"The watch was used as the timing device for the explosion – the bang."

She still looked confused.

"It was a time-bomb," said Crump, watching her carefully. "Made with a watch."

Her whole face opened with astonishment and she looked suddenly like an excited child.

"You say, made with *my* watch?"

Crump nodded portentously, his jowls flapping slightly above his collar with the motion.

"So I will never get it back?"

"I'm afraid it's now in very small pieces."

Elkie covered her face with her hands.

"My parents will be so angry – how do I tell them?"

Crump allowed a silence to fall around the girl's gently

139

renewed sobbing, then leant forward until his face was only a foot from her. She took her hands away, and he noticed the clear smoothness of the skin on her forehead, the over-wrought bloodshot eyes.

"Elkie," he said earnestly, judging the time was right for this avuncularly intimate touch. "It's very important that you answer this question."

She looked at him meekly and nodded.

"Did anyone else that you know of see you in that car? While you were parked there? Or while you were running away – did you see anyone else watching you?"

Her eyes went troubled again as she understood what she was being asked. The very thought seemed to cause her renewed horror. Suddenly she plunged her face back into her hands.

"I do not know – I am very ashamed." Her voice was thick and wet and stumbled incoherently. "I do not want Charlie to know this. I feel the whole world is watching me now, all this time."

"But did you *see* anyone? Anything?"

She shook her head wildly, silent except for the constricted gargling of her sobs. Crump leant back in his chair with a sigh of hopelessness. No good going on with this, he told himself. And still no bloody progress. The Chief; his wife; his heart. He rubbed his eyes briefly and stood up to leave. He envied the way Elkie could relieve her feelings by sobbing and weeping. Still, he thought eagerly, he could give his eyes a really good, energetic rub on the way back to town, forget about everything; provided that thick sergeant didn't insist on talking to him.

20

You could always tell that Saturday was Saturday at Upperdown. The boys were allowed to leave their shoes uncleaned and wear sweaters and pullovers rather than blazers for the four morning lessons – another of Bernard Briggs's symbolic little reforms. There was also a general air of high spirits and relaxation, and it was a notorious time for practical jokes – booby-trapping people's lockers, putting vaseline on door handles – and illegal sneak visits to town for cigarettes and pornographic magazines. By this particular Saturday, the unnatural excitement earlier in the week, culminating in the sacking of Melfort, had begun to recede, and the explosion had been widely replaced as a topic of conversation by the day's match with Bunyan's, the derby of the cricket calendar. And once again, a faultless blue sky canopied the English Arcady that was Upperdown.

Spider Webb was taking an early-morning stroll across Great Sward to sniff the air and have a look at the pitch. He was hoping for a bit of cloud to move up later on so that the new fast-medium man that he believed to be this season's up-and-coming secret weapon, Fanning-Bradshawe, could get the ball moving around in the air a bit. Not, of course, that anything could fully compensate for the loss of Melfort; but that could no longer be helped. Above all he was hoping to have a day off from the stresses, strains and constant interruptions of the week so far.

He had just passed the Colts Pavilion when a large figure hove into view from behind Sparrow Copse, evidently heading rapidly towards the main school buildings. It was Thickett, and he suddenly changed course and bore down upon Webb. The headmaster continued his nonchalant stroll, hoping it was all nothing to do with him, but began to feel increasingly like a small yacht in the path of a battleship.

"Morning, headmaster," panted Thickett heavily. "A word with you, sir, if you please. It's what you might call pressing."

Webb did not stop and turn until he was close up to one of Great Sward's large chestnuts, as if he sought protection beneath its heavy, low-sweeping branches. He looked dejectedly at the louring dark red face of the head groundsman.

"Morning, Thickett," he said, still hoping, against the obvious odds, to get away with light conversation. "Nothing to disturb the peace of this fine Saturday, I hope – pitch in good condition, you think?"

"I'm not thinking about the pitch, meself, at the moment, sir, although I believe it's one of the better ones we've prepared for this term, what with it being Bunyan's and all. I'm afraid there's trouble, Mr Webb, sir."

"Oh, dear, Thickett, that sounds unfortunate," said Webb, hoping he might only be about to bang on about his wife's bunions, as he did in times of stress. "Isn't it something that can wait?"

"It's something that 'as to be acted upon immediate, sir, in my 'umble opinion," said Thickett forcefully, his oaken chest still heaving with exertion and indignation. "It's to do with the hexplosion."

Webb felt as though his heart had dropped down through his shoes into the hallowed turf beneath. That 'hexplosion', as Thickett called it, was going to haunt him for the rest of his days, he thought despairingly: it would probably see him into an early grave. He bade an internal goodbye to the warm, green day of carefree cricket he had been looking forward to.

"All right, Thickett," he sighed. "You'd better tell me about it, then."

"Well, sir," said Thickett, leaning against the tree's trunk, where his brown, knotty arm immediately began to look like one of the branches. "The other day, like, the day it 'appened, Mr Briggs came over to my place and asked me to check everywhere and make sure none of my chlorate was missing, you know, what we use to kill the weeds 'ere and there, on the paths, and that."

"Ah, yes, that was my suggestion, in fact, Thickett. You can make bombs from the stuff, you know."

142

"Yes, sir, so I'm told, sir. So I give the job to young Blegly, and he goes round and checks the sheds and there's nothing missing. Until this mornin'."

"What do you mean, Thickett? Speak plainly, there's a good chap."

"Well, I was chattin' to 'im about it, Blegly, I mean, while we was going out to give the pitch a roll first thing, and 'e tells me 'e didn't check the little shed next to the garage where we keep the tractor and the mowers and that. I keep some of the stuff over there, see, to keep the weeds off the back of them buildings, but Blegly says he never even knew we kept any over there. I could 'ave given 'im a thick ear there and then, idle little bugger. 'E must 'ave known there was some, 'e just didn't fancy the bit of a walk."

"I see, Thickett, so what did you do?"

"I went straight on over there meself, sir, and lo an' be'old, it's missing – a whole bag of the stuff. I remember taking it over there at the beginning of term, and I only used it once, sir, just a tiny bit. There must 'ave been twenty pound of it left – and it's gone now. Vanished into thin air."

Webb heaved a still larger sigh. The sky had turned grey for him and his world was suddenly a place of trial and pain again.

"Very well, Thickett," he said wearily, his feet dragging as he started to walk reluctantly back to the headmaster's lodge to telephone Crump; there would be no time to inspect the pitch now. "I'll deal with it. Thank you for your efforts – most conscientious, I'm most grateful."

He had managed to raise a bit of momentum and was striding bad-temperedly past Century Copse, envisaging the whole day consumed by further dreary consultations with that buffoon of a policeman, when another large figure entered his view and seemed, in its turn, to be heading him off. It was Rhage, an unusual spring and force in his military gait, bearing down on Webb waving aloft a piece of paper. Damn and blast! Would nobody give him any peace this morning? What was it to do with him if Rhage had got a parking-ticket or something? Why couldn't these people take care of their own affairs?

Rhage, too, was highly indignant and excited.

"Headmaster!" he barked from a good twenty yards

away, still moving like an express train. "There is something urgent I must show you – absolutely vital – arrived in the post a few minutes ago. Confounded cheek, if you ask me – criminal, no less!"

He ground to a halt alongside Webb and thrust a large, half-crumpled piece of paper towards him. Webb held up his palms, however, declining to take it.

"What is this, Rhage?" he said irritably. "I've got quite enough on my plate already this morning, including a most urgent telephone call to make in relation to the police investigation."

"If it's the investigation you're interested in," growled a puce-faced Rhage, firmly taking one of Webb's wrists and putting the paper into his hand, "then I insist that you read this – this message, I suppose is what you'd call it. Outrageous! Worse than blackmail! I'd like to get my hands on this blackguard, whoever he is."

Rather than have his wrist broken, Webb accepted the paper, straightened it out with a reproachful glance at Rhage, and saw that it consisted of a message in letters cut from newspapers. Oh, no, it was all too tiresome, too predictable almost.

"*Dear Mr Rhage*," it read, with capital letters stuck literately in all the right places, "*or would Killer be more appropriate? You probably think you've escaped. But you haven't. This is a serious business, and the job will be done properly next time. Beware the fury of a patient man.*"

"Hmm," Webb emitted grumpily. "He *must* have been patient to cut all those letters so neatly out of newspapers – different newspapers, too, by the look of it. Some from the *Times*, some from the *Daily Comet* . . ."

"How d'you know what the *Daily Comet* looks like?" snapped Rhage accusingly, in the voice reserved for boys who overstepped the mark. "That bloody rag."

Webb coloured; he wasn't going to take that from one of his own masters, not even from Killer Rhage. He let rip.

"It so happens, Rhage, that I am currently in correspondence with the editor of the *Daily Comet* over the activities of one of his staff in respect of the school, of which I happen to be headmaster and the interests of which it is my duty to safeguard in whatever way I see fit; and in the course of this affair I have found it necessary to read that particular newspaper for professional purposes. Now, Rhage, if you're satisfied with that as an explanation, may we proceed to the matter in hand?"

Sucking in breath after this little tirade of self-importance, Webb held up the paper in one hand and struck it smartly with the back of the fingers of the other. Rhage, his own anger blown away by this outburst, stared at him in mild amazement: not like old Spider to go over the top quite so fast, especially on the day of a match, he thought. Can't have got rid of his two coils after breakfast.

"Quite so, headmaster," he said with feigned contrition. "I do beg your pardon. The letter, though . . . apart from the newspaper question, what d'you make of it?"

"You appear to have an enemy," said Webb in a voice which implied that he thought the person concerned had good reasons. "Any idea at all who could have sent it?"

Rhage shrugged.

"Must be the bomb chappie all over again," he said. "But I'm confounded if I know who it is. I've always considered that a chap doesn't make many enemies if he follows my sort of policy of playing everything above-board – firm but fair, that sort of thing. People tend to respect you, even if they disagree with you, not turn against you in this cowardly, foreign sort of way. Still, we seem to have an exception here. I suppose there's always got to be the one-off, the oddball who takes it all to heart and starts going off at the deep end."

Webb stared at him for a moment. Rhage had run Paine House firmly but fairly for the last twenty years, he thought: the boys all knew where they stood, and if they broke the rules they got swatted. But they were evidently dealing with a wily and dangerous criminal here, he had now concluded, and Rhage's lack of imagination was not going to be much of an asset. They didn't seem to have very many assets at all in this investigation.

"I was just on my way across to take an early look at the pitch," he said in an even voice designed to indicate that he at least did not resent making sacrifices. "When Thickett accosted me to say some chlorate's missing from a shed. I was on my way home to phone the police when I come across you and this letter. Obviously it's going to be a busy day. Would you care to accompany me to my study and speak to our Mr Crump about all this yourself?"

Rhage frowned.

"Crump?" he said disapprovingly. "Can't say I'm very keen – I had quite enough of that buffoon yesterday. Cracking up, if you ask me – looked ripe for a nasty attack of something. I was intending to go and take an early look at the pitch myself, actually."

"Right, good, yes, that's what I'd do if I was you," replied Webb in sudden, constipated fury, stamping off towards the lodge like a chastised child, with furious waving gestures of dismissal towards Rhage. "You just go and take a good look, take your time, while I do all the work. Fine, you go ahead. I am the headmaster, after all."

Rhage mildly watched his agitated, receding back. Trouble with Webb, he reflected, was he couldn't take the rough with the smooth, couldn't handle the occasional bouncer; and he sometimes wondered if the man really was fit to be running the whole outfit.

21

"It's not funny, Smithson, is it?"

"No, Blair."

"Then why are you sniggering, Smithson?"

"I'm not sniggering, Blair."

"Smithson, I have been watching you for the last two minutes and you have been sniggering. What's so funny, Smithson?"

"Nothing, Blair."

"You can't be sniggering at nothing, Smithson."

"Why not?"

It was a fatal mistake; the trap snapped shut.

"Ah, so you *do* admit you were sniggering, Smithson."

"No, I don't."

"Don't be insolent, boy. If I say you were sniggering, you were sniggering. And if you say it's possible to be sniggering at nothing, there's a clear admission that you *were* sniggering."

Smithson A. J. was struggling with four O Levels, while Blair was about to take several A Levels in mathematical subjects. It was an uneven match. Smithson's snub features knotted in confusion, and his moment of hesitation allowed the prefect to move in ruthlessly for the kill.

"I'm sorry, Smithson, but you can't get out of responsibility for your own actions. It's a basic moral principle, although I doubt whether such things as morals hold any interest for a yob like you, Smithson. I saw you sniggering, and I also heard you talking with your friend with the shag-spots here" – he gestured dismissively towards one of Smithson's colleagues who was looking away, hoping to avoid being caught up in this debacle – "about what happened to the cricket pitch. I can only conclude from your amusement that you're not interested in this afternoon's match. So I think you'd better report to me on the asphalt at two o'clock in gamesers and I'll arrange a little alternative activity for you."

Pain and anger swept sullenly across Smithson's face; he was looking forward to an afternoon lounging on the grass, sucking pineapple chunks and reading an Angelique book while leather clicked on willow; he hated running, and he could not suppress his feelings.

"You've just got it in for me, Blair," he burst out. "You've been giving me punishments for just anything this week, and I've hardly done anything at all."

Blair's eyebrows lifted in the mildest of surprise; the rest of his face remained pale and impassive.

"Got it in for you? Don't be ridiculous. That's a very serious allegation to make. I'm afraid that it's just that your behaviour is getting you into trouble all the time. Any other poxy little oik would get the same treatment for the same behaviour. It's perfectly fair, boy."

Smithson opened his mouth to say more, but Blair cut in again, sharply.

"Shut up, Smithson, or you'll be doing even more running."

And Blair strolled away, tall and nonchalant, leaving Smithson standing helplessly, mouth open like a frog, deprived at an airy stroke of his Saturday afternoon.

News of the vandalising of the first eleven pitch had spread swiftly round the school after Rhage had discovered it on his early-morning inspection. Storming back in outrage to inform the headmaster, the first person he met was the yellow-tracksuited Bernard Briggs, jogging in a portly manner round the perimeter road. After a short but brutal explosion, he subsided a little and asked in mild bewilderment about the meaning of the message so prominently spread from one popping-crease to the other.

"It's an American expression," gasped Briggs, hoping his face was not too red and trying to minimise his panting. He wanted Rhage to be impressed with his fitness.

"Ah," said Rhage, with distaste, as if that explained all the crudity and barbarism of the world.

"New York, to be precise," said Briggs, who had taken a

148

cheap plane-ticket across the Atlantic the previous summer and had picked up some of the lingo as well as the jogging obsession. "Every time New Yorkers don't like something, they say it sucks. Everything over there seems to suck, one way or the other. I believe the expression is creeping over the pond, now, actually, and certain elements of British youth are beginning to adopt it. Trendy, you might say."

"It also strikes me as singularly vulgar. What exactly am I supposed to suck, or be sucking? Eggs? My teeth? Is some lout trying to imply I've *got* no teeth? He'll think differently when I chew his ear off."

"No, you shouldn't take it so literally, Rhage – it's just an expression, used very loosely to denote, well, contempt, or hatred, I suppose. Obvious sexual overtones, too, one has to admit. I'm afraid someone's got it in for you, Rhage, as well as for the first eleven and cricket in general."

"Yes, and I've got a fair idea who that someone might be," said Rhage, boiling up again. "Damned little whipper-snapper, can't take his punishment like a man. Resorts to the revenge of the coward and the bully – sneaking round your back, stabbing you between the shoulder-blades, twisting your arm. Using degenerate American expressions. I should have given the little lecher the thrashing he deserved."

Bernard Briggs, who was not a large man despite his incipient pot-belly, took an involuntary step of caution backwards. Rhage's face was still crimson with indignant rage, and his large hands were clenching and unclenching below the leather-hemmed sleeves of his sports jacket.

"I suppose you mean Charles Melfort," said Briggs.

"Indeed." The word hissed through powerfully clenched molars.

"Ye . . . es," said Briggs slowly. He had always found Melfort a very personable and reasonable young man, whose panache he rather admired – even envied. He sympathised with his latest predicament, and found his chosen revenge fairly amusing, despite its seriousness and possible criminality; but then, he wasn't much of a cricketer. All the same, he decided against putting a word in for the boy with Rhage. The man was clearly prepared to do violence to anyone who challenged him in his present mood.

149

"Ye . . . es," repeated Briggs. "Well, I dare say there'll be serious repercussions. Nasty business – what'll they do about the match? Transfer it to the second eleven pitch, or Colts?"

"Yes," fumed Rhage. "Won't be the same, though – Thickett had worked hard to make it the best pitch of the season. A beauty, it was. And now that snivelling young puppy's ruined it – ruined! And he a cricketer himself – I don't know how he could do it. An Englishman! He'll roast in hell for this!"

"Yes, it's too bad," said Briggs unconvincingly, resuming his gentle jog with a vain attempt to look loose and athletic in his movements. "But a man's innocent until proved guilty, Rhage – cardinal principle of English law!"

"Nauseating little liberal," growled Rhage, resuming his purposeful stride towards Webb's house, nurturing and massaging his infinite outrage at the desecration. To strike at cricket was to strike at morality, nay, civilisation itself.

* * * * * *

Crump – resentful and dishevelled, the increasingly grey, soft folds of his neck exposed by an open shirt – stared disbelievingly at the pitch, disfigured by the stark black letters burnt into it.

"Killer sucks," he muttered under his breath. "Killer sucks – who's Killer, and what does he suck, if it's not a rude question?"

Webb and Rhage explained. Crump nodded. He sometimes found it hard to credit the goings-on at this place. It was as if it had its own codes of behaviour, its own language, like some lost tribe.

"Aha," he said flatly. "I see. And you say you suspect young Melfort of this act of mindless vandalism."

"We do indeed," said Rhage and the headmaster with one voice.

"And do you know where that young man is now?"

"Well," said Webb. "He left the school yesterday – picked up by his elder brother in a rather noisy and vulgar sports car. They must initially, we must presume, have made a detour to perpetrate this cowardly and despicable act, but they were proceeding thereafter, I believe, to their parents' home in London."

"You've got the address?"

"I have indeed, in my study, and I shall be happy to pass it on to you."

"Good. If your suspicions prove correct, we could have a charge of criminal damage on our hands. Personally, I don't believe the youth of today should be allowed to get away with this kind of vandalism, no matter what their parental background. At times like this, I'm inclined to feel it was a shame we ever did away with corporal punishment for young offenders – although I'm pleased to note you still employ it here."

Rhage looked at Crump: he was taking on life and shape, like some grey balloon being blown up. Rhage felt the beginnings of a new curiosity and respect. Was this really the same flustered and hesitant creature he had apprehended only two nights ago? He was evidently a potential ally to the sadly diminishing band of beaters in the world. Webb, however, shuffled from one foot to the other on the tightly mown grass of the infield.

"Well, of course, it remains a matter of some contention among my, er, colleagues, something we tend to leave to individual conscience . . ."

"I am certainly an advocate of corporal punishment, Mr Crump," Rhage cut in briskly. "And I can tell you frankly that I now very much regret the fact that I did not administer another thrashing to young Melfort at the same time that I informed him of his expulsion. I foolishly believed at the time that that punishment alone was large enough. Now" – he waved a slate-sized hand at the scarred pitch – "I realise how wrong I was."

Crump blinked fearfully at the sight of Rhage in warlike mood – something he had had enough of several nights before – and coughed uncomfortably.

"Yes, indeed. Well, Mr Webb. I shall depute one of my officers to go and interview Mr Melfort about this."

Webb's face clouded anxiously.

"But, Mr Crump, in view of the letter and the general, er, seriousness of the current situation, I do hope no energies are going to be diverted from the main, shall we say, thrust of the investigation."

Crump smiled at him, enjoying some minor internal consolation which soon became clear.

"Don't worry about that, headmaster," he said reassuringly. "I have just the right officer in mind for this job, one who knows about the inquiry in some detail but has been moved away to the, er, fringes. He'll enjoy the temporary diversion – and I'm sure young Melfort will as well."

He glanced at Rhage to see if he understood and appreciated the irony. Sure enough, Rhage's face also bore a slight smile.

"You mean, I assume, Detective Sergeant Slicer?" he said, with growing relish.

He did not know, of course, about Slicer's exploits with Elkie, for Crump had deliberately kept this from the schoolmasters. But he remembered all too well the night of the drainpipe-climbing and his shotgun arrest.

"I do indeed mean DS Slicer," said Crump warmly. "Our man with the brothel creepers and the photographic flash-gun. He and young Melfort have got a certain amount in common, anyway, and I'm sure they'll appreciate the opportunity of a further chat."

While Crump and Rhage exchanged the kind of expressions which used, no doubt, to tauten the faces and moisten the lips of spectators at the start of a cockfight, Webb scampered mentally after them, finally caught up, and uttered a nervous, embarrassed little laugh.

"Aha, yes, I do perceive a certain irony there," he said.

"They can compare notes," said Rhage, drily.

"They can compare . . ." began Crump, with the kind of lewd expression which looked exceedingly comfortable on his rubbery features.

"Ahem," interrupted Webb loudly and firmly, and began to usher the other two away from the ravaged pitch. "Now that we have a – relatively – innocuous explanation for the theft of the weedkiller, gentlemen, I suggest that we return to the potentially much more serious task of deciphering that extremely unpleasant little letter."

As the three men were walking purposefully along the main avenue before turning into Webb's front garden, they pared, in their preoccupation, little more than a glance for a coach which purred slowly past them, bearing the Bunyan's eleven round to the pavilion, its windows crowded with healthy-looking adolescents in blazers with gold-encrusted badges on the breast pockets. The three certainly did not look closely enough to notice the driver, whose peaked cap was pulled down hard over his eyes in a secretive manner. And they did not notice how this small, round-faced driver, for his part, watched them carefully and speculatively out of the corner of his furtive eye as the coach slid past.

22

What a glorious afternoon! The second eleven pitch had been skilfully tweaked into condition at the last minute by Thickett and the disgraced young Blegly before the two white-flannelled captains walked on to toss the coin under the blue-and-cloudy sky: the pitch played truly, but with an impish hint of perversity. It took a little spin, there was that trace of movement in the air so desired by the headmaster, and yet a versatile bat could still make strokes, take those scoring opportunities. The school was out in force and high spirits, and the applause rippled and echoed around the stately trees of Great Sward at every fine shot, every well-pitched delivery. As if to conclude the proof that it was a normal summer Saturday at Upperdown, that nothing was wrong nor ever could go wrong, Rattray was there in his usual place near the square-leg boundary. He reclined low in his favourite deckchair with his little white sunhat, reserved for cricket matches, pulled down on his lined forehead to shade his eyes. There was no visible sign of the injury to his soul sustained by the news of the desecration of the first eleven pitch a couple of hours before. He sat with his fingers interlaced on his chest and his joined thumbs pointing, steeple-like, up at his chin; the expression on his face was of ecstatic simultaneous contemplation of the outward ritual and the inner mystery of cricket, and he never moved, except, of course, for tea and cucumber sandwiches at four o'clock in the pavilion, with the players and other senior masters.

A careful observer would have noted that every fifteen minutes a panting boy, his pimply face red with anger and exhaustion, would skirt part of the outfield as he toiled round and round the school's perimeter road; this was Smithson A. J., labouring in purgatory for his bolshiness, his cheek, his slack behaviour and his general attitude. As he passed, he cast envious glances towards groups of his peers who lolled on the grass arguing, eating sweets and occasionally fighting. Every third or fourth time Smithson passed, Blair would languorously rise from his comfortable chair in the prefects' enclosure, mount a bicycle, and follow Smithson round for a circuit, hands off the handlebars and casually resting in his blazer pockets, letting fall an occasional exhortation or insult on the head of his sweating and defenceless victim.

Soon after three o'clock, Crump, having enjoyed Mrs Webb's delicious Saturday special of cheese soufflé for lunch – and failing to impress her with his table-manners – headed off back to town carrying the offending letter for forensic examination, three parts convinced already that it was another part of Melfort's revenge. If the young lout hadn't laid the explosion, as Crump had at first been convinced, he was certainly not above capitalising on the confusion and fear it had caused by sending this nasty, anonymous little threat. He'd have had time to prepare and post it, too, after his destructive little sortie to the cricket field – it was postmarked London, and could have been posted as late as nine o'clock the previous night. Now that his degenerate behaviour – drugs, sex, all the typical vices of modern youth – had finally got him kicked out of the school, he was taking every low opportunity available to him to hit back. Biting the hand that fed him, bringing more shame on his parents, who would now have the police calling at their house in full view of the neighbours. No doubt the fingerprints on the letter would confirm this in a matter of hours, Crump thought as he drove out beneath the Upperdown archway at the main gate. He was looking forward to putting his feet up in front of the television for the afternoon, and feeling strong enough in character for a change to face down any uxorial suggestion that there was work to be done in the garden.

At precisely this moment, Rhage and the headmaster were settling down to watch a critical and fascinating stage of the match. Crump had overstayed his welcome, kept them away from several hours of the game, and thoroughly unsettled their nerves. Upperdown had notched up a creditable 192, a notable feat without the scoring abilities of the disgraced Melfort, and the team's bowlers were locked in a tense struggle with the flower of Bunyan's batting strength. Fanning-Bradshawe, to Webb's delight, had already taken two important wickets with full-pitched balls which had shimmered in the air and sneaked below the bat. It was 56 for 4, and everything to play for.

"Not entirely happy with that sleuth Johnny," growled Rhage as the team changed positions at the end of an over.

"Oh, I don't know," mused Webb as the next bowler began his run-up. "Why not? I thought we'd sorted him out a bit, starting with the other day, got him on the right lines again. And that letter should give him a fair bit to go on. Oh, well bowled, F-B! Beat the bat again!"

"Can't put my finger on it," murmured Rhage, clapping desultorily. "Seems to be always barking up the wrong tree, if you get my drift. All that far-fetched stuff about Melfort being the bomber. Took him some time, too, to cotton on that the said Melfort was having illicits with Miss van H. She's leaving next Tuesday, by the way, earliest we could manage – boat train back to her degenerate countrymen. Chaps brought some hair-raising tales back from Amsterdam just after the war, I seem to remember. Hmm. That batsman could be rather useful, I'm afraid, headmaster. We could do with a man with an off-drive like that."

"I don't think he'll survive young F-B for long, however. Yes, I do see what you mean about Crump. He now seems overly keen on Melfort being the composer of this, er, threatening missive. Quite possible he's got the wrong end of the stick again, I suppose. Anyway, I thought you were all for him because he's a beater like yourself. Oh, well bowled, F-B! What a disastrous stroke! What did I tell you?"

Rhage fell back into silent thought as another crestfallen Bunyan's man walked back to the pavilion to slow applause, trying to hide his disappointment by fiddling with his batting gloves. Rhage winced at some internal realisation as the next gladiator walked out.

"Yes, I grant you, he seems to have the right idea in some ways. But I can't help feeling nonetheless that he's a bit short on the grey matter. Not the sort to be in a tight corner with – ten to one he'll be on to us in a panic before long when they tell him the fingerprints don't match those of the late lamented Melfort."

"Mmm. Crump wouldn't listen to me when I tried to tell him Melfort wasn't the literary sort. 'Beware the fury of an honest man', wasn't it? Doubt if they even mention Dryden in that English course for the scientific sixth – it is Dryden, isn't it?"

"So Ratters tells me – knew it straight away, of course, had to restrain him from quoting great chunks of the stuff. No, friend Melfort was more at home with inorganic molecular structures and Faraday's first law and that kind of stuff, not the great figures of English literature."

"What a fall from grace, eh, Rhage? Only a year ago he was set for great things – cabinet minister, perhaps, something like that. Come on now, F-B, do your stuff – see him off!"

"Fatal flaw somewhere, I'm afraid. Just needs a little chink, the poison gets through and bang! – another good man down. Oh, I say, well bowled!"

"What did I tell you?" remarked Webb smugly as the school clapped and cheered F-B's wiles. "Now for the hat-trick!"

Over near the tractor sheds where the weedkiller had been stolen, Smithson A. J. was gazing through sweat-misted eyes at a small man in a peaked cap who had stopped him and engaged him in casual conversation in a Scots accent. Only too glad of the opportunity to walk rather than run for a while, Smithson fell in alongside the man, who at one point, for no obvious reason, produced two five-pound notes from an inside pocket, turned them over and studied them, and then put them back inside his jacket again. He was the driver for Bunyan's coach, it transpired, and was very interested in the habits and gossip of the various schools he got to visit. Didn't like cricket, it seemed: preferred wandering round, chatting to people. He'd heard there'd been various goings-on at Upperdown recently, was that right? No, really? He was even prepared, you know, to pay small sums of money to people he found really interesting, and Smithson was rapidly falling into that category.

Smithson, loose-tongued and unsuspicious in his exhaustion, was quite happy to rabbit on and tell the man, who produced a notebook at one point, everything he wanted to know. So when he had completed his tenth circuit half an hour later, he headed for the tuck shop, promising himself a rare feast with this new-found wealth, so easily acquired. A couple of long Coca-Colas to get the ball rolling, he thought, then he'd move on to a brace of hot dogs. After that anything could happen.

The result of the match was perfection: Upperdown beat Bunyan's by 26 runs. Fanning-Bradshawe 6 for 78. A sterling performance against the odds; a sportsmanlike competition.

"Absolutely magnificent bowling," asserted Webb for the twentieth time as the defeated side climbed back into the coach in the fresh mid-evening after high tea.

"So you keep saying, headmaster," said a testy Bernard Briggs; he was very miffed that it had been his turn to stay and supervise the blasted tea when he could have been off to see the new Bergman film in Leatherfoot. He disliked cricket: he couldn't see the point, called it 'regressive', which none of the other masters bothered to try to understand.

"Oh, my God!" said Webb suddenly and inexplicably. Briggs looked at him sharply. The old duffer was getting more eccentric by the day.

"What do you mean, headmaster? Why can't we give thanks in the chapel tomorrow in the normal way?"

"That driver – no, it can't be, surely, he wouldn't dare, he wouldn't be able to do it."

"*Do* speak plainly, headmaster, I'm not a clairvoyant."

"What? Er, nothing, Briggs." Webb's brow was creased in evidently painful memory-searching. "It's just that the driver looked uncannily like a rather unpleasant reporter chap from the gutter press that I was obliged to throw off the premises in high dudgeon the other night. Oh, dear, that's going to upset me now. I had hoped for a serene ending to a near-perfect afternoon."

In the growing gloom, Bernard Briggs smiled an imperceptible smile of satisfaction. One more nail in his boss's coffin. He'd be in charge of this place yet, turn it into a model of progressive education, save the private sector from dying, like the dinosaur, from lack of brain and adaptability. No more cricket duty, for a start, or what the boss called 'little tasks' for him.

"I'm afraid I must ask you to do a little task for me," resumed Webb as the tail-lights of the coach dwindled down the dusky avenue. "We must have another special assembly tomorrow."

"We had one earlier in the week, sir," said Briggs, in a steaming pet now.

"I'm aware of that, Briggs," snapped Webb, anxiously on edge. "But the time has come for another appeal – not to say another warning – in the light of recent developments."

"But . . ."

"No 'buts', Briggs, please. Kindly do as I say."

23

To the casual observer, Rattray was sitting in his deckchair in the orchard on a beautiful Sunday morning, enjoying a quiet snooze in the sunshine before lunch. But anyone coming closer would have noticed something so absolute in his immobility that they might have gone right up to him and looked into his face, just to make sure that he was all right. They would have seen a horrible, deathlike opacity in the parts of Rattray's grey eyes which were visible beneath the half-open lids. Had they laid a concerned hand on his arm, or even stuck a pin in it, they would have got no response; and anyone unused to the quirks of Rattray's personality in general, and his dreams and trances in particular, would probably have panicked and run to fetch the doctor.

In fact Rattray's eyes were merely turned inward, hunting and rummaging down the dusty, gargoyled corridors of his maze-like old man's memory. Ever since Rhage had told him that line of Dryden, the line from the anonymous letter, a thinly connected chain of little bells had begun twitching and tinkling fitfully in the back of his head; and now, prostrate in the sun, he was working his way along the deep and secret trail of instinct leading from one slight, mysterious sound to the next. He was determined to find the knowledge which was tucked away – he was certain – in some remote and musty recess or crenellation. Just occasionally the stone-like set of his lips would fracture and a little grunt of effort or murmur of surprise would creep through them. Now and then a tendon would twitch beneath the brown-spotted parchment of the back of his hands. Boodle, asleep beneath the deckchair, now and then squealed gently, expectantly, and kicked his dwarf hindlegs. Slowly, a seasoned observer would have deduced, Ratters was getting there.

The scene now beginning was, he was sure, the one. It had taken place some ten years before, in the class of boys of the lower sixth who were studying scientific subjects, but came to Ratters for a small number of lessons in English literature each week. "After all," the headmaster had once feebly remarked. "We don't want our men of science to be unlettered philistines, do we?"

Rattray was taking them through *Absalom and Achitophel*, which was one of his favourite poems and which he considered served two purposes for this coarse-brained lot: it gave an opening to the tortuous and violent history of late seventeenth-century England, and it presented salutary arguments about the inviolability of Authority and the miserable consequences of Rebellion – both principles which, Rattray felt, should be drummed well into young men of all generations. And in the late nineteen sixties, with their social turbulence and revolutionary whisper, it was with special heat that he drove home Dryden's cautious and reactionary message:

> What prudent man a settled throne would shake?
> For whatsoe'er their sufferings were before
> That change they covet makes them suffer more.

He had just asked that rather lumpish-looking boy with the round face and spectacles – what *was* his name? – to comment on this passage, and he could now hardly believe his ears. The creature had risen to his feet and was delivering quite a little republican diatribe, casting his pebbly little eyes from side to side in the evident hope of drawing approbation from his colleagues.

". . . then you'd get no change at all, sir, good or bad, and it's by making changes that, well, new things are tried and, er, things get better, sir, and society advances, and, er, that."

The boy, noticing that his neighbours, far from giving him their approval, were giggling behind their hands and exchanging grins of complicit mockery, came to a hesitating halt. He stood there, confused, for a moment, withering under Rattray's stare of wild-eyed patrician contempt, then sat abruptly down.

"I take it you've finished what you've got to say?" Rattray

161

enquired icily after allowing the silence to continue for a few long moments more.

"Yessir."

"Quite sure?"

"Sir." The boy's white face had now gone quite crimson.

"Yes, well. I can see we have quite a revolutionary in our midst. Nobody's opposing change, boy, it's a question of how change takes place, whether or not the principles are right. And if you've read the whole of the poem, which I suspect from your oratory that you have not done, you would have read this passage against the background of the whole and taken a more measured meaning from it. It's the difference between ordered change, legitimate succession, and anarchy, which is change for its own sake, and which produces chaos. There seems to be rather a lot of that sort of thing about these days, and our young friend in the spectacles seems particularly infected by it."

Rattray peered out disingenuously over his half-moon, gold-framed reading glasses and asked: "Tell me, are all you scientists bent on wrecking everything? If I had my way I'd ship the lot of you out to Russia, I think. Your spiritual home, as far as I can see."

While the class tittered uneasily over this little jibe, Rattray leafed back through his well-thumbed Dryden.

"Line 531 et seq," he droned, "seem to describe the case of our young republican friend. Read, Freeman."

Freeman, an angular youth whose bass still occasionally slipped upwards into involuntary falsetto, rushed without punctuation through the lines.

> 'Gainst form and order they their power employ
> Nothing to build and all things to destroy.
> But far more numerous was the herd of such
> Who think too little and who talk too much.

Rattray had moved off his dais into the aisles between the desks and was now alongside the offender. He stopped the reader with a gesture of the book in one hand, and used the other to flick some of the speckling of dandruff from the still-blushing boy's shoulder. His bony face was full of distaste.

"Thank you, Freeman. I think that makes my point. Dryden, as usual, says it all much better than we can. Proceed carefully in life, in society, don't let the hotheads rock the boat, and don't go chasing down fashionable blind alleys like the Continentals, after the latest fad. Stick to the principles, the institutions, that have withstood the test of time and which provide stability. I think that's what we're being told here, isn't it, boy?"

"Yessir." The voice was husky, as if with threatening tears.

"And the ones who want change and revolution and power to the people – I believe that's the phrase, isn't it, on the demonstrations and sit-ins? – are mostly irresponsible anarchists without a thought in their heads, or people with a grudge against society, a chip on their shoulder. Monmouth, for example, Absalom in Dryden's poem, came to feel that life had treated him unjustly, that he should have been given better things. See yourself as a modern Monmouth, do you, eh, boy?" Rattray was bending now over the bowed-headed and humiliated figure. "Should have been born higher up the ladder? 'Why am I scanted by a niggard birth?' – that sort of thing?"

Almost before the sentence had left his lips, Rattray's head jerked backwards in sudden surprise; the book he held in his hand shot up in the air in front of his nose, somersaulted in a clattering of pages, and dropped heavily to the floor. Goaded beyond his self-control, the humiliated boy had struck upwards at the book and his tormentor, and then retreated immediately into cowed immobility at his desk, his head bowed slightly to one side as if expecting a blow to fall.

The heavy silence of held breath descended on the classroom; his classmates' eyes gleamed with the anticipated excitement of a small hurricane which they were confident would touch none of them. Rattray looked disdainfully from the boy to the fallen book and back again. Slowly he bent to the floor, retrieved the book, and walked back to his desk on the dais, face impassive, metal heels clicking on the dark, dented parquet. He sat at the desk and sighed deeply.

"I'm sorry you feel you have to disgrace yourself by behaving in this violent way," he said calmly, regretfully.

163

Rattray was a master in the art of punishing others by feigning deep and stoically–borne wounds. "This is just the kind of thing we're talking about, isn't it? Order and chaos? I think you'd better leave the classroom . . ."

"I'm leaving anyway," muttered the boy, clattering his way out from behind his desk and striding towards the door, large head bent forward on his too–small frame.

"Very well. I'm glad you have the decency to do the right thing. But before you go . . ."

The boy paused, hand on the doorknob, not looking at Rattray.

". . . just another little line from Dryden which is just as relevant in 1967 as it was in 1681, to remind you I won't take any more of this nonsense in future:

'Beware the fury of a patient man.'"

The boy – what *was* his name? – furiously pulled the door open, flung himself through, and slammed it behind him. Its glass panes rattled and the crash reverberated down the long, hard corridor outside.

"Yap! Yap! Yap! Yap! Yap! Yap! Yap! Yap! Argh! Argh! Argh! Argh! Argh! Argh! Argh! Argh! Angh! Angh! Angh! Angh! Angh! Angh! Angh! Angh!"

Boodle was awake and catapulting from beneath the deckchair, a projectile of flashing teeth, wiry hair and furious voice and eyes. As his pumping three–inch legs carried him off into the distance on some imaginary mission of canine murder, Rattray also opened his eyes and returned to the world around him. His features were set grimly.

"That boy," he muttered thickly, mystically. "The monumental brass of it . . . yes . . . 1967 . . . I must see the headmaster immediately!"

Rather more slowly than his dog, Rattray set off urgently in the opposite direction, his ancient yellowy–white flannels flapping round his stiff, stick–like legs. A sudden cloud crossed the sun, and a gust of shadowy wind blew all the fresh, clustered leaves of the orchard into an anxious, whooshing agitation.

24

Crump had just lost a protracted and bitter argument about the lawn, which had involved the exchange of some wounding conjugal remarks about halitosis on the one hand and the need for a face-lift on the other. He was standing at the hall mirror dejectedly contemplating the growing bags under his eyes before going out to the shed to see if the little bastard of a motor-mower would start. He was spared even putting it to the test: the phone rang.

"Bland here," said the voice flatly. "We've opened the laboratories specially for you, Mr Crump."

Crump controlled a rejoinder on the lines of 'So what, it's your job, isn't it?' and replied sweetly: "Oh, Major Bland, you don't know how grateful I am. I hope it hasn't all been a waste of time."

There was a silence at the other end. Crump visualised the stony, unmoving face and grimaced at himself in the mirror. As he put out his tongue, however, he noticed an odd, orange-coloured film upon it, and was studying it with such concern and alarm that he missed Bland's eventual pancake-flat response.

"Are you there, Mr Crump?"

"Er, yes, yes, so sorry, just, er – the dog's making a nuisance of itself." (The Crumps did not have a dog – Mrs Crump found them too messy.) "Would you mind repeating that? I was slightly distracted."

"I said, Mr Crump, that the prints on the letter do not, repeat not, match the prints which principally covered the door. In other words, it does not seem to have been handled by your Mr Melfort. The prints do not seem to match any of the other ones we were given last week. In short, you would seem to have a new arrival on the scene."

Crump stood for a second, staring blankly at his grey

image and feeling his spirits slither unpleasantly down inside his body and curl up dejectedly in his beige Sunday hush puppies. The small thread suspending his remaining hope that it could, after all, be Melfort, had now been cruelly sliced through. It was somebody else. The letter was no help. He could only guess at the author. Could it have been written by the anonymous caller, for example? He cursed Slicer again over the tape. And Bland was probably going to relapse into his usual slow-motion from now on as far as forensic work was concerned. There could be another outrage before he came up with anything more. Crump pulled himself painfully round to face this inner emptiness, and saw the irate features of the Chief swimming up at him out of the mists.

"Are you there, Mr Crump?" There was a trace of animation in Bland's voice: the man was actually displaying an emotion of some sort, albeit the negative one of irritation.

"Er, yes, so sorry," mumbled Crump. "I see – a new arrival on the scene."

"So it looks as if you'll have to start again from scratch, Mr Crump."

The hint of satisfaction, of schadenfreude, in the toneless voice pushed Crump suddenly over the narrow boundary between despair and fury.

"And why do you sound so *pleased*, Mr Bland? And what the fuck do you know about it anyway? I should have thought you would be pleased if you were getting results which were helping the inquiry forward rather than the load of crap you've given me so far. Or perhaps I've been mistaken all along and your interest is in the welfare of the criminal rather than the police?"

"I take no view on such matters, Mr Crump." Bland was as level as ever again. "I do the impartial scientific work, and hand it over to the likes of you. It's my job, is it not? Goodbye, Mr Crump, I'm off for a game of golf."

Crump put back the receiver slowly. He paused for a few moments to contemplate the worst possible fears which crept surrealistically into his mind – the whole of Upperdown tossed into the sky by explosions of seismic force, the white shards of stone glittering in the sunshine before toppling slowly back into the carnage of 500 sons of the rich and influential. He struggled with, and barely overwhelmed, an urge to curl up in a foetal position in the corner of the hall, pull the rug over his head, and pile the telephone directories around himself. Perhaps he'd better make sure they took a few precautions out there at the school. A powerful, instinctive certainty of disaster was taking hold of him. Copper's instincts? He was no longer sure. He took some deep breaths to make sure his voice was steady, then lifted the phone again, swallowing his pride in great indigestible lumps. He was going to consult the Chief.

*   *   *   *   *   *

Slicer sat in the unmarked Ford Escort, parked on a double yellow line in the elegant Kensington square, and peered up through the windscreen at the house. It was an imposing Georgian façade, four or five corniced and pedimented storeys of gleaming, glossy stucco. Pretty senior digs, he mouthed to himself in a posh voice, using the phrase he had overheard in a crown court as two top-drawer barristers discussed their country weekending haunts. Not the sort of address you usually visited when investigating a case of criminal damage. He decided to be on his best behaviour, and turned the rear-view mirror towards himself for a moment to practise a few smarmy facial expressions.

"Dreadfully sorry to intrude, sir, on your domestic privacy," he oiled at his image. "But your brat's going to get his collar felt."

Having amused himself for a few seconds in this way, he sighed and clicked open the police car door: better get it over. With any luck they'd be frightfully polite and offer him a drinky-poo in the drawing room. But as he put one leg towards the pavement, he stopped: the door of the house was opening, and two people came into view.

One of them he recognised: Charles Melfort, his rival, looking older now he was wearing casual civilian clothes instead of school blazer and flannels. The other he did not recognise – a small figure wearing a pale trench-coat, stuffing something which looked like a notebook into his pocket as he stood on the doorstep grinning obsequiously. As he turned and came down the imposing front steps, Slicer noticed the intensity of the expression of rat-like pleasure on the man's coarsely reddened features. He thought for a moment, then shrugged. It certainly looked as if they'd given *him* a drink, he concluded, and climbed out of the car with some anticipation.

* * * * * *

Smithson and Nimmo exchanged a last grim and pale-faced glance before Nimmo straightened his tie and his back, cleared his throat, and knocked boldly at the door of Killer Rhage's study. It had been decided at their brief emergency summit meeting in the bogs that he, being four places senior on the house list, would have to take the lead on this one.

"Come in," came the firm and familiar bark. A small tremor of fear ran down Smithson's spine and settled in the soft, fleshy part of his buttocks. Should he have tried the magazine-padding trick? Killer had caught Hanratty at that one and given him three extra strokes for it. Nimmo opened the door and they stepped into the study, where the cosiness of worn rugs and armchairs was rather offset by the forbidding regimental and military souvenirs lining the walls, including a Luger in a glass case reputed to have been taken from a dead German, despatched by Killer with a bayonet soon after the Normandy landings. Rhage glanced up briefly from his marking of the third form's geography essays: the amount of red ink being spread upon them suggested either that they were rather primitive or, worse, that Rhage was in a bloody mood.

"Yes, you two, what is it?"

Nimmo stepped forward, but the price of keeping the tremor out of his voice was that he found himself unable to come to the point.

"Well, sir, we thought that, well, after this afternoon and everything, with the headmaster calling the special Sunday assembly and all the warnings and everything, about another bomb and all that, sir, we thought we'd better come and see you, sir. We weren't quite sure that we should, sir, but we thought we'd better. We wondered about it quite a lot, sir, sort of couldn't make up our minds."

Rhage slowly put down his pen and looked at them, a terrifying composure and calmness on his craggy face.

"Don't waste time whiffling, boy," he commanded. "Get to the point."

'Whiffling' was known to be a beatable offence in its own right when Rhage was in certain frames of mind. Nimmo came to the point, but this time his voice quavered a little.

"Well, sir, the headmaster said we should report anything suspicious, absolutely anything, and, well, we did see something, down in the tunnel, sir, the other day."

They now had Rhage's full attention. He hadn't expected anything to come from this feckless crowd in response to the head's rather dramatic and panicky appeal to the school earlier in the day. He'd expected this lot to have forgotten all about it by now, and jogging a schoolboy's memory was not, in his experience, an easy thing. His eyebrows had already risen slightly as he registered the out-of-bounds offence they had already confessed; but he decided to let them finish their story before he took them up on that – there just might be something in it which would stop Johnny Terrorist having another bash at him, and he was all for that.

"Go on, boy," he growled.

"Well, sir, we were down in the tunnel, in one of the little cupboard-type places, actually, and we heard someone walking along it towards us. We kept quiet and hoped he would just walk past" – Nimmo's voice was cracking and squeaking now – "but he didn't, sir, he stopped and opened the door and sort of, well, *looked* at us for a while . . ."

"It was the same day you came back from hospital, sir," broke in Smithson with impatient irrelevance. "He was sort of laughing, wasn't he, Nimmo?"

Nimmo threw his comrade-in-crime a look which said 'Shut up, you fool, I'm handling this.'

"Shut up, Smithson," said Rhage, his features now thunderously severe. "Let Nimmo handle this. At least he's got some brains."

"He didn't say anything, sir," went on Nimmo. "Just sort of looked at us for a moment, and nodded a bit and sort of laughed, and then closed the door and went away again. It was weird, sir, really creepy."

"Did you see him well enough to describe him?"

"Yes, sir," they said together.

"Right, stop there," commanded Rhage. He strode round them to the table by the door, lifted the phone and dialled three figures. It was rapidly answered by a voice which came over loudly enough for the boys to overhear the conversation which followed.

"Headmaster, it's Rodney Rhage here."

"Good God, Rhage, aren't you aware that it's nearly nine o'clock on a Sunday night?"

Rhage looked calmly at his watch.

"Eight thirty-two, to be precise, headmaster, you're exaggerating again. However, it is something rather important. Concerns the investigation."

"Quite frankly, Rhage, I'd rather leave it until the morning unless it's something absolutely imperative. I've just had Ratters with me for over an hour – he's been in and out all day, raving on about how he knows who did it. Had a brainstorm sitting in his deckchair, it turns out, and he's decided it was someone in one of his classes ten years ago. Something to do with the wording of the letter to you, you know, the bit about the honest man. Quite frankly, old boy, I'm at the end of my tether."

"Make your way over here, headmaster, and I'll pour you a stiff whisky and soda and give you a little more news. PDQ – I'm afraid it is imperative."

"Oh ye Gods and little fishes. All right, Rhage, I'll be with you in a minute."

"By the way, what've you done with Ratters?"

"We compromised – I said I'd tell the police about it officially if he could remember the name, and he's disappeared into the library to go through all the records. Quite frankly, I wouldn't mind if all those tons of dusty volumes fell on top of him and cracked his daft old . . ."

"I *do* have boys with me at the moment, headmaster, and you're coming over loud and clear," Rhage cut in firmly, nipping in the bud this lapse in masterly esprit de corps. "I'll expect you in a few minutes."

Rhage put down the receiver and gazed grimly for a few seconds at the two boys, silent and subdued on the carpet before him. Then he contemplated his Luger on the wall for a while. Smithson's buttocks began to tingle slightly again.

"I'm not going to ask you why you were down in the tunnel," he said finally. "Because I already know. I suspect it was for exactly the same reason that you got up early and were wandering around the school grounds on the day of the explosion. You've already been punished for that, and now you're up in front of me again. Your foolishness and blatant lack of self-discipline astonishes me. You seem determined not to stop breaking school rules by smoking cigarettes, and so I shall make it my business to compel you to stop. However, we have a rather more important matter on our hands at the moment, so this particular subject can wait. Sit down, both of you, until the headmaster arrives."

The two boys did so, and stared at their shoes. Rhage, ice-cool, resumed his marking of books until they heard agitated footfalls approaching and a flustered-looking Spider Webb knocked and bustled into the room. Rhage took control of matters before the head could launch into another nervous bout of verbal incontinence.

"Sit down, headmaster. These two miscreants saw a suspicious character moving about in the tunnel several days ago, and their conscience has overcome their cowardice, thanks to your appeal to the school this evening. Tell the headmaster what you saw, Nimmo."

Nimmo did so, his voice calm now with the flat hopelessness of the boy who has been drained of all suspense, and even fear, now that he knows quite certainly that he is going to get beaten.

"And the description?" prompted Rhage.

"Well, sir, he had these funny glasses and rather staring eyes, like a fish or something. And a sort of blue overalls thing, you know, a bit like some of the workmen wear."

"Big? Small? Medium?"

"He was sort of medium, and his head looked sort of too big for his body, if you know what I mean."

Rhage turned to the headmaster to see a look of horror growing on the other man's features. His face was draining, changing, chameleon-like, from agitated pink to ghastly white.

"What's the matter, headmaster? You look as if you've seen a ghost. I'd better get you that scotch straight away."

"No, no," said Webb, waving him back to his seat. "This is quite uncanny, extremely serious. That's exactly the same description that Ratters gave – the spectacles, the large head, the big round eyes. I don't like the sound of all this, not one bit, Rhage."

Rhage's jaw was grim.

"Better get on to your Mr Crump. After all, he's all we've got."

"Yes, indeed," replied Webb, eyes now roving round the room wildly. "May I use your phone?"

While the headmaster talked to Crump, Rhage dismissed Smithson and Nimmo with orders not to go to bed yet but to wait in the dayroom in case the police wanted to interview them. They sidled glumly out, realising they would have to wait for their beating until tomorrow; a night of horrible anticipation lay ahead of them.

"Well, what does your Mr Plod say at Brigade HQ?" Rhage asked as Webb put the phone down with a shaky hand.

"Sounds as if he's going to pieces," said Webb, slightly confused at the idea, as if policemen ought never to do such things. "Said he was calling his Chief Constable immediately, putting it in the hands of the Yard, all sorts of things I didn't quite understand. Panicking, if you ask me. Talked about something called the Special Assault Group."

"Ah!" said Rhage, brightening suddenly. "That sounds more the ticket."

"Who the hell are they, if I may ask?"

"Special unit from Scotland Yard – deal with all the big terrorist jobs in town. Military approach to things, useful chaps to have around in a scrap. I've been hoping for something like this all along, between you and me. Some of these police forces have seen the light recently, you see, and got themselves properly tooled up – none of this Dixon-of-Dock-Green stuff when you're dealing with dangerous reds and mad mullahs, eh?"

Light but brisk footsteps approached outside the door, and there was a febrile knocking. Webb put his travailed head in his hands.

"Oh, no," he groaned. "Not Ratters again."

Ratters almost fell into the study, clutching and waving
dusty green-bound volume of the 1967 Upperdown List.
is eyes were wider than ever, his hair bristling stiffly above
s crimson-edged ears.

"Loomes," he quavered. "Known to one and all as Pronk.
aine House 'sixty-three to 'sixty-nine – must be nearly
irty now. English abysmal, science subjects outstanding.
murderous philistine, in other words – couldn't take his
ryden, and now he tries to slaughter us all like sheep to get
is own back. A patient man! A homicidal barbarian, I
ould say!"

Rhage had moved forward to steer the stumbling Ratters
a deep armchair, before he fell down in a fit: there were
ready little wedges of foam in the corners of his mouth,
d his face was a disturbing mauve colour.

"All right, Ratters, old boy, everything's under control,"
urmured Rhage, returning to his desk and retrieving a
ottle of whisky and three tumblers from his bottom drawer.
t's in the hands of the right chaps now. Loomes, eh? Yes,
remember him well. Pronk Loomes. Rather odd type, I
em to recall. Staring eyes, bad at games, not very popular."

The headmaster had his hand up to his face to cover its
itching. Rhage glanced at him with contempt as the
olden whisky glugged out generously. A spot of real
xcitement, he thought, a chance to get properly stuck in,
d the Field Marshal goes into shell shock. A fine example
the troops. Ratters, slurping his drink, was now mum-
ling crazily to himself.

"Get this down you, man," he snapped at Webb, who
ut out a trembling hand to receive the tumbler. "And pull
ourself together."

"I can't bear it," snuffled Webb. "What have we done to
eserve this? What will the Governors say? We're all going
die."

25

The next day – the new week – dawned with the same serene brilliance as the day of the explosion. The songbirds stirred early in the hedgerows and copses, and the herdsmen on the school farms drove their charges, swaying and grumbling, through lightly dewed green fields to milking-time. The earliest train clattered past in the distance on its way to Victoria, and the faint vapour trail of a fighter-bomber from the nearest United States air base climbed silently into a perfect blue sky. All seemed right with God, Upperdown and the world, which to many people were more or less the same thing anyway. But a trained observer of the surrounding countryside would have soon discovered that something was subtly – and lethally – wrong.

The Special Assault Group had arrived swiftly and spread through the school like a virus in the middle of the night. As one of the black–clad groups of officers entered Paine House even Rhage had to consciously prevent himself from shrinking back against the wall alongside the headmaster and the cowering Ratters. They came in pouched and padded overalls, their eyes as dark and murderous as gun muzzles and their mouths like chinks in heavy armour. Beside them, incongruously, their Labrador sniffer dogs panted, smiled and drooled amiably. The men had been briefed beforehand and their words were few, tight and terse. They took their powerful flashlights down into the tunnel with them and in minutes had found the command wire which led them to nearly a hundred pounds of high explosive, neatly and professionally packed beneath the floor of Rhage's study – accessible from the tunnel – and round the foundations of the house.

An impassive bomb–disposal man immediately came back upstairs and, instinctively addressing himself to Rhage rather

174

than the crumpled-looking Webb, ordered the evacuation of the whole of Paine. Fifty yawning and shuffling boys in dressing gowns were moved along to Wilde House, where they lounged irritably in the dayroom and eventually started mounting raiding-parties on Wilde's dormitories. Then the same nerveless officer had neutralised the detonator. Two men were sent to find the other end of the command wire. Running silently, their torch beams jerking crazily in front of them in the darkness, they followed it down into the furthest, dampest branch of the tunnel. It led, sure enough, through a neatly drilled hole in a heavy glass skylight near the gymnasium, and then a hundred yards along the grass verge of the road to a man-made nest in the copse by the lake. There, in an old ammunition box carefully concealed under the grass and leaf-mould, was a small black canister with a plunger running into it, a pair of powerful binoculars, and a groundsheet: the tools of a carefully prepared private apocalypse.

And so it was that, by morning, the hideout and the rest of Upperdown lay in a concealed ring of steel. Men with blackened faces and rifles lay under piles of undergrowth in and around the copse by the lake. Several snipers, wearing earmuffs against the thunderously reverberating commands of the bell, were in the tower of Big Hall, scanning the school severely through their binoculars, which were even more powerful than those found in the hide. In the lanes approaching the school, sharp-eyed men sat in ordinary family cars, pretending to read newspapers. Others were concealed in cupboards near to all the fourteen entrances to the tunnel from the houses, gym and kitchens. Several more were deployed in the tunnel itself, one of them carefully examining a suspicious pile of cigarette ends in a musty cubby-hole almost underneath Paine House itself. Century Copse concealed a van-load of elaborate equipment – night-time cameras, rope-ladders, strait-jackets, body armour, riot shields, an arsenal of guns, helmets, grappling-hooks, and a bank of sophisticated communication equipment linking with Scotland Yard, Whitehall, MI5, and a betting shop in Catford.

"I say," murmured Nogge doubtfully when Rhage indicated the van to him as, begowned and with hands clasped behind their backs, they walked up to morning chapel. "Anyone would think the third world war was about to break out."

"Don't worry, Nogge. These chaps know what they're doing – strategy of minimum force needs plenty of back-up, y'see."

As Upperdown serenely continued its daily round, under strict instructions to act normally, the SAG spent all day cramped, aching, deafened or bored, waiting for the homicidal ex-public schoolboy to return to his elaborate and demented act of revenge. By mid-afternoon, an inspector in charge of the van was losing heavily on the horses and getting increasingly restless.

For Sergeant Slicer, however, things were rather busier. Once again, Crump had passed out the legwork to him; Crump was certainly in no fit state to do much himself, bunkered in his office back at the station, perspiring and trembling every time the phone rang, and wondering whether the Chief or his heart would get him first. By 8 a.m. Slicer had been halfway up the motorway to Northampton to visit the company where Loomes had, according to urgent midnight inquiries, worked ever since leaving London University. The local police force, meanwhile, had been asked to trace where Loomes now lived and, if he was there, pull him in; but their dozy attitude had not impressed even Crump, who was fatalistically expecting something very nasty to happen very soon. Despite the defusing of the explosives, his dejection was complete.

26

Oh, yes, sir, Mr Lazenby's expecting you. Please come is way."

With a glittering carmine smile, the receptionist rose and d Slicer down a highly polished corridor towards the silent epths of the administrative headquarters of Luconi Ltd. er high black heels tilted her buttocks upwards, and they ppeared to rise a little, in turn, as if to offer themselves to ne following Slicer. Despite the early hour and his bleary ondition – or perhaps because of it – he had to force himself ot to reach out and fondle the tantalising fruit. He was, ter all, very partial to buttocks.

They glided upwards in a silent lift, the girl smiling quietly nd staring antiseptically in front of her as Slicer greedily took er clothes off with his slightly bloodshot, sleepless eyes. hen, along another corridor, through an anteroom, and nrough a large, wooden door into an office of pastel carpet nd chrome and leather furniture. A man with an erratically alding head, thick glasses, a thin and unpredictable mouth, nd an untidy pot-belly, rose to extend a sticky hand and wave licer to a seat. When Lazenby himself sat down again, he most disappeared into the depths of his leather chair. He ooked at his visitor with ill-concealed truculence.

"I understand you want to talk to me about one of our nployees, Mr Slicer. May I ask what this is all about?"

Slicer registered the defensive hostility of the man and ttled on the oozing-easy-charm approach which he ormally used for people who thought they had a position nd dignity to protect.

"Yes, certainly, sir. It's rather an urgent inquiry, as a natter of fact, which is why I asked for an appointment at nch short notice – and I'm very grateful, by the way, that ou agreed to see me."

Lazenby gave a slight, acknowledging nod: Slicer saw the slight break in the permafrost and knew he had chosen the right strategy for this particular customer.

"You're familiar, I'm sure, with the Upperdown explosion?"

The nod: he was.

"There's a possible connection, I'm afraid, between your Mr Loomes and the Upperdown affair. I'm here to try to eliminate him from our inquiries."

There was an indecipherable glitter from behind the big lenses.

"I hope you're not suggesting our man did it – are you?"

"We're not in a position to make any such suggestions at the moment, sir," lied Slicer. "We're obliged, however, to follow any possible leads we have. The culprit may try again, you see, sir."

"I must inform you, Mr Slicer, that Mr Loomes is on two months' leave following a bereavement, and I cannot be sure of his whereabouts. I understand his family comes from Stoke-on-Trent. What 'lead' brought you to Mr Loomes, anyway, if I may ask?"

Slicer hesitated. What lead did they actually have, apart from the half-baked insights of a geriatric schoolmaster and a sighting by two kids? He toyed maliciously for a moment with the idea of saying just that, but knew it would be counter-productive with this prickly twit.

"I'm afraid it might be unwise to reveal that kind of operational detail at the moment, sir. All we're trying to do is build up a picture, if you see what I mean."

This seemed to anger the managing director, who shifted violently around in his leather swivel-chair.

"I see. You want us to tell you everything, while you tell us nothing," he said in a voice taut with repression. "Right. Fine. Police work, I suppose. Doesn't sound very fair to me though."

Slicer waited for the agitation to subside, then said gently, "It may seem unfair, sir, but I assure you we're acting in everyone's best interests."

Lazenby finally reached forward and took a file from his desk. He opened it.

"Well, Mr Slicer, I've got our personnel people to bring

ne Mr Loomes's personal details. Not a lot we can tell you
eally, although we have a policy of co-operating with the
olice. Joined us straight from university, worked his way
p to a respectable technical position, quiet sort of chap,
eeps himself to himself . . ."

"Anything about his home life, company he keeps, that
ort of thing?"

"This is a confidential file, Mr Slicer."

"We're investigating a serious crime, sir."

"Yes, I see, right, fine, so we just hand everything over,
o we? Is that it?"

"If you wouldn't mind, sir."

Slicer firmly, slightly, tightened his grip. Firmness, he
ad realised, was something Lazenby understood, in spite
f his blustery protests.

Lazenby tossed the file towards Slicer ill-temperedly, got
p and paced agitatedly around the room while the detective
ead greedily. Amazing what they kept on their people,
hese firms – pity they didn't record whether or not they
vere homicidal maniacs. The phrases from the annual
eports on Loomes leapt out at him one by one.

"Excellent task fulfilment . . . slightly unpredictable
nanner . . . an innovative year . . . personality does not
ltogether fit in . . . undoubted technical competence . . .
loes not conform to parameters of eventual senior man-
gement material . . ." Ah! What was this? "Special report
y corporate welfare officer, psychological services divi-
ion." Dated a year ago.

Slicer's eyes skidded hurriedly down to the section marked
conclusion': this looked more like it.

Loomes's performance in the counter-insurgency weapons
systems section is technically impeccable, but my investi-
gations have led me to the discovery of certain qualities
of personality which make him unsuitable material for
advancement into areas of higher managerial responsibility. Certain aspects of his private life indicate the defici-
encies: Loomes married early and unsuccessfully, and
since the time of his divorce has lived alone in a small flat
with frequent visits to his ageing parents in Stoke-on-
Trent. His social performance is uneven, in that he

alternates between attempts to ingratiate himself with senior personnel – something which, by all accounts, seems to have the effect of alienating them – and near-violent rejection and condemnation of them. In psychological terms, a paranoid personality; in layman's terms, a chip on the shoulder.

Confidential interviews with the subject and his colleagues suggest the following as the essential structure of his psychopathology: lower-middle-class family with ambitions for brighter than average son, with great financial sacrifices made to send him to a public school. Intense pressure resulted on him to succeed. Indications of intense but unsuccessful attempts to gain acceptance from peer group at school; rejection was probably on grounds of class, social style, accent, mannerisms etc., etc. Indications of retreat into world of study and discipline – a form of self-imposed penance for failure to 'do well' – punctuated by gauche forays into the social surroundings he still aspires to. Over-attachment to parents, motivated by guilt, continues into adult life and probably helps account for the failure of the marriage, with a severe personal crisis likely to follow their demise. The net result is the kind of personal instability which would make for inconsistent management performance, as a result of fluctuating attachment to overall goal definitions, i.e., the production and sale of counter-insurgency and security systems. Signed, E. Howlett-Molar, senior confidential assessment officer, corporate psychological services division.

Note: As a personal observation, the original mistake was made when he was pushed into a public school, without the necessary social background.

Slicer glanced up and was surprised to see Lazenby hurriedly draining a glass of amber liquid. He glanced at his watch and saw it was not yet 9.30 a.m. He wondered for a moment about Lazenby's attachment to overall goal definitions, and whether he would survive the scrutiny of the corporate psychological services division.

"May I ask you, sir – do you know Loomes personally?"

"No, not really. Know of him, of course, seen him about the place."

Lazenby was noticeably more talkative already, his gestures looser and the line of his mouth more relaxed.

"Not the sort of chap you'd really want to mix with too much," he slurred on. "Bit awkward – I'm sure you know the kind of thing. Stripes on his shirt a bit too wide, somehow, if you see what I mean."

Lazenby paused and his eyes, already slightly red, slid up and down Slicer's sharpish suit.

"No," he resumed after a moment, half to himself. "I don't suppose you would. Anyway – peculiar chap generally. Either sucking up and being a trifle smarmy, or getting a bit aggressive – especially after a few drinks."

"Quite, sir," replied Slicer, glancing pointedly at the empty tumbler in Lazenby's tubby, short-fingered hand. "That's more or less what it says in his file."

"Oh, does it? Haven't read it myself – that line of country is more for the personnel bods. I do remember, though, seeing Loomes behaving rather erratically at a dinner–dance we held for the management at Christmas – came by himself, for a start, which was a bit odd, by any standards, and was wearing a rather ill-fitting dinner-jacket with an extremely loud bow tie. Someone made a rather amusing remark about it, if I remember rightly, called him a butterfly boy or something harmless, and the fellow turned nasty – insulted someone's wife, if I'm not mistaken. Had to be asked to leave. All more or less blew over in the long run, of course, but that sort of thing does linger on a bit, you know."

"I see, sir. And here, in the company, did Mr Loomes have access to explosive materials?"

"I'm afraid that's classified information, old boy."

Slicer sat patiently for a moment and waited for Lazenby's loquacity to overwhelm his discretion as he paced, portly and agitated, around the office. It did.

"Matter of fact," he blurted. "We've got an unfortunate occurrence on our hands – shortfall in material in the section where he worked. Happens every so often, nothing really new about it. Usually turns out to be a stocktaking error or something of the kind. Trouble is, it doesn't look like it this time. Especially not now you mention, er, other possibilities."

Lazenby glared at the impassive Slicer, biting off the

added words 'Damn you' under his breath. The whisky glugged generously into the glass. He paused in mid-swallow and waved the bottle interrogatively at Slicer, who shook his head.

"What possibilities do you mean, sir?"

"Why, that the damn fool's made off with the stuff to start acting like a bloody terrorist and blowing things up. Chaps running amok and causing explosions – we can't afford to have that sort of thing here! Just because nobody wants to give him a game of squash, or whatever his bloody grudge is. He'll have to go, you know – we're a respectable security equipment company!"

* * * * * *

Webb's eye was caught by the pile of newspapers on the doormat as he came down the last flight of stairs. The *Comet* – he recognised it by its stentorian typography – was lying folded on top with part of its splash headline visible: the words 'Top School'. Webb paused, immediately suspecting the worst, gave an involuntary little moan of appalling foreknowledge, and pulled his dressing gown closer around him, as if to hide himself away and protect himself. His instinct was to back off, pretend the papers were not there. But he forced himself to approach, one slow step at a time, like a disposal man approaching an anti-personnel mine. Halfway there, he saw the little box below the headline which contained the words which confirmed the awful truth: "EXCLUSIVE", it read, "by Robbie MacPherson"; and beneath that: "the only reporter inside Upperdown".

Webb's fingers felt like pencils, nerveless and unresponding, as he picked up the *Comet* to confront the entire front page. A bold message at the bottom told him that he was now holding "Britain's fastest-growing newspaper – FIRST with the news, FIRST with the girls, FIRST with the sport: your bigger, better, sexier, roaraway *Comet*." He winced and raised his vision again to the main story.

"SEX AND DRUGS SCANDAL AT TOP SCHOOL" read the three-inch capitals; then, in lower-case type, "MP says dope in dorm 'not cricket'. Exclusive by Robbie MacPherson, the only reporter inside Upperdown."

Another moan left Webb's lips, more abandoned this time, as if he had been firmly punched in the solar plexus. The text read:

Amazing scenes involving drugs and sex take place regularly behind the closed doors of one of Britain's public schools, we can exclusively reveal today.

In a shock dossier compiled in a searching *Comet* investigation, we disclose high living and low morals at £2,000 a year Upperdown.

Only last week Upperdown, where the rich and snooty send their sons, was the scene of a mysterious explosion which devastated a master's home and injured three.

Now the *Comet* probe exposes the scandals behind the terror blast – with senior pupils watching colour TV and seducing au pair girls while masters are powerless to act.

Police are working on the theory that the blast could be an 'inside job' – carried out by a desperate man who knows the school well and harbours a grudge.

A local MP said yesterday: "I'm amazed. Nobody wants Tom Brown's Schooldays back again – but it's like the Ritz in there."

Turn to centre pages.

Webb whimpered as he shuffled the pages through fingers still stiff with shock and anxiety. The Governors, he thought; the Prime Minister; the parents; the staff; the public, even! Oh God! The centre spread had a large picture of the school, taken from its grandest aspect, a fuzzy picture of himself, taken God knows when, frowning like a gorilla above the words: "Webb – out of depth". Then there was another of Charles Melfort, neat and crisp, with the words: "EXPELLED – Melfort" beneath it. Webb raised his eyes and cursed aloud. Melfort! He should have known! Suddenly abandoning his non-violent principles, he found himself wishing fervently that Rhage had given the whelp such a thrashing after the last little episode that if he'd spoken to the gutter press at all it would have been from a hospital bed. (He himself would not have done the beating, of course.) He pressed on with the story, every syllable hitting him like a jab below the belt.

We can now reveal that:
- A senior pupil made love to the housemaster's au pair girl – in the housemaster's own bed!
- That wild 'pot' parties are held in the small hours;
- That group sex with gymslip girls takes place on the library floor during school dances;
- That senior boys bribe juniors in return for homosexual favours;
- That boys stole sports goods and sold them to local criminals;
- That staff are under orders from headmaster Archibald 'Spider' Webb to cover up scandals and head off inquiries by the press.

Only on Saturday, when blackboard rebels stole weedkiller and wrecked the cricket pitch by writing obscenities on it, a senior police officer said: "It could have been any of them."

Webb paused and snorted with outrage: that little whelp Melfort had wrapped them round his little finger, trying to put everyone off his trail! But there was worse to come.

A 'get-tough' policy put forward by the old guard has been vetoed by Webb, reported to be under the 'liberal' influence of trendy deputy head Bernard Briggs, 36.

One traditionalist told the *Comet*: "There's nothing wrong with this place that six of the best wouldn't cure. But our hands are tied."

The boy who used the housemaster's bed for torrid sex sessions with curvy au pair Elkie van Horning, 19, has now been expelled.

He is Charles Melfort, son of wealthy banker Gerrard Melfort. Charles told the *Comet*: "I lived the life of Riley – booze, drugs, anything I wanted.

"Some of the masters were in on it all – that's why they couldn't stop it. They smoked cannabis confiscated from the boys.

"I'm rather glad it's all over, really. I wasn't getting

much of an education there. I'm thinking of going into newspapers."

Another boy, who must not be named for his own protection, said: "People drink and smoke all the time. Some of the older boys hire the 'squits' for sexual services."

Webb's eyes glazed with despair as he weakly retreated a few steps, sat on the bottom stair and lowered the paper, slowly, as if he was putting down his own career, to the floor. Then he put his head in his hands. A vision reappeared inside his eyes of that runt of a reporter screaming at him as Thickett pulled him out of the room: "I'm going to expose you to the British public . . ." He remembered with disgust the beery breath, the spittle, the white gummy substance in the corner of the little madman's eyes. He jumped up in a sudden rage and stamped his slippered foot with a muted thud.

"I'll sue them," he said wildly to the matching hunting prints hanging in the hall. "Highest court in the land . . . deny it all, write to the *Times*. Can't let them get away with it . . . power without responsibility . . . prerogative of the harlot . . ."

The kitchen door opened and his wife put her mild, greying head round it.

"Are you calling me, darling?" she asked anxiously. "Your eggs are boiled, you know – I don't want them to go hard."

Webb dropped the paper and walked obediently into the kitchen. At least, he consoled himself, at least they hadn't got hold of that ghastly business the other night with policemen shinning up and down drainpipes and guns being pointed at people by his own staff. But then, Melfort wouldn't tell them that, would he?

27

Crump, looking as grey as a lump of putty, joined the hard men playing cards in the SAG caravan at about lunch-time: he'd had a miserable morning discussing the latest moves with the Chief, who clearly took the view that if anything went wrong from now on it was going to be Crump's fault. The SAG men more or less ignored him, and he sat quietly in a corner feeling his chest gingerly for any signs of pain or palpitation underneath, and wondering pessimistically how it was all going to end. Depression sat on him like a heavy black cloud. At ten to one, the green telephone on the communications console rang discreetly, and the granite-faced sergeant handed over the receiver with a stare of contempt.

"It's for you, *sir*," he growled.

At the other end of a crackling line was Slicer, faint but firm: Crump's contempt for the man was forgotten now in his eagerness and anxiety. His pride had been crumpled and thrown away.

"Ah, Slicer, anything turned up at all?" he croaked.

"We were right about the explosives, sir," said Slicer, unaccountably deferential. "Made off with a fair whack of high-quality stuff from Luconi – had access to the high-security storerooms, apparently, and now he's buggered off on two months' leave because of his old lady snuffing it. They didn't say anything about losing the explosives because they thought it was a stocktaking error – I ask you, anyone would think we were talking about plasticine."

"Go on," urged Crump painfully.

"Also, they had no reason to think he'd scarpered with it. According to the M.D., who's something of a headbanger himself, by the way, Loomes was a bit of an oddball. Good at his job and that, and mostly well-behaved, but now and then gets out of his pram and starts upsetting people. Unpredictable, know what I mean?"

"Local force any help?"

"Nah, not really. I'm speaking from the local nick now, matter of fact. They've been round, searched his bedsit, found a couple of things – bound copies of the school magazine bang up to date, apparently, a map of the area, loads of letters from his mother telling him to change his socks and work hard . . . he's our baby, all right."

"Well, we're after the right man, if that's what you mean . . . there's an alert out for him all round the country."

"Yeah, thanks to Ratters the wild-eyed guru rather than us, that is . . . Still, better not go into all that right now. Fact is, he's disappeared from his home and the local boys haven't a clue where he might be apart from lying low down near the school somewhere. Neighbours are fuck-all help – say he kept himself to himself and that sort of thing."

"Right, then, Ron" – it was very rarely that Crump had used his colleague's Christian name since the inquiry began – "perhaps you can continue up to Stoke and find out if they've got anything on this nutcase. I've asked the force up there to have a sniff around, too, see what they can come up with."

The precise words of Slicer's reply, the tone of which unmistakably indicated resentment and protest, were drowned not only by the whistling and crackling from the telephone line, but by a sudden loud report from outside the SAG caravan. Even before its crash and echo had died away, all but one of the men in the van had stampeded, grabbing articles of weaponry and equipment in their headlong exit, shaking the thin floor in a clatter of heavy boots.

Confused, Crump looked round, but was distracted by the angry tirade still coming down the phone.

"Sorry, Slicer, I can't hear you – something urgent's blown up at this end . . . What? . . . What? . . . No, not another explosion, just a gunshot or something. I must go, call again later, will you?"

When Crump put the phone down, the door was still swinging gently from the salvo of fired-up policemen who had just shot through it, and the remaining officer was talking intently and gently into a microphone.

"Red Claw to all units," he intoned. "Red Claw to all units. We have action. I repeat, we have action. Maintain full alert. Red Claw to all units . . ."

Crump tapped him on the shoulder, intending to ask where everyone had gone, but the officer gave him a glance which stated that if Crump didn't get off his back he was going to get his neck snapped with a single clean blow. Rather frightened and indignant, Crump stumbled out of the caravan to look for the 'action'. He walked stiffly out of the copse, blinking, into the sunshine of the main avenue. It seemed to be full of young boys chattering excitedly as they ran through the gap between two of the boarding houses towards Little Sward. In the distance he could hear what sounded like the yelping of a dog. Crump stumbled after the boys, as quickly as his twitching heart would allow.

He neared a growing, milling knot of people at the edge of Blunt's Copse, the cluster of chestnut trees behind Paine House.

"It's Boodle," squeaked one of the junior boys, eyes gleaming with excitement, and tie awry. Boodle? Who the hell was Boodle? Another of those batty old masters? Crump hadn't heard of any Boodle.

"Is he dead?" asked another schoolboy with what sounded distinctly like relish. Oh no, Crump pleaded with God, not a death, that's not fair, you can't do this to me, the Chief had warned him he'd be to blame.

Some of the boys were turning and pointing up at the school bell-tower two hundred yards away. Crump also looked round, nearly losing his balance and falling. That must have been where the shot came from . . . some bloody, trigger-happy madman!

Panting stertorously, his face the colour of dry ashes, he pushed his way to the front of the gaggle where three of the SAG officers were kneeling over the prostrate body of a very small dog. The white, wiry fur of one of its forelegs disappeared into a mangled, bloody mess below the knee. Boodle was no longer yelping, but lay still, rolling his eyes pitifully.

"One of the lads in the tower must have seen something moving in the target area and let rip," one of the officers was saying to another in hushed but admiring tones. "Hell of a good shot from that distance."

"Well, they've got the telescopics, you know," said the other grudgingly.

"Trouble is, there'll be hell to pay over this," said the first. "Headmaster's wife probably sleeps with this little runt or something – hello, what's this?"

The officer looked round just in time to see Crump clutch convulsively at his chest with both hands, roll his eyes horribly upwards, and crumple slowly to the ground like a large beast with an iron bolt in its brain. His grey face came to rest a foot away from Boodle's tiny, wounded body.

* * * * * *

At first Rhage did not even realise there was somebody else in the room with him. The alarms and excitement of the last few days meant he was seriously behind in his geography marking, and he had come into his study to spend the final hour of the evening as productively as he could. The life of the school, after all, had to go on. Gradually now, without shock, he became aware that the final mellow beams of the sun, filtering into the study between the bars of the work-men's scaffolding still standing outside, were falling also on another person standing quietly by the door. When the feeling grew to a certainty, he calmly put down his pen and looked up.

"You came in very quietly," he remarked, holding his voice in a conversational tone and his face into impassivity.

Loomes said nothing and did not move; he just smiled. It was a brilliant smile, wide and charming and unexceptionable in itself; but put together with the rest of the face – with the strangely bright, milky eyes hidden deep behind the thick, round glasses, with the curly hair standing roughly away from the large, round head, and with the monumental immobility of his gaze and his bearing – it was a smile which proclaimed unequivocally and with a kind of wild, abandoned pride: "I am stark, raving barmy!"

Rhage folded his large hands cautiously on his blotter, cleared his throat, and glanced up at the Luger in its glass case: where the hell was the SAG? The SAG's reputation with Rhage had collapsed like a house of cards after the Boodle incident. Cruelty to human beings was quite normal,

189

in his book, but cruelty to animals was beyond the pale. Now he thought: typical bloody policemen, never there when you need them. Probably gone off to crash one of their fancy vehicles or amuse themselves with a full-scale dog shoot on the North Downs.

"How did you get into the school?" he enquired, following snatches and twitters of little, nervous voices from the back of his mind saying things like: 'act normally', 'humour him', and 'don't antagonise him – he may be dangerous'.

The staring smile continued unbroken, and Rhage was about to haul out another, more neutral, conversational gambit, when Loomes suddenly spoke.

"Easy," he said, in his rather high-pitched voice with its trace of Staffordshire vowels. "They had guards on my little hide and all the entrances to the tunnel, so I got off the bus at the main gate and walked in. Policemen are very stupid, you know."

His smile returned, and he gestured at the door, adding: "I've locked it and got the key in my pocket, by the way."

Rhage hesitated, realising how trapped he was, and wondered whether he should agree about policemen and their intelligence, thus trying to win the lunatic's confidence by showing him he was on his side, or contradict him in order to reassert the voice of authority and start gradually bringing him round to his senses. Before he had come to any decision, though, he realised that his uninvited guest was, almost imperceptibly, holding a package out towards him.

"I've brought you a present," Loomes said with apparent innocence, looking alternately, unblinking, up at Rhage and down at the shoebox-sized parcel which he held reverently before him in both hands, like a sacred offering. "It's the last bit I've got, but there's quite enough to do the trick."

Rhage suddenly felt as if a chilled fluid was running through his veins, and lifted a hand up to his still-scorched cheek in memory of the last explosion. His mind swam off again among the crashing of waves and gunfire and the cries of mutilated men on the beaches of Dieppe. He gave his head a little shake to jerk him back to concentrating on the dangers of the present. Loomes, his smile intensifying to the point where his whole face seemed luminous in the growing gloom at the far side of the study, suddenly lifted the package to his ear and listened, as if to sweet and distant music.

"Tick–tock," he said, and uttered a disturbingly high, sibilant giggle. "Five minutes to go. And if I drop it, it'll go off straight away, you know. So don't try anything."

"I'm afraid I'm not quite with you," said Rhage, with feigned calm, trying to focus his inner ear on a little voice which was unconvincingly squeaking: 'don't panic'. "Five minutes to go until what, precisely, Mr Loomes – it is Mr Loomes, isn't it?"

Suddenly Loomes stopped smiling; the moon–face was instantly brooding and intense, the glow switched off.

"Ah," he said. "So you *do* recognise me? That's something, I suppose. Seeing I've picked you out."

"Oh, yes," said Rhage breezily. "You're not quite such a mystery as you might think. Rather gave yourself away with that letter, I'm afraid. Your one wrong move."

"What d'you mean?" snapped Loomes, threateningly, hands tighter round his parcel.

"Oh, just that Mr Rattray remembered one of the phrases in it, something about patience being a virtue, or something similar, and traced it to some, er, difference of opinion he'd had with you. Amazing memory, as you probably know, old Ratters – stretches back for years."

"Amazing bastard, he is, too," grunted Loomes sulkily. "He's got a lot to answer for, that one. I considered doing him instead, but I decided in the end people would take more notice if it was you."

Rhage's eyes slid nervously to the white hands, podgy but with delicate fingers, which were palping the parcel fitfully.

"And how did they find the stuff in the tunnel?" Loomes asked, truculently.

"Well, it seems two of the boys saw you down there . . ."

"But they were smoking!"

"Yes."

"Surely they didn't own up? They'd have got beaten for being down there!"

Rhage dragged a conciliatory smile on to his numbing lips.

"Ah yes! But times are changing, Loomes – not as harsh as in your day," he said, knowing as he spoke that the partial truth of this statement was not due in any extent to his own efforts.

Loomes grunted again, his eyes roving aggressively round the study, as if registering the unchanged details and remembering everything that he had hated so much, beneath his eager conformity. Suddenly he looked up, as bright and smiling again as when he first entered. Where the hell were the SAG, thought Rhage desperately, glancing at the telephone on the little table near the door.

"Oh, well," said Loomes cheerfully. "Even I can make mistakes, it seems. I counted on those two keeping quiet. And I should have known that line would have jogged old Ratters's memory. But don't worry, there's no escape this time."

Rhage cleared his throat again, more thoroughly and carefully this time.

"Look here, old chap," he ventured, his voice quavering just a little now that all the background voices seemed to have chickened out and left him alone in the fire-zone to rely on his own resources. "Why don't you sit down and talk it over? You have my word that we'll all take the sympathetic view. After all, you'd never get away with it, you know."

"Get away with it?" The big face clouded again as Loomes hurried to clear up this misconception. "Oh, no, I'm not trying to get away with it. I'm coming with you, you see . . ."

"I'm not quite sure what . . ."

"Pee–oww–ooohhhhh," Loomes interrupted with a gentle, wondering voice-imitation of a large explosion, slowly stretching up and widening his arms, the parcel in one hand, to indicate the scale of his little final solution.

Rhage sat silently. Forget the police, he thought dejectedly: what were definitely needed here were the men in white coats with big hypodermic needles. What had he done to deserve being locked in his study like this with a bomb-toting psychopath? They should have got this lad into the Army for a year or two – that would have brought his dangerous ideas under control.

"Still," said Loomes, brightly. "I don't mind a bit of a chat for the next minute or two. I suppose I owe you some sort of an explanation for all this."

"You could say that," remarked Rhage drily, beginning seriously to contemplate the thought that he really was going to meet his maker this time and trying vainly to console himself that he'd had a good innings and given a reasonable account of himself. Loomes, meanwhile, walked across the room in his strange, duck-like gait and sat in the leather armchair under the window, setting the parcel delicately on the little table beside him. Rhage measured the distance with his eye; he was well out of lunging reach, and the desk between them made it certain Loomes could dash the parcel to the floor before he could possibly reach him. He would somehow have to talk him out of it.

"What do you want to know?" said Loomes brightly, like a studious child ready to be tested on its homework. "Why I'm doing it, I suppose."

Rhage nodded, noticing Loomes's clothes for the first time. Even he could see that they were strangely awkward and unfashionable garments: orange-brown cotton trousers with bell-bottoms that seemed to end halfway down his shins; a shiny, powder-blue nylon roll-neck sweater; and a pair of scuffed suede slip-on shoes with elastic sides. Even ten years ago, when such clothes had currency, he would have looked incongruous.

"I selected you, I'm afraid," Loomes was saying cheerfully, "because I decided that you represented what was at the centre of it all."

"All *what*, if I may ask?"

"It," said Loomes, gesturing widely around his head. "The whole set-up. The system, if you like; the way it all works. As I say – it."

"You've got some sort of grudge against the school, is that it?" twigged Rhage, leaning earnestly forward. "I can't recall you having a particularly unpleasant time here, Loomes, no worse than anyone else. In fact, I checked my records earlier on and found that I never even gave you a beating. Quite a low score in the punishment book generally."

Rhage tried a grimly humorous smile and added: "Not many boys can go through Paine and say that."

But Loomes was not amused.

"It's not funny, Mr Rhage," he admonished angrily, seriously. "It's not direct punishment like that I'm talking about. The point is, the system you ran, which punished everyone for existing, more or less, for being different, forcing everyone to be the same . . ."

"Nonsense, old chap. Everyone's encouraged to be an individualist here, you know that. Why, look at some of the characters the school's produced, some of the country's great eccentrics, Alf Choker, Sir Gerard Whybrow . . ."

"And me!" broke in Loomes, with a smile like a searchlight being switched on. "Ah, yes, I'll be well-known after this, won't I? Now I've done something wrong. Oh, yes. I'll have my picture in the papers all right, even though everyone's always sniggered at me up to now. That's the trouble, you see. I was always trying to be one of them, one of you – it was the only way to get on at this place, it was the only thing they were interested in. It's the same outside as well."

His face fell and he fingered his chin as if it was an unfamiliar object he had just discovered.

"And somehow I could never get it right – they'd always be looking down their turned-up noses at me, pushing me about, raising their eyebrows at my accent. Then my dad died, and then my mum, and I soon realised it was all their fault. They wanted me to do it, and I never realised it was all something that didn't matter . . ."

"Precisely, old chap, absolutely," broke in Rhage, heartily. "So why don't you just relax and be yourself and just, er, hand over that parcel. Or if you like, just let us out of the study and we'll leave it to go up by itself, eh? And you have my word we'll take . . ."

"The sympathetic view? Don't be silly, Mr Rhage. That lot out there are so trigger-happy they'll have me like they had Boodle. I know about that already, you know – news travels. And keep your eyes off that telephone."

Rhage brought out a red handkerchief from the top pocket

of his sports jacket and dabbed at the sweat forming on his forehead. It was a hot evening, he thought desperately – or was he afraid?

"Look here, old boy," he coaxed. "Why don't you tell me all about it, eh, man to man, and it won't go beyond these four walls. Just, er, disconnect that thing, er, there, and I'll give you all the time you want. All night, if you like. We'll talk it over together."

Loomes shook his head without hesitation and glanced at his watch. His face was beginning to look crumpled, like that of a tired child.

"'Fraid not, sir. Only two minutes to go. And I just don't care any more, you see. I've stopped trying to be what they, what you, want me to be. Only trouble, it's too late to be anything else – I've forgotten what it was like to be normal, probably never was normal. I came too early to this place with its" – his face distorted with revulsion – "codes of behaviour and cold baths and its punishments and beatings and wank-brigades and fagging and boot-licking and its horrible rituals and obsession with smelly sports and the hidden buggery that goes on – oh yes! – and all the sadists and perverts who come here as masters and turn out more sadists and perverts who, who *masquerade* as the pillars and standards of society, and, and, that old bastard Rattray, using bits of English so-called literature to push his daft ideas down your throat . . . and you don't learn anything except how to keep your lip stiff and your arsehole tight. Anything that matters, anything serious, like, like, God, say, or death, or infinity, is just skated over, all rather embarrassing, that sort of thing, people's feelings, isn't it?"

Loomes, with reddening face and twisted mouth, struggled to string together and spit out his litany of humiliation and failure, his resentment of all the forces he had tried for so long to placate, and which he had now decided to try to destroy. As he spluttered on, cornered, discreetly homicidal, and probably mad, Rhage's eye strayed cautiously from his adversary's face to the frame of the window behind his shoulder. Was it moving, or wasn't it? It had been slightly open to let in the scent of the early rose blooms in the garden outside, but now the catch had been lifted off its hook and the gap was three inches, four, five . . . Rhage could feel his heart beating a little faster, warming his veins again. Better keep him talking – look hard at his face, concentrate.

". . . and as for *talking* about it, Mr Rhage, I had plenty of jumping through hoops like that. They sent me to a psychiatrist, you know, to try to straighten me out. I've had the drugs and everything, until I realised that it wasn't me that was up the creek and round the bend, it was them . . . They were just trying to shut me up and knock me into shape, make everything more convenient for them, and I wasn't going to have that. I decided on action . . . and after the first bomb failed . . ."

"How did you plant that one, old boy?" Rhage enquired, straining to keep his voice even; the window was definitely fully open now, framing the purple velvet of the evening sky, gridded by the scaffolding. Keep him talking, he urged himself. Concentrate.

Loomes relaxed a fraction, giggled conceitedly.

"Easy," he said. "I know my way around this place, you know. Through the back door, up the fire-escape stairs, borrow the key from the hook inside the head prefect's cubicle, through to the landing, place it carefully outside the door. Thought I'd kill two birds with one stone, you see."

"Quite literally," said Rhage indignantly. "I can see I was one of the birds, as you call them, but who or what was the other?"

"That mucky little Dutch bird. First au pair allowed into the school, according to last term's *Upperdowner*. I saw her round the place with your kids when I was doing my preliminary surveys. Then I saw her again, you see, one night, down in the lay-by with a bloke. I was looking for a place to set up my little hide, you see, when they arrived in his little car. She put up a struggle, mind you, and she got away in the end. But I thought she deserved it, too."

A look of confusion was on Rhage's face: this was new and inflammable stuff to him. Was he really being told that the little hussy had been flouting herself around with others as well, even before this whole thing with Melfort – or, worse still, at the same time? This was getting worse than ancient Rome.

"What's all this, Loomes?" he barked, reverting suddenly to the role of interrogating housemaster.

"D'you mean to say you don't know, sir?" Loomes's eyebrows rose high in surprise as he, on his side, reverted unconsciously to schoolboy forms of humility. It was as if he felt obliged to confess everything in full detail, and receive his final punishment in the place where punishment had become an essential part of his life.

"Then you don't know about my phone call to Mr Crump?"

"What phone call?" Rhage was distracted again as he glanced at the window, then quickly tried to keep his eyes off it. Some large implement had now been raised into the aperture and was being slowly, silently, moved forwards into the room. It looked suspiciously like a cricket bat; the SAG certainly seemed to carry an odd variety of weapons – but you never knew what the police were up to these days. Loomes, meanwhile, gave a delighted little giggle at the memory.

"It was lovely, that," he said. "Really put the cat among the pigeons, pretending to be one of the ground staff, you see, or a local yokel out on the prowl. He didn't know if he was coming or going, didn't poor old Crump, fell for it hook, line and sinker."

Rhage knew nothing about this. He felt his concentration going, his mind swaying. Don't look at the window, he told himself, keep him talking, anything, think of anything.

"And all that stuff in the tunnel?" he blurted suddenly, rapidly, with the relief of returning presence of mind. Loomes smiled again with self-satisfaction.

"Aha," he said pompously. "You have to remember that I've got ten years' experience in the arms industry, Mr Rhage. On the research side, of course – they wouldn't let me into management because they thought I was a weirdo, not smooth enough, you see, not public school enough. Good joke, that. No, I rather enjoyed all that stuff setting the wires and cables – what militarists like you would call hush-hush stuff, I suppose. So, those juniors gave me away, eh? Still, doesn't matter much." He paused and glanced at his watch. "Our little alternative plan seems to be going very smoothly. The letter was just to tease a little, just to string you along – pity it rather let the cat out of the bag . . ."

"I see," said Rhage, staring at Loomes, who was now wheezing and hugging himself, half-laughing in some weird self-satisfaction. Then his eyes were attracted to a fast movement at the window.

The cricket bat suddenly reared high above Loomes's head, paused for a distinct but indecipherable fraction of time, then came down suddenly and fiercely, hitting the large, fuzzy skull with the sharp, hollow crack of a good off-drive struck in the meatiest part of the willow.

Loomes's glasses fell forward on to his knee, and for a split second Rhage was able to study directly the curious grey-green glacier paleness of the eyes, frozen in a look of question and surprise; then his face suddenly lost all shape, like crumpled paper incinerated to ash, his head fell forward on to his chest, and his large, short body relaxed heavily into the chair. In the sudden silence, Rhage could hear the faint ticking from the parcel.

A head appeared in the window through which the cricket bat had now been withdrawn. It was Charles Melfort. Rhage stared at him, nonplussed, blinking repeatedly.

"Quick, sir," shouted Melfort urgently. "Out through the window before that thing goes off!"

Melfort stretched a hand through the window-frame. All Rhage had to do was dodge round the desk, take a step-up from the arm of the chair which bore the inert body of Loomes, grasp the hand, and with one bound he would be out of danger. Indeed, he had reached the stage in this strategy of lifting his foot to the arm of the chair when he paused. Instinctively, he knew there was something wrong, and as he glanced sideways at Loomes, he knew what it was: his conscience was uneasy. No matter how far a chap's actions had put him beyond the pale, set him outside civilised society, one could not just leave a chap to be blown to bits and burnt to a cinder.

"Come on, sir," yelled Melfort, waving his helping hand.

But already Rhage was bent over Loomes, manhandling him like a bag of salt to reach into the pockets of his trousers. The thought crossed his racing mind that it was an action which would in the normal way of things be open to misinterpretation in an institution such as Upperdown, but he scrabbled on nonetheless. The key wasn't in the first pocket he tried. The ticking of the parcel, a foot away from his right ear, was very loud now.

"Leave him, sir," Melfort's voice came from the window. "He's a nutcase, sir, he tried to kill you!"

Rhage glanced up at the agitated Melfort, his face serene with resolution, as he hauled the body sideways to reach the other pocket.

"You know that's not on, Melfort," he said, the calmness of his voice broken only by one or two grunts of effort. "And if you're the man I thought you were all along, you'll get in through that window and help me get this fellow out."

The second pocket yielded the key, which was warm from Loomes's leg and which had become entangled with a half-empty bag of sticky toffees. Like a child still, thought Rhage in passing. Then in two strides he was at the door, thrusting the sticky key in and turning it. He threw the door open. Melfort, landing lightly on the floor, already had Loomes's ridiculous, unfashionable feet in his hands. With a nod of silent, soldierly approval, Rhage seized the shoulders. Shuffling swiftly, they were out of the room, through the front door of the house, and lying behind the low garden wall when the bomb went off. The window-frame spun slowly out towards them; then came the bang, the tinkling of the fragmented glass, and the painful bump of pressure in their ears. Then there was the long, rumbling, crumbling noise as most of that part of the front wall of Rhage's house which had not been damaged by the earlier explosion slithered and tumbled on to the front lawn, bringing the scaffolding down with it.

As the smoke gusted grittily over them, Rhage turned to Melfort, who was lying the other side of the insensible Loomes, with his head well down.

"What the hell are you doing here, boy?" he snapped. "I thought I expelled you last week."

"'Fraid I left a few things behind the other day, sir, I thought I'd call and collect them," panted Melfort. "Reckoned I'd be able just to dash in and get them. But I'd just got my cricket bat and togs out of the changing room, sir, when I saw him sneak into your study. Thought I'd better investigate, sir."

"Well . . . thank God you did, I suppose." Rhage's voice wavered for a moment in the weakness of relief, and his head sank forwards towards the ground. But it snapped quickly back up again with the force of a particularly urgent memory: his face, illuminated by the fading dusk and the fire getting under way in the ruins, clenched in anger and distaste.

"I don't know how you've got the nerve to show your face here again, Melfort," he crackled. "After that outrage – that sacrilege – on the first eleven pitch . . . don't try to deny it, Melfort, I know it was you. I thought you were a cricketer, not a coward."

Melfort eyed Rhage's clenching fist, and edged sideways away from him, finding a use for the first time for the 'leopard crawl' which every Upperdowner had to learn in the Combined Cadet Force.

"Yes, well, sir," he said uncertainly. Fragments of brick dust were settling on his face, giving it an acned look. "It, er, wasn't my idea, actually."

Rhage summarised his contempt for that particular excuse with a vicious snort which set the nearby marigolds a-flutter once more.

"No, really, sir. It was my brother Nigel who came to collect me, you remember, and he'd just come back from the States. He had some duty-free with him, sir, and we decided to do a little farewell tour of the grounds, sort of nostalgia . . ."

"I remember that good-for-nothing brother of yours," cut in Rhage. "Congenital bolshie – should have been strangled at birth. So I suppose he brought back that disgusting expression along with the cut-price booze?"

Melfort nodded ruefully.

"We did get a bit, well, blotto, sir, I'm afraid."

Rhage struggled to his knees, suddenly feeling that lying on the ground was not the most advantageous posture for administering a dressing-down. The fire had a good hold on his study now, but he was oblivious: another more burning question had occurred to him.

"And I suppose you've come back to see that, that . . . girl

200

gain? Don't give me that tommy-rot about collecting
ogs."

"Well, yes, sir, as a matter of fact I did call in to say
oodbye." Melfort employed the leopard crawl once more.

"Climbing up that bloody drainpipe again?"

"Yes, sir." Melfort grinned in spite of himself. "But no
oliceman in tow this time, sir."

Rhage was about to raise the question of that morning's
sue of the *Daily Comet* and the source of its information,
vhen a sudden flurry of heavy footfalls in the growing
arkness behind them drowned his words. It was quickly
ollowed by an ominous silence.

"Hang on to your hat," muttered Rhage grimly, falling
ace down to the ground again and putting a protective arm
ver the still-unconscious Loomes. "Here comes the Special
ssault Group."

And for the next half-minute they pressed their fingers
nto their ears and their noses into a still sweet-smelling
ower-bed as the massed firearms of the SAG pumped
everal hundred bullets into the bombed-out study, whose
mouldering curtains flapped eerily in the light breeze. "Just
n case," as the officer in charge confided to them later.

28

Rattray was never quite the same after Boodle's amputation.
It was as if one of his own limbs had been removed and he
was no longer his complete self. He considered that his little
dog's front paw had been lost in the service of the school, and
the police now replaced Moscow and Bernard Briggs as the
chief villains of his dreams and fantasies. But there were
fewer of these now, and before long he began to lose his
maniacal edge in favour of a new detachment and serenity.
After a last burst of flame, his fire was damped to a comfortable glow, and he seemed to welcome the arrival of a respected, if eccentric, old age. He could be seen every day for years
after, in the woods and hilly fields surrounding Upperdown,
with Boodle gamely running and sniffing and hunting round
for rats on three frantic tiny legs instead of four.

Webb, of course, felt he came out of the whole thing quite
well, in the end. He had kept a cool head – he told himself and
anyone who expressed even the slightest interest – he had
liaised sensibly with the police, and his alertness to what he
called "currents of feeling" in the school had been decisive in
tracing the criminal. The terrible flaps, the fear of blame, the
almost insurmountable desire to bury his head beneath the
bedclothes each morning and refuse to come out, the irritable
reluctance to listen to Rattray's near-clairvoyant insights – all
these melted conveniently out of his memory before the warm
glow of success. He even made his peace with the *Comet*,
which published a splash story headlined 'Banished Hero
Saves School – Head Pledges: Rot Will Stop'. There were
pictures of him smiling determinedly and of Rhage, looking
uncomfortable and self-conscious, with his arm round
Melfort's shoulders. There was also, after the trial, a background article on Loomes – 'Loner Nursed Secret Grudge' –
including interviews with his neighbours ("He kept himself to

himself"), his employer, Lazenby ("A good employee, but a bit of an oddball socially"), and a former schoolmate, now a banker ("Pronk Loomes? Good God. Always sucking up, then turning nasty if you laughed at him").

Rattray, of course, considered that Loomes should be hung, drawn and quartered at Tyburn – although he managed to admit that he himself had contributed to the provocation by savaging him in the 'patient man' episode. Fortunately, though, the courts chose not to apply this solution. Rhage at first pined for a military procedure, something along the lines of a court-martial and a firing squad, but concluded after some honest paternalistic heart-searching and some conversation with his softer-hearted wife that a good talking-to by his commanding officer and a few weeks in the glasshouse on hard rations would have done the trick. Both Ratters and Rhage rather scorned Webb's wishy-washy approach, which conceded that the poor boy had been under a great deal of strain, especially taking into account his family background, and that he had had, well, rather an unfortunate time at Upperdown. To admit this, the old guard felt, was to start to open the gates to the enemy.

"It's absolutely the wrong way to look at things," said Rhage firmly when a group of senior masters were sitting in the deepest armchairs of the staff room discussing it one day. "If this episode proves anything, it proves the folly of that sort of liberal approach. It's precisely when you start listening to the so-called point of view of anarchists and subversives and madmen of this sort that they take advantage and start trying to destroy society. They have to be dealt with firmly. That's the lesson we should learn from the Loomes affair – and from the whole of the history of this country over the last fifteen years, if you ask me."

"A return to sanity!" proclaimed Rattray, index-finger raised and eyes rolling. "No more liberal studies, no more welfare state and free love, and the return of capital and corporal punishment. That's what we should stand for – the return of traditional values."

It was left to Bernard Briggs to point out, with a certain tentative satisfaction, that there was a slightly hollow ring to all these protestations. These were men clinging desperately to the wreckage, he implied. He pointed out the paradox that Melfort, who had daringly preserved traditional values in the human form and substance of Killer Rhage, had earlier flouted them openly, shamelessly, practising free love, inhaling exotic foreign stimulants, and defying the laws of both God and Mammon. The tide was strongly against Briggs, however; a silence of stern disapproval descended and a dozen hard eyes fell heavily upon him.

"Quite honestly, I don't see what relevance that has to the principles of the thing," said Rhage, rather coldly. Briggs felt he had just been put on a list of some kind; he consoled himself with the private insight that Upperdown, like the country it served, was still regretfully looking over its shoulder at past distinction instead of facing a changed modern world, and that the twisting of the neck distorted its vision somewhat.

Nobody at the school had quite known what to do about "poor old Crump", as he quickly became. Their contempt for his failure – for the way he had barked up wrong trees, neglected to see what was plainly displayed before his eyes, and keeled over at the crucial moment – was tempered by a certain pity for the heart attack he had suffered in trying to serve Upperdown. All in all, though, Boodle's sacrifice probably received greater honour. Eventually Webb took Crump some flowers, overcoming a feeling that it was perhaps not quite manly – Rattray insisted that they should be taken to him personally lest they mistakenly find their way to Loomes, who was languishing in the same hospital at the time with a fractured skull and a police guard.

To Webb's great surprise, he found Crump high-spirited and cheerful in his weakness as he handed over the wilting asters.

"You're extremely perky, old boy," he said, failing to conceal his slight resentment. He liked the recipients of his magnanimity to be suitably craven and dejected, which was perhaps why he had become a public schoolmaster in the first place.

"I most certainly am," croaked Crump enthusiastically; he had lost a lot of weight. "This is the end for me, you know."

Webb's face clouded with false sympathy. This was more like it.

"Surely not that bad, is it?"

Crump gave an impatient, feeble wave.

"No, no. I'm not kicking the bucket yet, I can assure you. What I mean is, I'm out – a Blighty One was what they used to call it in the Great War, I believe. Early retirement on health grounds, a nice little pension, bungalow up in Lytham or Morecambe. And the Chief can go and chase his ruddy tail."

"Oh, I see," said Webb stiffly. "You're contemplating an end to a distinguished career, eh? Can't say I blame you. I feel a bit like that myself sometimes."

While Crump's ambitions thus foundered on the rock of the Upperdown Affair, as it later came to be known, the career of Charles Melfort, by contrast, took off from it as if from a springboard. He was lionised by the newspapers so fulsomely that the relationship was eventually consummated, by mutual agreement, with the appointment of Melfort as the youngest gossip writer on the Cedric Temper column of the notorious *Daily Post*. A little help from MacPherson clinched this particular deal. A discreet offer that bygones should, in the light of events, be bygones, that his expulsion should be converted to a short rustication and that he should quietly return to Upperdown to take up the cricket captaincy, was turned down without hesitation.

"It's people like Loomes who seem to need an extra dose of the place to teach them some manners," he remarked cryptically to Webb on the telephone. "Not me."

Melfort quickly learnt the internal politics and tricks of his newspaper in particular and Fleet Street in general – so well, in fact, that when his prosecution for criminal damage to the Upperdown first eleven cricket pitch came to court, he skilfully turned it to his advantage. He ensured that it received maximum media attention and, wearing a flamboyant bow tie in MCC colours, gave a brilliantly disdainful performance in the witness box, principally to the effect of pouring witty scorn on Detective Sergeant Slicer. The papers loved it. Melfort left court with a £500 fine, which he paid on the spot with a flourish and a cheque from one of the smaller and more exclusive banks, and a one-month suspended sentence; Slicer left with smarting pride and a boiling temper which caused him to drive his black Alfasud so aggressively on his way home that evening that he knocked down an old lady on a zebra crossing and ended up on a serious criminal charge himself.

"I don't know," sighed Webb, sitting down to breakfast in the dining hall after reading the papers on the day following Melfort's case. "At this rate we're going to get a reputation for turning out charming cads – not quite the thing to attract the more solid parents, I fear."

"Either cads or raving lunatics," corrected Rhage, taking a large helping of fatty school bacon. "I don't know, though – maybe it's better than turning out a production line of grey nonentities."

"I'm not so sure: why can't we achieve, well, normality – something down the middle? One moment we're turning out someone like Melfort, who breaks the rules and then goes off to rule the world, most probably – rather depressing, isn't it? – then another time it's a raving lunatic like Loomes who tries to kill all of us off. There's no *consistency* any more, not like there used to be."

"I think there might have been an intake problem with Loomes, which makes him a bit of a one-off," said Rhage, chewing reflectively and staring out over the noisy babble of the hall. "Trouble is, I suppose, we're losing control – can't keep the rest of the world in its place any more. It's coming in the blasted windows at us, one way or another. Ask your Mr Bernard Briggs about that. I say, bacon's rather tough today."

He paused to swallow, and looked a little guiltily at Webb before continuing.

"I might as well tell you, headmaster, that I've had an invitation to lunch at the Ritz with Melfort after the term's ended. I find the attack on the pitch very hard to forgive, but I might as well tell you that I have, in fact, accepted."

"Good God." Webb put down his knife and fork and stopped chewing his fried bacon. "What on earth are you doing that for? You'll only end up in that dreadful column of his and the school will be dragged further into the gutter."

Rhage laughed indulgently.

"Oh, no, nothing of that kind, I assure you. We've got a gentleman's agreement of no publicity. He asked me to go so we could complete the burying of the hatchet, as it were, nd, well, I couldn't see why not. So I said yes. Never been o the Ritz before, as it happens."

Webb stared at Rhage for a moment, then morosely esumed his breakfast, struggling with a feeling which he nsisted was disapproval but which felt strangely like envy. o Rhage was going along for the ride, joining the gravy rain late in life.

"Well, I hope you don't get food poisoning," he said. "Hasn't it been taken over by Arabs, or something even vorse?"

There was a pause. Rhage's eye took on a distant look, s if he was reflecting on some Kiplingesque inner truth. Compassion and violence lived alongside each other in the :ast-iron recesses of Rhage's heart.

"Mind you," he said. "I've been wondering about poor ıld Loomes."

"Poor old Loomes? What do you mean, man? The idiot ried to blow you to bits, not once but three times. A langerous criminal lunatic."

"I know. But a C.O. still has a kind of responsibility for ıne of his men who goes off the rails. Perhaps you never ıppreciated that, headmaster, having no experience of higher Army command. You can't just turn your back on people when they stray from the straight and narrow."

Webb looked at him, struggling to find a way of showing his anger at the impugning of his leadership skills, and wondering if Rhage was a candidate for inheriting Ratters's mantle, now that the old man was declining. He also wished, as so often, that he'd chosen a quiet breakfast at home instead of doing his duty in hall.

"Well, I'm afraid he'll be in Broadmoor before long," he said, with poorly concealed satisfaction.

"Yes," said Rhage, renewing his flagging assault on the rubbery bacon. "I must go and visit him."